Praise for Kate Watterson's *Frozen*

"Beware. *Frozen* will have you shivering."
—Sandra Brown,
New York Times bestselling author

"Gripping, atmospheric, and fabulous!"
—Carla Neggers,
New York Times and *USA Today* bestselling
author of *Saint's Gate*

"Watterson's evocative prose brings to life a Wisconsin winter where the most dangerous threat isn't the cold but a cunning killer who will leave you chilled to the bone." —CJ Lyons,
New York Times and *USA Today*
bestselling author

"A tale of psychological suspense that builds to a chilling ending . . . will keep you turning the pages late into the evening." —Jamie Freveletti,
international bestselling author

"Taut, tense, and completely original—I couldn't put it down! Kate Watterson is a terrific storyteller and this compelling page-turner will wrap you in gripping suspense until the very last page."
—Hank Phillippi Ryan,
Anthony, Agatha, and Macavity
award–winning author

TOR BOOKS BY KATE WATTERSON

Frozen
Charred
Buried

BURIED

Kate Watterson

TOR®

A TOM DOHERTY ASSOCIATES BOOK • NEW YORK

BURIED

Copyright © 2014 by Katherine Smith

All rights reserved.

A Tor Book
Published by Tom Doherty Associates, LLC
175 Fifth Avenue
New York, NY 10010

www.tor-forge.com

Tor® is a registered trademark of Tom Doherty Associates, LLC.

ISBN 978-0-7653-6962-8

Tor books may be purchased for educational, business, or promotional use. For information on bulk purchases, please contact Macmillan Corporate and Premium Sales Department at 1-800-221-7945, extension 5442, or write specialmarkets@macmillan.com.

First Edition: January 2014

Printed in the United States of America

0 9 8 7 6 5 4 3 2 1

To the ghost in Brown County. I am glad we get along so well.

ACKNOWLEDGMENTS

My thanks always to Kristin Sevick and Barbara Poelle for fabulous guidance, with humor thrown in along the way.

BURIED

Prologue

White jagged streaks split the sky and the deafening blast, only a few seconds later, meant the lightning had hit all too close.

These early fall storms could be really nasty.

Time to get off the water.

Roger Bridges nudged the canoe toward the bank, paddle dipping fast, his back hunched as the storm roared in.

He fought his way under an overhanging branch because he had no choice—by now the lake was wild, the wind coming from the north, waves hitting the sides of the craft, slapping water upward into his clothes and face. The roar of the wall of rain swept in like a force of enemy aircraft, low and hollow.

Dragging the canoe out wasn't the easiest maneuver, but he'd paid three hundred bucks for it and wasn't about to let it go just because he was going to get wet.

He'd seen the piles of thunderheads but figured he'd have time—wrong on that score.

What the hell was he thinking? This was Wisconsin, and the weather was about as predictable as a cornered rabid badger, and the hail was coming sideways and hurt.

He banked the canoe, dragging it up, rain coming down hard now, his hair dripping into his eyes . . .

And that was when he fell into the grave.

Chapter 1

SEPTEMBER 1957

She was cold. Shivering. Her body reacted to every sound in the creaky old house. The wind was rising, whistling through the eaves, and the old birches outside groaned and protested in a primal whine.

The one board in the parlor always complained when stepped on just right and she made that mistake, the protest loud and damning.

No.

The floor was chilly, but she was freezing already, so it didn't matter.

This wasn't perfect, but she didn't want perfect, she just wanted it over. Lies were tiresome, there was just no two ways about it. A burden, something to cart around with you all day and take to bed at night. Her mother had always said so, and she was beginning to agree.

Around the corner there was an oak sideboard, massive, with pretty dishes and an engraved silver coffee urn, looming in the filtered light. There was an old sofa, a carriage lamp, and the smell of roses lingered from a vase full of blooms from the garden, but the flowers were starting to wither, so the sweet odor was tinged with decay. Accidentally she bumped the table and a few of the petals fell, whispering against the polished wood.

The knife was in her hand. Not heavy—a lightweight steel made for fileting fish, curved, the blade Finnish, something she'd gotten actually from her father, inherited when he died. There was a hint of rust along the edge because she didn't oil it like he had, but it was still as sharp as death.

And death was part of this chill night.

SEPTEMBER, PRESENT DAY, ONEIDA COUNTY

The day was cold and Detective Ellie MacIntosh winced and adjusted her collar in the mist. Raindrops were even gathering on her lashes. So much for Indian summer. The entire week before it had been in the seventies, but that party seemed to be over. The leaves were starting to take on just enough color to indicate summer was going to fade before long. It looked like it might be an early fall.

"What is it I need to see again?" The question was reasonable because it was hardly the right weather for a stroll through the woods. Damp, too cool, the pine needles underfoot slippery, the trees dripping.

"A hole." Her grandfather stopped as if he wasn't entirely sure where he was going, and then veered off a little to the left. "Over here."

That didn't really fill in the blanks. She carefully stepped over a fallen log with fungus the size and shape of human ears on the side. "Excuse me, but, we are out in this to look at a hole? Can you be a shade more specific?"

He glanced back. His face was reddened by the crisp breeze and his pale eyes direct. The cold wind ruffled his white hair. As usual, he wore a plaid shirt, a tan coat over it, and his jeans were so worn they must have been three shades lighter than when he originally bought them. His boots were covered in mud, but it was wet out. "Just follow me, Eleanor."

Fine.

She disliked her given name, but could hardly tell him that since she'd been named after his mother, so she instead glanced around the wooded hill. At the bottom of the slope there was the same lake she'd swam in as a child so many times, and right now it held a flotilla of fallen maple leaves, starting to gather in a circle thanks to the wind, the water swirling. The trees were turning early, not a good sign. It had been awhile since they'd had a truly frigid winter by Wisconsin standards.

Mystified, she watched her grandfather tramp between a ridge of white pines and slender birches and followed.

What is this?

Her first glimmer of what was really happening made her stumble over a small rock. She was no longer paying attention to the terrain, her foot sliding on the hill before she caught her balance with one hand behind her, skidding on the fragrant pine needles.

What was in front of her was not a hole. Well, it was, but it was roughly square and reminiscent of something grimmer than that generic label.

The partially revealed outline in the moist soil was of a human skull, and one fragile, broken hand didn't help the situation. The grinning skull had a missing tooth, and a wash of horror swept through her despite a career in law enforcement and experience with more than a few gruesome sights.

Not a hole.

A grave.

"What the hell?" She hadn't meant to blurt that out, especially in front of a man she revered, so the question was quickly amended. Her grandfather was more than a little old-fashioned. "I meant: What on earth? When did you find this?"

"This morning. And I didn't find it."

Her grandfather was breathing heavily enough that she felt a flicker of worry. "Are you all right?"

The nod he gave was curt. "The storm must have washed it out. That rain came through like a runaway locomotive."

No doubt a correct conclusion. When the front swept in, it had arrived with a vengeance as the temperature plummeted a good forty degrees. It would warm up again, but not today.

She certainly felt cold through and through. A frigid droplet trickled down her neck.

"It looks old to me." He stared at the skeleton, but stood a few feet away.

If he meant those brittle bones, it looked 100 percent, extremely dead to her. The age would probably have to be determined by a forensic anthropologist, but impossible to gauge on a wet hillside half covered in dirt.

But definitely in the dead category.

"It obviously isn't new, but old is a relative term. At a glance a buried skeleton is not in your provenance of expertise or mine either, for that matter."

That was putting it mildly. He leaned on a walking stick he often carried but never used. "So, what now?"

The phone call that had summoned her up north hadn't exactly prepared her for this, but he had never been a talkative man, which was why she had dropped everything and made the drive from Wausau where she'd been visiting her sister. Jody had agreed. If Robert MacIntosh called, it was urgent. That he'd specifically asked Ellie to come alone made sense now. If he wanted help, he needed it, and this seemed to bear out that conviction. She managed to ask calmly, "Have you called the police?"

"I called *you*."

"Not quite the same."

He looked at her, his face not precisely amused, but still the corner of his mouth lifted. "You are still a detective for the Milwaukee police, right? Big-city law enforcement. The only person I know who has shot more than one man. So who else should I call? You *are* the police. So technically, I have called them."

The testiness in his voice was a surprise, but maybe he was more rattled than he cared to admit. The reference to two recent cases and the way they'd been handled made her experience a moment of chagrin, but it had been all over the television so she knew he'd heard about it. She didn't really think he was being critical as much as asking for her help in a roundabout way.

It was a little interesting to her they had never discussed what happened. How was that conversation supposed to go anyway? *Hey, Grandpa, did you hear about me shooting a serial killer?*

Not her style, and actually, not really his style either. They were politely close, if such a thing were possible. She adored him, but the affection was implied since he didn't wish to talk about it, so she didn't bring it up.

It was hardly as if she'd never seen a dead body, but the outline of the half-turned skull got to her. It was maybe more the lonely spot and the bleak, gray day. "I am a detective, but this is not my jurisdiction either. How about 911? Lots of people use it, especially when they find the evidence of a crime."

"Do I have evidence of a crime?" The shrug he gave was pragmatic, but she thought he looked a little pale except for his cheeks being reddened by the sharp breeze. "Make them all rush out here for what? There is no one to be saved and it seems to me time doesn't really matter much to those old bones. Waste of tax dollars to have everyone come with screaming ambulances when it is obvious whoever is buried here can't be helped."

There was validity to that logic—though she didn't agree completely. Her job as a homicide detective was to help, even if it was to only obtain justice for the victim. They both stood for a few moments staring at the half-exposed skeleton. "No, he or she can't be saved. I'll concede that."

The trees wept, her coat was soaked, and this situation was beyond the scope of her experience, even as a law-enforcement officer. She was far too used to blood and death, but this was not her usual kind of case.

Not her case at all, in fact.

Ellie let out a slow breath and reminded herself that he was eighty-plus years old and maybe he didn't realize that since she now worked in Milwaukee this was not going to be her investigation. She unclipped her phone from her pocket. "Let me get the sheriff's office and they will have someone here as soon as possible. It will probably be just a deputy at first and then the coroner as soon as he can respond. At that point, they can decide what to do next. I can't really do more than that."

It took two transfers but she finally got through to the correct department once she explained the situation, and the dispatcher promised to send out an officer. Since it wasn't exactly an emergency, Ellie just gently pushed the button on her phone when the call was done and moved a few steps closer. "Any ideas?"

"About what?"

"Who it is?"

Crouching down, her grandfather frowned at the skull as if he could possibly recognize the person, his face pallid in the late afternoon light. "Don't think so. This is land our family has owned for many, many years."

Ellie glanced around and immediately started processing the scene in her mind. It seemed like a strange place to bury a body. On a steep hillside? The slope was at least at a thirty-degree angle. Then again, it wasn't easy to walk on either, so discovery would be unlikely. "You said you didn't find it. Who did?"

"Kid fishing on the lake in a canoe stumbled across the skeleton trying to get off the water as the storm rolled through. Roger Bridges. You've met his parents. Stepped right on it, or so he says. Scared him half to death."

Human remains had a way of doing that to you. She winced inwardly. She believed the part about him taking refuge on the shore, but that Roger had contaminated the scene would not help forensics when the team came in. It looked like maybe he'd cleared away some of the dirt with his hands too, probably because he couldn't quite believe it. "Why didn't *he* call the sheriff's department?"

As if it made perfect sense, her grandfather explained, "Because it is on my property. His folks have a place across the lake. If it hadn't started to rain so hard so fast, he would have gone back to their dock. This is closer. Roger came to the house, and when he told me about it, I really didn't believe him at first either. Told him it must have been a dead deer or something. Once the weather settled down, I came out to look. Then I called you. I knew you would have a handle on how to take care of it."

Exasperated, she searched for something respectful to say. *Take care of it?* That answer was easy. Try calling for local law enforcement, which is what should have been done in the first place.

Her grandfather straightened. "Should we go back to the house? Kind of wet here and I could make a pot of coffee while we wait on them."

"I . . ."

She stopped in the middle of her sentence. Something wasn't quite right.

Just the two of them. The wind eerily rustling the leaves, the water silver and rippling, and a very dead silence.

Ellie thought uneasily: *You aren't surprised enough*.

It wasn't anything in particular, but she knew Robert Lawrence MacIntosh, and she felt it. Part of her job was reading people and it was just *there*.

Whoever lay in that grave, he just wasn't surprised. Felt the need to report it because this kid knew, but really hadn't wanted to call it in.

What the hell?

He stood there, this strong, kind man she'd known ever since the day she was born, his gaze averted as he turned, a lock of white hair blowing across his brow.

Were it anyone—*anyone*—else, she would start a rapid-fire litany of questions, but she found she didn't want to ask them.

"You are a police officer," he said it as if it gave him some sort of anchor. "A detective. When something like this turns up, what happens next?"

The breeze made her shiver almost as much as the sight of those bleached, deserted bones. "When the deputy arrives he'll ask about the victim. Do you know who it could be, that sort of thing."

"Thought that might be it. Then what?"

"They'll exhume the body from the makeshift grave. I predict there will be crime scene techs all over as they look for clues, but it also looks to me, from an inexpert view because I am not a medical examiner, that this body has been there a long, long time, so I doubt they'll find anything. Most of the evidence will have deteriorated."

She stopped, took in a breath. Because she was a police officer, and because this was not just her job but a sudden immediate problem she had never seen popping up on her horizon but was still there, staring her in the face, she weighed her next words. She tended to try to meet problems head on. "As I said, they are going to ask you, so let me ask first. Do you know who this might be?"

"I can't say that I do."

But he didn't look her directly in the eye as he spoke. Instead he gazed out over the rippling water of the gray lake.

Dear God, one of the people she respected most in the world was lying to her.

She remarked very quietly, "I would love a cup of coffee."

Detective Jason Santiago had been out of uniform for years now, but the rhythm of it came back naturally.

Officer Danni Crawford got the message from dispatch just as she was pulling out of the parking lot where she'd answered her last call, which proved to be simply a report on an unruly customer at a pharmacy. The man could not get his Schedule 2 meds filled for a few days and was starting to feel the pangs of withdrawal from a very strong narcotic if his erratic behavior was an indication. A few words with him and looking into those bloodshot eyes, Jason was reminded how little he liked the ramifications of addiction. The unruly customer was convinced finally that screaming at the pharmacist was not going to get him anywhere but into a jail cell and he'd left peacefully enough.

Job done. Problem solved, at least to the extent that Crawford did not have to haul anyone off in cuffs. Jason, just along for the ride because he was still officially on medical leave, was amused when she pleasantly asked the manager of the store—who was hovering uneasily and was the one who had called the police—who the hell thought twenty-four-hour places that could dispense narcotics were a good idea?

Corporate, he'd answered. Truthfully, he looked tired with his rumpled shirt and askew tie. Then he added, "And I couldn't agree more with you, Officer."

She wasn't enthusiastic about her reassignment to this late shift, but beggars really couldn't afford to be choosers she told Jason as they went out to get back into the squad car. Promotions required sacrifice.

"Don't I know it." Recently he'd taken two bullets in the line of duty.

Danni shot him a sidelong look as she started the vehicle. "Yeah, I guess you do."

She was pretty enough, brown hair, pulled back at

the moment in a no-nonsense ponytail because she was on the job. Danni was a little overweight, but there was nothing wrong with something a man could hold on to was always his attitude. Besides, though he doubted many people would believe it, he valued personality above physical beauty and she was, in short, a nice girl and a good cop.

Her radio sputtered and she answered.

The dispatcher said urgently without a hint of the usual boredom, "We've got a shooting and we think there's possibly an officer down. The phones are lighting up. How close are you to KK?"

KK meant Kinnickinnic Avenue. Jason's heart rate shot up. *Officer down*. Close, but it was a fairly long street . . . *officer down*?

"Minutes away," Crawford said, her voice catching. "What do we have?"

"Shots fired at what seems like a routine traffic stop. We aren't sure what happened, but we need as many officers to respond as quickly as possible."

It was a Saturday, and the street would be busy. "Give me the address. I'm close. I'm already driving."

Maybe it was just as well Jason had asked, out of sheer boredom, if he could ride along.

KK had recently become retro chic and there were nice but quirky restaurants and little shops where tourists and locals browsed. The sound of sirens shrieked everywhere as they sped along and it wasn't hard to figure out exactly where they needed to be.

The man sprawled in the street in a spreading pool of blood was definitely in uniform, his hat lying a few feet away, one arm flung out, the other limp at his side. His patrol car was parked, but the door was still open.

"Oh God." Danni's voice echoed horror. "Jason, oh God. I think it's Chad."

She didn't quite get the car in park before she was out and running. He did it for her, feeling the jerk as the transmission locked, a chill creeping over his skin.

She shouldered her way through the crowd, Jason following, and knelt by the side of the fallen officer. With shaking hands she sought a pulse as the sirens neared.

Jason also recognized him with a shock that froze his muscles.

No ambulance with even the most skilled emergency personnel was going to save him, he realized, looking down at his still face. The man was dead.

And Chad Brown and Danni had dated, for what? Four years now?

Jason reached down and touched her shoulder. "Hey."

Danni started trembling uncontrollably. She crawled to the curb and vomited, her body reacting to her emotions so powerfully she couldn't help it.

This is not happening, Jason thought numbly.

Chad Brown. Jesus, it *was* Chad.

Danni and Chad had never said they were serious, but Jason had seen firsthand how comfortable they were with each other. Lovers, friends, colleagues . . .

As she dropped her head, probably to keep from passing out, in the distance, someone said, "Ma'am—Officer—you okay?"

"I've got this." Jason's voice was curt but he was

hurting too, in shock, a little paralyzed by what had happened. "Hey, hold on. Come on, Danni, he'd want you to keep it together."

"I know." She wiped her mouth with the back of her hand and sat up, but she was starkly pale and trembling.

Definitely not fit to be in charge. He said quietly, "Stay here. This is a homicide anyway. Let me handle it. Right?"

He did. Producing his badge—no one needed to know he wasn't officially on duty—firing off questions about witnesses, directing the other officers arriving on the scene to look for casings in the street, ostensibly taking over even though he really didn't have the authority at the moment, but someone needed to besides the pale-faced officer who had just emptied her stomach into the gutter.

She crawled back to the body and touched Chad's face.

When she looked up, her face was streaked with tears. "I've been trying to drop the weight, you know? I kept telling him no engagement until I lose twenty pounds. He always said he loved me just the way I am. To stop worrying about it so much. Why did I worry?"

Man, if there was anything he was bad at, it was a moment like this. Jason crouched down next to her and said the most profound thing he could think of.

"Whoever did this is fucking going down."

Chapter 2

The creak gave away there was someone on the stairs. It must have because she heard the movement above as the bedsprings groaned, and then the sound of feet on the floorboards.

The electricity was out, but that happened often enough this time of year and she had a kerosene lamp. There was dark, and then there was the utter black of the north woods on a night with no moon. Later she would light it, but for now she was content with the darkness. It served her purpose well.

Utterly still and pressed against the wall, she strained to hear.

Her fingers gripped the knife so tightly her hand began to ache.

The room was dead silent. Not even the rustle of a piece of paper.

Chief of police Joe Metzger said slowly, "These are the events as we know them. Officer Chad Brown stepped out of the vehicle with the intent to approach on what he called in as a speeding stop. The driver didn't move but the passenger engaged, getting out even after being asked to stay seated, and he hit Brown with three rounds to the chest before the officer could even draw his weapon. At this point, our perpetrator apparently got back into the vehicle and they drove away."

Lieutenant Carl Grasso asked neutrally, "Witnesses?"

"We have a description of the vehicle from a person who was passing in the other direction, but that's about it. A lot of people heard the shots and ran to look, but when I say fleeting, I mean fleeting. It was a flash in the night. Brown had called in the stop, but the car didn't have plates, and obviously there was no chance to get the registration. Beige doesn't really give us a lot to go on."

Ellie frowned. The shooting was all over the news, but this was the first chance she'd had to hear details from an accurate source. "What about ballistics?"

"We rushed it through. It's inconclusive that it is exactly the same gun, but it is the same caliber as the last one anyway. A .45 Glock. I don't like the pattern similarities."

"Second cop hit in two weeks." Grasso didn't precisely smile but his mouth curved in an ironic arch. He was in his early forties, a touch of gray at the temples, his history with the Milwaukee PD not exactly pristine. Once upon a time he'd been the division's most successful homicide detective until he'd been transferred to vice for a suspicious incident. He'd recently been temporarily reassigned as Ellie's new partner and she wasn't positive she was thrilled about it. He asked in a cynical tone, "Coincidence?"

Metzger shook his head, but then he sighed and rubbed his cheek, slumping in the chair behind his desk. The chief was thickly built, a former marine who rarely cut anyone slack, and a decent politician. Ellie liked him with certain limitations. He didn't handle media attention too well. It annoyed him, and it showed. He was no-nonsense, and abrupt if pushed, which was fine with her. She preferred the real deal to the smooth-over.

He said shortly, "A fluke, not a hit, if I had to call it, but I don't know. That's why we are having this meeting, just the three of us. I want to think I'm just fishing around. Maybe it is just two incidents that happened and are not at all related."

Now that is interesting.

"I'd like to believe you're right, but I have an ugly feeling this is a vendetta." Grasso wore a thousand-dollar suit and a skeptical smile. He had his own money and didn't do the job for the salary, so the clothes didn't make the man necessarily. As of yet, Ellie hadn't decided how she felt about him.

As distrustful as she was of Grasso, she had the same feeling about a possible revenge scenario. "We've had a department-wide very high mortality rate for the past two years, sir. I mean one of the highest in the nation. Might even get us first prize in a contest we never wanted to enter, much less win. We need to look at it."

"Could be inside." Grasso's voice was even and pragmatic.

She didn't agree. "Give me one solid reason why someone with the metro MPD would want to kill off random officers. Or better yet, give me something to connect the cases."

Metzger placed his hands on the blotter in front of him, his chair creaking as he leaned forward. "Honestly, I know all the officers under my command pretty well and some of them better than pretty well, and I can't see this is inside. That means it is *outside,* and we need to stop it right now. Cop killers are like suicide bombers—they just don't care or they wouldn't do it. If we catch them, they are going down, and they know it. When you have nothing to lose, you don't *care* who you hurt. But it is well-known Fielding and Brown were friends. So we have two officers taken out under similar, albeit not identical, circumstances, and they are closely connected to each other. It makes me nervous. Do you know why? Because I don't think the usual criminals concern themselves with the social habits of their targets. It just seems likely to me one of two things happened, and I don't like either option. Care to hear them?"

Ellie would have pointed out that suicide bombers killed random people and perhaps this particular person was targeting cops, but she didn't open her mouth. Grasso could be right.

There were times when it was better to sit back and stay quiet. "Yes, Sir."

"Our first casualty was killed at home and off-duty. Whoever broke in shot him execution style and did not kill his wife or his son." Grasso looked thoughtful. "He was undoubtedly the target, and whoever pulled off the hit did it smoothly and with a professional edge. The shooting last night was just as clean. Fast, probably planned, and they were out of there before we could as much as blink. Organized crime?"

They were still getting a measure of each other, but Ellie had learned Carl wasn't shy about his opinions. Maybe she liked that, and maybe she didn't.

Chief Metzger didn't seem to agree. "Carl, it doesn't feel right. This is my concern. They were both involved in something, and it got them killed."

"I never got that from either of them," Grasso objected.

"Neither did I. That brings up my second concern."

They spoke like two longtime friends and she wasn't in the club.

"Which is?"

"One of them got the other one killed in some way. What if the information came from one of us?"

"A police officer?" she interjected.

Metzger rubbed his forehead. "I don't know. Carl is right on both counts about Fielding and Brown. I'd prefer if you proved me right about it being outside, but most of all, just come up with something we can work with, okay? I don't want to hear on the national news that Milwaukee has a cop killer on the loose."

Ellie couldn't help it, she had to ask. "Is there some reason we are being given this case?"

And the private briefing?

"You aren't being given this case. I assigned Hamish and Rays."

She had to admit, she was a little confused and it must have showed.

The chief blew out a frustrated breath. "Here it is in a nutshell, MacIntosh. You haven't been with the department long enough to have a personal vendetta, and Carl knows exactly how to investigate something like this." His smile was thin. "Let me put it this way; I trust *you* to make sure he toes the line, and I trust *him* to babysit you through the process of an unofficial internal affairs investigation. No one gets a whisper of what was just said in this room, and I want it settled fast and quiet. You report only to me, and you work your other cases as usual. This is extra duty; I am not going to deny it. You'll have to operate under the radar of everyone else in this precinct."

Grasso stood. "I'm more than fine with it."

Well, shit. No pressure.

"Me too." She nodded. What else was she supposed to say?

"Okay," Metzger said, his expression strained. "Just do me a favor and catch these sons of bitches quietly and quickly." He didn't bother to say good-bye, just left the room abruptly.

They walked out together, the hallway long and empty, though there were a few detectives still at their desks.

This wasn't a complication she needed. The call from Metzger had come at an especially bad time; she'd had to leave before the coroner had finished the initial examination of the lakeside grave. It wasn't like there was anything she could do in an official capacity, but she had worked up north before taking the job in homicide in Milwaukee, and even though her grand-father's property wasn't in the same county as her former department, she knew some of the officers.

What the hell was going on up there?

For that matter, what the hell is going on down here?

Grasso asked neutrally, "Should we go talk about this?"

What she really needed to do was call her grand-father.

Damn.

Quite frankly, the last thing she wanted was for her partner to get wind of the investigation up north, especially when she had no idea what to make of it herself.

The math was fairly simple. One skeleton on her grandfather's property, no suspects, and no leads . . .

But still . . . there was now a cop killer evidently on the loose—or maybe the killings weren't necessarily connected until it could be proved otherwise.

So she equivocated. "I've got something personal to handle. How about tomorrow? It's getting late and I drove down all the way from Oneida County for this meeting."

"We have a few issues to discuss, not the least of which is how we are going to handle this investigation quickly. We worked pretty well together on the Burner case. Let me buy you dinner, okay?"

Dinner out with Carl Grasso? No. She wasn't at all in the mood to go someplace with the bustle of people everywhere, but maybe he was right, they needed to at least discuss strategy.

Last she knew, Bryce was making lasagna. She drew

on the advantages of knowing she had a hands-down good dinner waiting. At the moment she didn't even want to think about whatever was in that grave.

It wasn't impossible. She *could* handle these two situations at once.

Or at least she hoped so, but she couldn't handle sitting in a noisy restaurant trying not to worry.

So she asked abruptly, "Do you like Italian food?"

He shrugged. "My last name speaks for itself. What do you think?"

That actually won him a small smile. He was right; stupid question. "If we need to talk, I agree, let's do it over dinner," she said in resignation. "I appreciate the offer to go out, but I prefer a quiet table to a busy restaurant, and quite frankly, I've had an interesting day. If you want antipasti, stop and buy some. I'm officially inviting you to dinner."

"Your place? Okay."

"Not exactly."

Grasso looked amused. "Where?"

"I'll text you the address."

"Wine?"

"Absolutely."

"Sounds good."

She reached for her purse and slung it over her shoulder. "Eight o'clock."

Chapter 3

It was much more than she expected.

The fear evaporated during the act, like a vanishing fog once the decision had been made. It was eerie, as if she could see beyond herself, beyond the moment, to when it would be over, resolved in her mind, settled in the most definitive way possible.

She'd lifted the knife, and then lifted it again, and again . . .

Her hands were absolutely steady when she poured kerosene into the lamp from the can, and lit it.

Carnage.

Blood was everywhere. Bedding, floor, even some splattered on the window, running down in gruesome crimson tributaries. When she'd sensed it was over, when the resistance faded, she'd kept on, but she wasn't sure why. Now the knife was on the floor but she couldn't for the life of her remember dropping it. Her *dress was drenched, the feeling warm and the copper smell cloying. Oddly she welcomed it even as she realized she hadn't planned for it. Her clothes were ruined. She would have to burn them.*

But she was done and it was finished.

The grocery store was crowded, but he hardly noticed.

Distracted, Carl Grasso got a basket, tossed in a loaf of French bread, and thought about two murdered cops and a possible connection.

Why?

He picked up kalamata olives, roasted red peppers, balls of mozzarella, and some salami for the suggested antipasti. His mother had served it often, especially at parties. He remembered his childhood very clearly— like a movie that played in his mind. Nice house because his parents did well, pool out back, which made him a popular kid, and he'd remembered grade school and high school with a sort of nostalgic acceptance of the privilege of it all. His parents had been very much in love with each other, and in retrospect, maybe it was just as well they died together. He couldn't imagine one living without the other.

Balance, he'd learned, was everything.

A little tap on the shoulder to remind him of that fact might be in order, Carl thought as he studied a rack of red wines, settling on a bottle of Chianti. The temporary reassignment to homicide as MacIntosh's partner was a gift, and he needed to treat it as such, so he also needed to do the job with speed and precision.

However it all had played out, he had one true gift.

In his mind's eye, he wondered if he already understood this killer to a certain extent.

He'd always been able to do just that.

It scared him little it came that easy, but there was *the* reason he was a very good cop. He really could think like a criminal if he needed to, and never more than right now.

"Excuse me."

"No problem." He glanced back and stepped aside for an attractive, dark-haired young woman who smiled at him apologetically and gestured toward the stack of cheeses, realizing he'd been standing there absentmindedly, basket over his arm, blocking her view.

As usual, he was still thinking about the case.

Killing a cop; bad idea. Killing two? Double trouble. Life without parole if convicted. Wisconsin didn't stick a needle in your arm, but neither did the state smile upon murder of its law-enforcement personnel. Big risks, both killings, but well planned.

The woman lingered, and she sent him a sidelong glance and smiled again. "Do you know anything about cheese? I'm supposed to bring some to a party and I haven't a clue. I know it is a sin in this state, but when it comes to anything that says processed cheese food, I am an expert. Otherwise, not so much. All cheese wisdom is welcome."

Carl laughed. She had warm brown eyes, nice smooth skin, and wore formfitting jeans and a soft sweater over a T-shirt. College student maybe . . . she had that fresh look, as if the world hadn't quite let her know yet that it could be a very, very bad place.

Too young for him. He was forty-two, she was

maybe mid-twenties, but he wasn't immune to the slightly flirtatious way she was looking at him.

He asked, "What kind of party? Something given by one of the faculty so you need to impress?"

The look slid into a surprised stare. "As a matter of fact, yes, something just like that. A cocktail party given by the dean. You a mind reader or just a really good guesser? I'm a graduate student."

"The way you dress, the bracelet"—he pointed at the band around her wrist—"and the processed cheese all gave it away. Only starving college students eat that crap. Not to mention that you have a backpack instead of a purse in your cart."

"Most people aren't that observant."

"But I am not most people. Back to the problem at hand." He turned to the deli case. "Let's see. The water crackers, definitely. And the Brie. This one." He selected one that was just on the edge of being too soft, which meant it was perfect. "It breaks the bank a little, but you are out to impress, right? This English double-sharp cheddar layered with Stilton is another one that does not come with a foil wrapper around it in a box, and I promise, you will get raves. It isn't cheap either, but a little goes a long way. Hope that helps."

"It does. Thank you." Then she said facetiously, "Any thoughts on what I should wear?"

Good question. It gave him permission to do a slow perusal of what was a very nice figure. "I'm pretty sure you can choose whatever you want and wow them. The shorter the skirt the better. I'm a leg man."

"Thank you again." She held out her hand and there was a hint of a blush in her cheeks. "I'm Lindsey."

He shook it. "Carl."

"Nice to meet you." She gazed at him curiously. "You were pretty deep in thought there a minute or so ago and that is one very nice suit. Now it is my turn. Lawyer?"

"No, I'm a lieutenant with the Milwaukee Police Department. And if you are wondering what I was thinking about, I was wondering what would make you kill a cop, much less kill two."

Her eyes widened. "Oh . . . okay. I guess I see that now. I saw on the news . . . it's terrible. No wonder you were a little distracted. You don't have the safest job in the world, do you?"

"Police officer? No."

"But you make a difference."

The vote of confidence was appreciated, but he had his moments when he wondered. The place hummed around them with the sound of carts being pushed and elevator music. He smiled without humor. "Why *specifically* kill a cop?" Staring at a display of Dutch cheeses made from sheep's milk, he came up with nothing. The purpose was out there but he hadn't stumbled across it yet. The perpetrator was determined but not vicious. Vicious would also have killed the first victim's wife and child as they slept, but Fielding's wife and son were still alive.

No. This one was in control, and yet with a specific goal in mind.

He was getting lost in the case again and Lindsey was still right there, gazing expectantly at him as if he was supposed to say something else. He gave it a shot. "But pretty girls going to a party don't want to talk about murder."

Except one pretty woman, who wanted very much to talk about murder.

MacIntosh tended to be aloof, and to be truthful, he didn't mind that at all. He knew he had a reputation for being distant himself.

Beyond a shadow of a doubt, if this case was solved quickly and it even partially involved him, he could be back on homicide for good. He probably needed to get going.

"It was nice to meet you, Lindsey." Carl turned away toward the check stands.

She stopped him with a hand on his sleeve. "Hey . . . this is kind of impulsive, I know, and maybe you're busy, but the party is tomorrow night. Any chance you're free?"

"I doubt it." He thought about two dead cops. "I'm sorry."

"Well, here's my number, just in case." She reached into the backpack and tore off a slip of paper, and then rummaged for a pen with a playful smile. "For the record, I like older men. Give me a call."

If she could be impulsive, apparently so could he, for he took one of his cards from his pocket and handed to her in exchange for the slip of paper. "Maybe we can get together for a drink sometime."

The house smelled fantastic, like oregano and garlic and rich tomato sauce, but Ellie knew her appetite was going to be sketchy at best.

Bryce Grantham was intuitive, and that was good, but it could be a problem too. He took one look at her face as she walked into the kitchen and faintly raised his brows. "Wine?"

"I'd kill for a glass."

"No such extreme measures necessary. I opened a bottle about ten minutes ago when I got your message. So," he said in his calm way, "you came back early. Your text said something about a second homicide."

Or a third if the skeleton on the hill counted. Not connected, but all in her proverbial lap.

Hell yes to that glass of wine. Thoughtfully he'd set out two glasses, but they would need a third, though she hadn't informed him of that yet. She poured a Pinot Noir generously, and took a sip as he watched her with a slightly puzzled expression.

"Mind clueing me in?"

He had positively the sexiest eyes she'd ever seen. Dark, intense, and at the moment openly inquiring.

Ellie set her wineglass on the table and adjusted it with a careless rotation of her fingers. "We had a special meeting called. Metzger wanted me there."

"About?"

"The shooting of a patrol officer yesterday evening."

"I don't think I realized that had happened."

She shouldn't be surprised. He spent a great deal of time designing computer software, which was his job, and the rest of almost every waking moment working on a novel that he admitted was his real dream.

Right. She understood. When she moved to Milwaukee in the spring she'd made one of her dreams of becoming a homicide detective come true as well, but it was about as different as night from day. Bryce Grantham—Dr. Bryce Grantham—had a Ph.D. in literature, and she often wondered if two people could be more different. Her dream involved tracking down killers. His involved a literary novel about a family in the mountains of West Virginia.

Not quite the same thing.

And he was the only male she knew who did not watch much television. No ESPN or any of the usual suspects.

"We are wondering if it might be connected to another homicide involving a police officer that happened just a short time ago, but not sure. I hope you don't mind, but Lieutenant Grasso might join us for dinner so we can talk it over."

"Might, or is?"

She had to smile reluctantly. "Okay, fine, I invited him. Sorry. I should have called first but he wanted to go out so we could discuss the case, and I am really not in the mood for a crowded restaurant. I knew you already were fixing dinner. *Do* you mind?"

He moved easily between the oven and the polished counter, lifting his shoulders in a negligent shrug. "Since you and I couldn't possibly eat an entire pan of lasagna it's fine with me. Besides," he added with absolutely no inflection, "I wouldn't mind meeting the competition."

Ellie had to admit to a certain sense of consternation. She stopped, arrested with her glass halfway to her mouth. "What? I hardly know him."

His smile was rueful. "I'm starting to get the give and take of our relationship and no matter how I look at it, there are going to be other men in your life who play a pretty powerful role. It is an interesting dichotomy. I want them there, and yet I don't. Explain to me who is more important than the person who might just save your life? We all don't play on the same field. I wouldn't mind taking a look and seeing if Metzger made a good choice. I hope Grasso is trustworthy."

Ellie quirked a brow, amused and a little touched. "You think you'll be able to judge that better than the chief of police in a major city?"

Bryce flipped on the oven light and peered through the window in the door. "I think I'll be able to judge it better when it comes to *you*. As a citizen I certainly can't say I don't care about his abilities as a police officer—I want him to be out there doing his thing, hands down—but I am more interested in discerning if I trust him with your well-being."

"Maybe. But he isn't 'the competition.'"

He straightened, picked up a head of garlic from a small bowl on the counter, peeled away the paper, and set two cloves onto the cutting board. Taking the broad side of his knife, he smashed them. "Really? He'll be spending more time with you than I will."

Their love affair was a little one-sided if she counted the hours she spent at work, but then again, not everyone had the advantage of being able to work from home like he did. Neither did they officially live together yet, but she had the feeling that was the next, cautious step. Bryce, once divorced, wasn't pushing, and that was fine with her, because she still was adjusting to her move down south to an entirely different environment.

In the end, they'd both made concessions, but neither one was used to it. Ellie got out the plates and rummaged in the drawer where he kept the cloth napkins. "This isn't a job interview."

"Let's face it, it's a pretty intimate relationship. I wasn't all that excited about Jason Santiago either. Remember?"

Her former partner had been shot in the line of duty during their last case, which involved a series of murders and arson. Grasso was his replacement until Santiago returned from medical leave.

"I remember." Rain touched the window with a muted sound as Ellie unrolled the place mats and then set out the plates, trying to figure out how to respond. "*You* have an ex-wife."

"Guilty as charged."

"I suppose I'll always be a little bit jealous of her."

Understatement. It cost to admit it too. Suzanne Colgan-Grantham was not her favorite person.

"I can't see why, since we can hardly speak two civil sentences to each other."

She carefully placed a fork on a napkin. "You *chose* her. I didn't choose either Santiago or Grasso."

"I still maintain your relationship with both of them is very close and requires an inordinate amount of trust."

"And I maintain that this particular discussion has no purpose."

He laughed at that. "Point taken. Fine." Then he sobered. "I'll be very polite to Lt. Grasso. Something else is bothering you anyway. Care to share?"

How the hell does he know . . .

"A lot is bothering me. What makes you think it isn't him and that crazy person out there killing police officers?" She was curious and disconcerted.

"Ellie." His tone held reproof.

Okay, fine, he *knew* her. It wasn't fair to have an argument just because she was worried.

"My grandfather called while I was at Jody's house. He insisted that I come to his lake property at once. There was something in his voice . . . I went."

"Is everything okay?"

"I have no idea. He found a grave and I assume he spent a great deal of the day knee-deep in sheriff's deputies."

For dramatic effect, she could win an award. Bryce stopped and stared, his expression reflecting shock. "What? Did you just say a grave?"

Ellie took a little pity and explained. "There were some bones on the hillside. It didn't take much to see it was a grave of some sort, but without forensic input it's very difficult to tell if they were five months old or had been there for a hundred years. Understandably, he was shaken and I helped him by calling the local sheriff's department. At this time we have no idea who it could be."

"I think I can see why you've been so remote since you came home."

"This isn't my home."

The words just came out and she didn't mean to

say them so frankly, she just was having one hell of a day.

Bryce took a second to process after that comment. He said mildly after a moment, "If you ever want it to *be* your home, we can discuss that, but in the meantime, when is our guest arriving?"

"Eight."

"Let me put in the garlic bread."

Bryce never fought. He didn't operate that way, which, in her opinion, was why his marriage to an attorney failed so miserably.

She was worried that a cop wouldn't work out all that much for him either. That was also as close to an official invitation that had ever been offered for her to move in. Maybe they *would* discuss it later, but meanwhile she had three dead bodies to help find justice for, which might be too little too late, but was *something* or else her job was pointless.

He slid a foil-wrapped loaf of bread from the refrigerator and put it into the oven, then looked at her. "This is bizarre. Any idea who it could be?"

"No, I sure don't."

"Hasn't your family owned that property for a long time?"

"Yes. Over half a century."

"Surely there is a frame of reference then. It obviously happened before the property was sold to your grandfather."

Grasso would be there in ten minutes, tops, and she didn't want to discuss this in front of him. "Without a clear time of death how can you speculate on that? Before or after, I don't know. That spot is kind of remote."

"I suppose you can't, but you've been to more than a few crime scenes and if the grave isn't fresh, that means it is old."

He was right. Nothing wholesome about the location. There was too much of a hint of homicide about—the skeleton and the water-soaked hole that had washed clean except for those bleached bones . . .

"Pretty old, I'm guessing," she conceded, "though I'm hardly a medical examiner and I didn't dig it up or anything. Maybe they'll find something to identify the victim. Scraps of clothing or buttons to indicate the time period."

As usual, Bryce could sense her discomfort. He said in an infuriatingly calm voice, "Ellie, people die. It happens now, and when it happened way back years and years ago, sometimes they were just buried. This could be nothing."

"No gravestone. They didn't do that often."

"Gravestones were a luxury at one time. Yes, they did it now and then."

True, but . . . She should never say this to another human being, yet Ellie took in a breath and then blurted out, "I think *he* knows who it is."

"Your grandfather?"

"Yes, Bryce, who the hell else? Robert Lawrence MacIntosh."

"Why? I thought you just said he had no idea."

"That is what he told me."

"You think he wasn't being truthful?"

The lasagna smelled really fantastic, perfuming the whole room. She controlled the impulse to be short, which Bryce didn't deserve just because she was distraught over a family issue. "I just feel something is off. And yes, people die and are buried, but usually not without a coffin on a hillside in an unmarked, shallow grave."

"That's a valid point."

"Thank you."

"Sarcasm is a must?"

"You act as if—" she stopped and reminded herself that this was her problem, not his. Taking another controlling breath, she said much more calmly, "I am going to recant my former statement and say that I didn't like how he acted when he showed me the grave. Can we at least concede I make my living by reading not just facts but people?" She swiped her hand through her hair. "Look, he didn't act right. Bad English, I know, but accurate. Can you cut me some slack here?"

"I will always cut you slack. You need look no further." He said it matter-of-factly, as if he hadn't just offered her a promise very few human beings gave each other. The hell of it was she thought he meant it. "So what felt so off-key?"

She looked toward the window, her voice hollow. "He always told me I should tell the truth even if I didn't like the consequences. I don't think he was following that particular rule. I have absolutely no reason on the face of his green earth to believe he would ever, ever lie to me, but I think he did."

Casting back, she recalled grandfather's inability to

look her in the eye. Were he less honest, there would be no problem.

Some people were not cut out to be criminals.

Others were.

The doorbell chimed.

Chapter 4

*K*illing wasn't the hardest part.

The shovel had been at the back of the shed and difficult to find, as she'd been trying to do it all in the wisp of a dawn that threaded the sky with ruby and pale white as the sun struggled to overcome the night.

The body was much heavier than expected, and even wrapped in a bed sheet, there was still a sickening trail of blood on the stairs. Literally a dead weight, it had to be taken out and buried. Planning for that hadn't been done well.

Sweating and breathing hard, finally she'd decided on the wheelbarrow, tipping it forward and righting it after two tries before pushing it down the lane.

Toward the hill.

The lake would be perfect, but the body would surface, she knew that. An old man had drowned in the *river near town last year. It was thought he was prob ably drunk, but no one could find him until the corpse had lodged under the bridge three days later and the police determined he'd been shot and robbed.*

All those stab wounds . . . no, it wasn't worth risking.

She had someone to protect besides herself.

Carl arrived a few minutes late.

Punctuality was important to him, but then again, he hadn't planned on chatting with a pretty girl in the supermarket either.

What a nice distraction and a legitimate excuse.

He recognized the upscale neighborhood. Some of his parents' friends had lived nearby he realized as he berthed his expensive sedan behind an equally pricey SUV. Nice big house, huge grassy lawn, mature trees.

Ellie MacIntosh didn't live here. He'd already gotten her address—and driven by it because he was into details—a generic condo she only rented, but public records indicated she owned her house up north, and given the economy, it wasn't surprising she hadn't sold it yet.

So this pricey place must belong to Grantham, at one time suspected of being the most vicious killer alive in the state of Wisconsin. He'd been in some pretty prestigious company, Carl thought as he got out of the car and slammed the door. Jeffery Dahmer and Ed Gein were hard acts to follow.

To be honest, given his own history, Carl could

hardly fault her for what might seem like a questionable career choice. He'd stepped over the line and he
would never—not ever—admit or apologize for it.

"Lieutenant." She came to the doorway and inclined her blond head. She didn't fit the part of a homicide detective in his mind, but seemed to do the job
competently. An interesting partner for sure. In every
single way she held a knife to his balls. Not her doing, but the MPD wanted to know if he was fit to
play with others again, and she would be the one re-
porting to the chief.

So he'd enter the game.

"Detective." He held up the red wine by the neck of
the bottle. "I come bearing gifts."

"My favorite kind of visitor." She stepped back, but
they were still wary of each other—of that he had no
illusions. Maybe he didn't even blame her.

"Please come in."

He glanced around the two-story foyer and murmured, "Nice."

"Not mine, but thank you. This way."

Suspicion confirmed. He was, after all, a detective.

Leather couches, some scattered dark tables . . .
probably not her choice, but Carl noted it as he followed her into what proved to be a large kitchen that
reflected the same masculine taste with poured cement
countertops and polished floors. A dark-haired man
was chopping vegetables on a wooden board and he
stopped and lifted the knife. "Hi, Bryce Grantham. I'd
shake your hand, but you'd smell like onions for a
week."

When he indicated the scattering of peppers and

tomatoes, Carl simply smiled in polite acknowledgment. "No problem. Thanks for having me."

"So you are Lieutenant Grasso." Grantham flicked him another glance as he deftly chopped an onion.

Definitely assessing.

"And you are Grantham."

"Both infamous," Ellie said dryly, deftly peeling off the foil over the top of the wine. "The two of you can skip the male posturing, okay? Please tell me this won't be the most uncomfortable dinner ever. I've had a long day."

Now *that* was frank.

Carl watched her quick, efficient movements. "I will endeavor to be on my best behavior."

MacIntosh was more delicate than the robust women he usually was attracted to. Maybe it was his Italian heritage, but he wanted a woman who would maybe take a swing at him if she was really mad, but . . . he really admired the compelling color of her hazel eyes.

"Santiago called me."

His brows rose. "How is he doing?"

The cork popped out and she reached for a glass, pouring the wine without letting it breathe. "Doing well but his convalescence is getting to him. He was riding around apparently with one of the patrol officers who answered the call when Brown was shot."

"Metzger didn't mention that," Carl said.

"I get the impression the chief doesn't know," Ellie lightly rubbed her forehead as if she might have a headache. "I wondered how Santiago was going to handle being off the job once he started to feel better. The officer is a friend from his days in uniform."

"Well, that's kind of an interesting twist. Quite frankly, I wasn't aware Santiago had friends."

"I realize he can be abrasive, but he's an excellent cop." MacIntosh said it sharply.

Santiago had saved her life. No wonder she defended him. Actually, Carl *liked* that she defended her partner, considering he currently held that position.

"Having met him only briefly, I can state unequivocally that he is a very blunt man." Grantham reached for a platter in an overhead cupboard. Carl approved of the kitchen. Functional and yet stylish and modern. Maybe he should redesign his house again. He had the money, just not the inclination.

He said neutrally, "Knowing that, it seems like Santiago might well be a good source for the investigation. It's a place to start. Whether they like him or not—and my impression is some do and some don't—he knows everyone in the department."

Ellie handed him a glass. "The wine has a nice bouquet, by the way. Thanks. Have a seat and go on. I am not quite sure how we are supposed to handle this. I can't see how we can ask a bunch of questions without word getting around pretty fast."

Grantham just looked resigned at the conversation, which didn't surprise Carl all that much. He'd seen that same expression before. Police officers were not necessarily the best choice in lovers.

She must be worth it.

He found Ellie intriguing too, but that didn't matter. She was clearly involved with someone else.

"Not everyone joins the force as a detective like

you did." He smiled ironically and took a sip, choosing a chair at a table set for three. The wine *was* nice; smooth and rich. "You know that. Jason just moved up a little quicker than some others."

"He seems like a survivor."

That was true enough. If the world was coming to an end, Carl would want Jason Santiago at his back. He gazed at her across the table. "I'm being serious. My first idea is that we go talk to him. Someone shot him in the chest, but his brain works just fine. He might remember something we can use. He would know, for instance, if anyone had a beef with Brown or Fielding."

"At least that is a game plan." She nodded. "I wonder about the first killing. It bothers me more . . . sometimes officers on patrol get shot—not as often as some people might think, but it happens. What doesn't happen is that someone breaks into your house and executes you in your sleep."

"I couldn't agree more." He gazed at her, feeling like he always did, that he should never be sitting and enjoying a glass of wine when there were mysteries in this world like the one they were discussing that needed his attention.

"I say after dinner maybe we pay Santiago a visit and see how he's doing."

He did three push-ups and then gave up, knowing he was skirting the edge because he'd warned about doing too much too fast . . . this rehab crap was killing him. Jason wandered to the sliding doors that led to his balcony and looked out, seeing the empty pool below. The cover was on, and it looked dingy under the security lights. Just after Labor Day. Pool closed for the year.

Depressing, he decided, though he could have sworn that just this past July, all the little kids swimming there, splashing around and screaming at the top of their lungs, had annoyed him.

Actually, they hadn't, he had to acknowledge. He'd liked the noise and laughter. What *really* annoyed him was not being in action.

Someone was killing cops. He wanted to know why.

The first case had caught his attention—of course. The officer's name was David Fielding. Young, still on the street, and squeaky clean as far as everyone knew. He'd make no apologies for how police officers reacted to one of their own going down—hey, it was a dangerous job and if everyone deserved protection, so did those who offered it. They put up their lives as an offering to society, and when they were taken, it was a big deal.

So some nut job breaks into an officer's house and kills him . . . not perfect in an imperfect world. It had all earmarks of a professional hit, and everyone in the department had been stunned.

The second killing set off all kinds of bells and whistles.

First of all, Jason knew the guy really well. He didn't have a lot of buddies—some, but he spent most of his time on the job—but Chad had qualified as a friend. They used to go and grab a few beers and play some pool now and then. When he started dating Danni, Jason had been happy for them both.

The other night had been pretty immediate, and not in a good way.

Every once in a while cops lost it. They all were, after all, human beings. But Danni had really come apart at the seams and he'd been glad that at least he'd been there to help until other units arrived. Calmly interviewing possible witnesses while her lover lay in a pool of blood was not possible.

The wounds drove him up the wall, itching and nagging him half to death. He paced the balcony in a way he was sure gave his neighbors pause, but he couldn't help it. The confinement was sending him over an unknown edge he didn't know existed. When he'd first come home from the hospital he'd been pretty weak and sore still, content to sit around and watch cable and DVDs as the pain meds had kept him pretty mellow. But he was paranoid about addiction—he'd seen way too much of that during his time on the street and he'd weaned himself off as soon as possible.

All he wanted was for the doctor to sign off so he could go back to the precinct, even if it was desk duty.

The inactivity was worse than the wounds.

A sound registered even as he moodily leaned on the railing and he realized it was his cell phone, sitting in on the coffee table. He moved to get it, stifling a wince—the push-ups *had* been a bad idea—and looked at the display.

MacIntosh calling. Really?

"Well, fuck me, if it isn't my favorite partner," he

drawled, just to be abrasive and because he knew the foul language was a sore point between them. "Kind of late. Shouldn't Barbie be in bed with Ken by now?"

A little out of line. Yes, she was blond and shapely and Grantham was a good-looking guy, but he should think before he made cracks like that. Her personal life was her own business.

His ex-girlfriend was right. He *was* an asshole. He'd been hoping to hear from Ellie, actually. The Brown murder had him wound up and he had been wondering who was assigned to it.

"It's nine o'clock. Sorry to call so late." Her voice was cool. "Up for visitors?"

Hell yes. He stifled the profanity and said instead, "Absolutely. I'm bored out of my mind."

"I won't be too flattered then at your enthusiasm, but Grasso and I wouldn't mind talking to you for a few minutes if you are okay with it."

"Fine by me."

"Good, since we are already on our way."

In the ten minutes it took for them to get there he did put the dirty dishes in the dishwasher and at least glanced in the bathroom. No underwear on the floor— good. On the upside, a disabled bachelor wasn't all that tidy, but an extremely *bored* disabled bachelor cleaned now and again just for something to do. The place didn't look too bad.

Why he cared, he wasn't sure. Appearances had never been very important in his upbringing. There actually hadn't been any consideration for that at all. His mother had walked out when he was young and his old man had tolerated his presence until he was eighteen, then tossed him out and proceeded to drink himself into an early grave. End of story.

Not a lot of glamour in his past.

MacIntosh was a bit different. He wasn't sure about her childhood, but she'd hunted down a serial killer who had been terrorizing northern Wisconsin for over a year and the blaze of glory had landed her in Milwaukee as a detective in homicide. At her age that was a little young, but he couldn't deny that she'd also been instrumental in hunting down the murderer who had popped up on their radar a few months ago, so she seemed to be two for two.

Well, not completely accurate. They'd caught him together. The only difference was Jason also got two bullets in the chest, but that hadn't been her fault. Not at all. They made a good team.

Go figure. He'd been pretty pissed off over being assigned with Miss Northwoods, but together they'd made a decent showing on a pretty high profile case in that they'd caught the killer.

Of course, right now, Lieutenant Grasso was her new partner.

Damn. It chafed to be out of the loop. Plus, he felt a little edged to the side, like Grasso might fill his shoes.

Why did they want to see him?

He couldn't wait to find out.

Chapter 5

It wasn't deep enough, but maybe she could do something later. Makeshift was the best she could do in the haze of the dawn, the sun reflecting on the lake in a crimson shimmer through the trees. The branches would be bare soon, skeleton arms lifted to the sky.

Afterward she went into the house. The bedroom was a gory display of torn sheets and the rug was ruined, soaked with blood in one corner, and she wondered how much it would be noticed that it was gone.

One person might think it was odd, but that was just a chance she had to take.

Gray light, the scent of water and fecund odor of rotting leaves . . . The image was not going anywhere soon and Ellie tried to shake it off even as she walked up the echoing, untidy stairway to Jason Santiago's apartment. She gestured at a tricycle sitting by a doorway, small pink tassels on the handlebars. "I have a fair idea of what his salary is, so even if we aren't exactly rich as police officers, why does he choose to live somewhere like this? It looks like a lot of young families live here."

Grasso shrugged. "I can't speak for him, but my guess is that if he picked somewhere quiet, he would really be alone."

That was profoundly honest. It sounded like Grasso knew exactly what he was talking about. She shot him a sidelong glance, couldn't get anything from his expression, and murmured, "Please don't make him more human on my behalf."

The man walking up the stairs next to her said neutrally, "We're all human, MacIntosh. Even the bad guys."

That statement was bland enough but caught her mid step. She faltered for a minute, looking back over her shoulder, hand on the rail. "Point taken. I wasn't trying to criticize him, I was just wondering."

"I assume he feels comfortable here."

She wasn't as convinced. Santiago lived in an apartment building that obviously, from the playground equipment and pool, had a ton of small children. It didn't fit the man she knew, but whatever. She was there about two murders, not his choice in lifestyle.

The building wasn't new, the carpet in the hallway a bit worn, but it was cheerful enough and there was a faint hint of someone somewhere baking a cake maybe . . . the scent of chocolate just a tantalizing background nuance.

Fine, maybe she could buy it. Ellie knew enough about her partner that his past *might* make him seek out a family atmosphere. He answered the door on the second knock, and for someone who had two bullet holes in the chest not all that long ago, he looked pretty good. He'd let his wavy-blond hair go without a haircut for a while, but who could fault a small detail such as that when he was recovering from multiple gunshot wounds? He had very blue eyes, almost startlingly so, direct and clear, and he wore baggy cargo shorts and a faded T-shirt.

She hadn't seen him since he was released from the hospital and felt a bit guilty about it, but to say they were friends would be stretching the truth. However, they did seem to work pretty well together, maybe even *because* of their disparate personalities.

"Hi," she said with a genuine smile. "You look good. Once again I hope you don't mind us dropping by."

For a moment he propped himself against the doorjamb, and folded his arms across his chest. "It's kind of an interruption if you want the truth. I was about to watch an episode of *Gilligan's Island* that I've seen thirty-seven times or so in my lifetime, but what the hell. Come on in." He stepped back and held the door. "Hey, Grasso, how is it hanging? The two of you together, this must be official police business. If you're here to search my place for porn, you'll find some, but it's all legal."

"I'm not vice right now, Santiago." Grasso laughed and followed her in.

"Good, but don't get too comfortable."

Yes, that was the Jason she remembered. Nor was his apartment a surprise, even if the family style building had been unexpected. There were some mirrors on the walls with beer company logos and half-naked women, a plaid couch in red and brown that looked comfortable but not even close to new, a coffee table that might be nice if dusted—but it wasn't. The open sliding glass doors to the balcony showed two plain plastic chairs. Aside from a couple of *Sports Illustrated*s next to a recliner and an obscenely huge flat-screen television, the place really didn't say too much about the man who lived there.

She handed him a small wrapped dish. "I brought you some lasagna. You told me once you don't like to cook."

"Thanks." For a moment he looked uncharacteristically serious, but it faded fast. "Real food, huh? I might go into shock. It doesn't help that the doctors haven't cleared me to drive yet," he said sardonically. "Luckily, there's always pizza delivery and a Chinese place about a block away. Did you know you can order boxes of mac and cheese from Amazon and they ship it? No shit. This is a great day and age to be an invalid. Have a seat."

"We'll try and keep it brief." She chose the couch—it *was* comfortable if not aesthetically pleasing. "We want to talk about the shooting. You were on the scene."

"Chad . . . I liked him. A lot." Jason nodded and sat down in the recliner, his breath going out in a long huff of either pain or anger. "Those fuckers."

Irreverent was an understatement when it came to Santiago, but in this case, Ellie didn't disagree. "We wondered if you could talk to us about him a little.

The second cop to fall in a homicide in a week. The chief is worried."

"He should be." The words were forceful. "Goddamn it, Fielding had a wife and little kid. The department should not be burying two good cops so close together. Both were straight arrows. What the hell? Fielding especially . . . it looked like someone came after him with a purpose."

"It just seems like a straightforward hit." Ellie kept her voice even. "Any idea why?"

"None. And I've been sitting here thinking about it a lot. Even more since last night."

"Why exactly were *you* there?" Grasso asked.

"Danni called me to see how I was doing. I asked if maybe she wanted a little company on her shift. It isn't like I'm a civilian or anything." Santiago shrugged, but his eyes were distant. "It was probably better I was there for her sake, but I am not sure about mine. He was a friend. I wish I'd not seen it firsthand."

Ellie would probably be wishing the same thing.

"The way Fielding was murdered really makes you think. It wasn't a lot different with Brown. We're wondering if they were both into something that came back and bit them."

"If you think he was dirty, think again. No way." Santiago shook his head emphatically. "Chad was a good guy. A good cop, for that matter. If you believe this is mob or gang related, it isn't, because he was not on the take in any way. Besides, I thought Hamish and Rays had the case."

Grasso had stood by the open glass doors, his hands

casually in his pockets. He didn't answer the implied question. "Yes, Hamish and Rays have it. No one has mentioned organized crime. Some reason it came to mind?"

Jason rubbed his chest. It looked like an absent motion, as if he did it often. Ellie well remembered the night he was shot. "The first homicide was definitely a hit, I'll give you that. I didn't know Fielding enough to vouch for him. Seemed like a good guy, though," he said, his expression thoughtful. "Obviously Metzger thinks they are linked together? I'm not sure I disagree. I take it you don't have the actual investigation but he wants you to poke around. Why?"

He had a quick mind, she'd give him that. Besides, she'd only joined the department a few months ago and he knew—like Grasso—the chief a lot better. "You tell us," Ellie said, her gaze intent. "You've worked almost every single division in the MPD. Anyone have a problem with either of the officers who were killed?"

"He thinks it's *inside*?"

Grasso looked impassive. "No, he doesn't. He just wants us to make sure the problem isn't internal but he doesn't want an official IA investigation."

"Oh yeah, that's sweet. Nothing like being a narc. Let me know how it turns out." Santiago got up restlessly. "Anyone else want a beer? I cut off the pain meds a few days ago and I'm starting to hurt. I also need a minute to think about this. Who drove?"

"I did," Grasso said dryly.

"Good. You get to be the sober one."

"Lucky me."

"MacIntosh?"

She declined. "You go ahead . . . I had some wine with dinner."

When he came back, he handed her a cool bottle. "Leinies. Have one."

He'd already opened it, so she reluctantly accepted the offering, more concerned with his attitude than with the beer. "What about this would make you think the chief would be concerned so quickly? You came to that conclusion pretty fast."

Santiago looked at her as he settled back into the chair, his gaze sardonic. "I have no idea. That bothers me because I'd like to think he and I aren't like-minded people. What did he say, and I mean *exactly*."

Grasso spoke in an emotionless tone. "Know anyone who might want to hit both of them?"

"Off the top of my head, no." Santiago tipped the beer back, tilted it forward, and then tipped again, his throat working. When he was finished, he said, "Maybe it just is what it is and they aren't related."

Ellie said neutrally, "You really think Chad Brown was clean, and maybe Fielding just ticked off his neighbor or crossed the wrong junkie on the street?"

"A junkie would have robbed his house." Her former partner shook his head. "I see Metzger's concerns, though. It was too slick. Too professional. They didn't kill Fielding's wife or kid. Only pros do that. They aren't paid for the wife and kid, so why risk the prison time, you know?"

She didn't know. The entire conversation left her cold. "Why would *anyone* do it? Why would someone kill Officer Brown? Any ideas there?"

Santiago popped up the footrest on the recliner. He had on flip-flops with small palm fronds on the straps. "I can do some digging. From here. I swear I won't compromise the investigation, but you are right, I know everyone in the department, good and bad. If there's something going on, I might actually be able to find it. After all, I'm a detective, right?"

"So we've heard." Grasso was joking but dispassionate.

"You've been investigated." Ellie glanced at her current partner. "So that process is not new to you, which I would guess is why Metzger chose us." She transferred her gaze to Santiago. "You, on the other hand, are considered rogue material. I am just going to suppose I've landed in such lauded company because I shot a man to death in the line of duty and because of that particular incident find myself in this predicament. I'm not all that fond of either of you right now."

"Predicament?" Santiago looked amused. He glanced at Carl. "Are we entitled to be insulted? Because I just can't decide. And, MacIntosh, *you've* shot more than one suspect. Remember the man who kidnapped the niece of a federal judge? You're no angel."

Oh, yes, she remembered. "He lived. Besides, he tried to bludgeon me to death."

"Still counts, sweetheart."

Outside someone had started to play basketball on the lighted court down below. She gave a short laugh. "Okay, so none of us here have any reason to throw darts at each other. Can we talk about *this* case?"

"Fine by me."

"So we've all shot suspects and I am not sure that

it is a brotherhood I want to belong to, but none of us have ever gone after a cop, and none of us would."

"Never say never."

Surprisingly it wasn't one of Santiago's flippant remarks, but Grasso who said it. Dryly, he added, "Look at Reubens. Sometimes it is hard to tell the white hats from the black."

"What is up?" Ellie was really searching, trying to stay focused, but honestly, she was distracted by lakeside skeletons and hidden graves. "Is there something going on, or is Metzger just paranoid?"

"Nope." Santiago set aside his beer, blue eyes serious. "I don't like it either. Fielding and Brown knew each other pretty well. Makes you wonder if they both stumbled over something. It isn't always what you know, but just sometimes what someone *thinks* you know."

Chapter 6

It drizzled, but maybe it was just as well.

No one was on the lake, not even a light on in the cottages across, mist over the water floating like gray ghosts, moving wisps in the uncertain light.

The branches were still there, scattered in a haphazard fashion over the stones she'd found and labored to move, but something had been at the grave. There was fresh dirt clawed out of one corner and she could see a glimpse of white flesh.

It was what she'd feared all along and a surge of panic ran up her spine, quickly tamed as she took in a deep breath.

Scavengers were fine as long as nothing pulled the body from the ground. The faster it was gone, the better.

She just needed to make sure it stayed buried.

The boat. Maybe she could pull that old rowboat up over it, but leave it tilted just enough.

That might just work.

* * *

Ellie sat outside the office and waited. The receptionist glanced at her now and then, but she just ignored it and assumed it was because the woman knew she was a detective. On her last visit she had handed over her card, but that had been official business.

Now she was a patient, though she really didn't like to think of it that way.

"The doctor is ready to see you."

Was *she* ready to see the doctor? She wasn't sure, but this was not a decision she'd made lightly.

Dr. Lukens met her at the door, eyebrows raised. "Detective MacIntosh. Come on in. Imagine how surprised I was to see your name on my appointment schedule."

Ellie's first thought was Georgia Lukens had a nice tan. Tropical location maybe? Sandy beach, plush towels, frozen drink in hand? Sounded good. Must be the case, because she hadn't gotten it in southern Wisconsin. Though it had been a record-breaking summer, it had been way too hot to sunbathe, and then it had abruptly cooled off considerably. Tall, leggy, with a no-nonsense haircut that showed off the fine bones of her face, the psychiatrist had on very little makeup, the sum of the parts completed by tailored slacks and a jacket. Her smile was unreadable. Dr. Lukens said neutrally enough, "Have a seat."

The office Ellie followed her into had paneled walls, two oak bookcases, and a few too many plants, so there was the hint of damp soil in the air.

"I am not sure I want to do this." Ellie remained standing, wondering if she'd made the right decision in coming.

"Fine. Just fine." Dr. Lukens sank down into the leather chair behind her immaculate polished desk. "Now you really have me curious. I'm all ears. What is on your uneasy mind?"

"*My* uneasy mind?" Ellie went ahead and sat down too.

"People without problems rarely visit me, at least not at the office. Last-minute uncertainty is not an uncommon reaction, but you made the appointment for a reason. Tell me what it is you want to discuss. Ever since my secretary said you called, I have been tossing the possibilities back and forth. Is this about the Northwoods Killer, or the Burner? Either way, if you are struggling, we can talk about it and work it through. Post-traumatic stress disorder is a viable condition, Detective MacIntosh."

Ellie regarded the woman across from her with a level look. "I want to believe that you are a good enough clinician that you know that is not why I am here."

"True enough. You can kill without remorse."

Put so frankly, that was a bit shocking. Ellie said carefully, "If the person places me in that position where there is little choice, yes. I think you know that very well."

"Is that why you chose me as your therapist?"

"I am not sure I even need a therapist."

Maybe the tension indicated this wasn't the best idea she'd ever had.

Georgia Lukens entwined her hands and rested them on the desktop. "Look, Detective, let's begin again. Obviously something is bothering you or coming to me would not have occurred to you in the first place. Let's discuss it. Anything you say is confidential, so you can speak freely. I think I do know why you chose me. We have a rather unique bond we may have not intended to forge, but it exists."

When she'd made the appointment, Ellie had wondered if it wasn't worth it to talk to someone to try and figure out if her issues with committing to a relationship were really related to her job, or to something else. She tended to blame her hesitation on the dark side of mankind she saw all too often, but then again, maybe it was *her*.

But now her focus was skewed to another problem that needed her attention, and maybe her relationship with Bryce could wait a bit. Perhaps that *was* the issue. There was always something else.

"I'm having a problem dealing with someone I love very much."

"Okay. That happens to all of us. What are we talking about specifically?"

"I don't know the facts. I have a few of them, but the background story, no. I do not want to stir up a hornet's nest if it isn't necessary, but I also am hanging out in the breeze."

"This is someone you don't feel comfortable talking to, or you think they won't be comfortable talking to you?" Dr. Lukens gazed at her inquiringly.

That was an interesting question, but maybe accurate. Slowly, Ellie confirmed, "Both, at least in the context of a certain problem. In truth, I'm not comfortable giving *you* exact names, so I am not going to, but I'll relay the gist of it, and maybe you can help me sort out how I feel about dealing with it."

"I wouldn't dream of doing otherwise. Outline the problem and we'll go from there."

She hesitated, then sighed. "I'm working another case. One that is really involved, but this dilemma is personal and entirely different. Look, recently I think someone I am very close to lied to me about something important."

"The very attractive Dr. Grantham?"

It was startling that this woman knew Bryce's name, but then again, they did not have the most low profile relationship in the great state of Wisconsin. "How do you know that he and I—"

"After the Burner case it was mentioned in a newspaper article by some very clever investigative reporter that you were involved with a former suspect in another case. Don't worry, just a sentence in the article, but I notice details."

That wasn't the best news ever, but it probably was impossible to keep your personal life completely secret, no matter who you were. "No, not Bryce," Ellie was able to say with quiet conviction. "I don't think he's ever lied to me. Or if he has, I have not yet caught it."

"Yet?"

"I'm suspicious by nature. Comes with the territory. We can talk about Bryce at a different appointment."

"It sounds like we should." Lukens leaned back, fingering a pen, her brows lifted. "I guess I assumed that the two of you have a complicated relationship, but maybe I see too many patients who have had bad experiences. Obviously, from the tone of your voice, you have a lot of confidence in him. So let's move on."

"I have a lot of confidence in quite a few people, some of which might be a mistake." She exhaled and ran a hand through her hair. "But, no. Strike that. I have every confidence in *this* person and yet he's lying to me."

"Motivation?"

"Now you sound like a police officer."

"No, now I sound like a therapist. You feel betrayed for some reason."

Did she? She wasn't at all sure about the terminology, but she did need some answers. "I am someone to whom he could tell the truth. He knows that. He doesn't want to. The realization struck a somewhat ominous note."

"So you think he was lying. Maybe you should explain why you think he isn't being honest."

"It was a feeling. Not very scientific but I do know this person well."

"I can tell you from experience human behavior is not an exact science. Let me ask you this: was he protecting *you* from the truth, or protecting himself?"

Food for thought. It took her a second, but then Ellie swallowed hard. "I don't see how either could apply."

Lukens's fingers toyed with the edge of her blotter now that she had put down the pen. "Okay again. Why would he lie? Do you have a theory?"

"He doesn't want me to look closer."

"You say it with conviction. Into what?"

Nope. Not going there. Ever. Once the words were said, they couldn't be taken back. "That is not part of this discussion."

"I believe at this moment it would be fair to say you wish me to shoot blind into a dark alley. Would you do that? Look, Detective MacIntosh, you came here for help, and I am more than willing, but could you solve a case without information? Help me out. You need to at least give me some evidence we are discussing something worth our time and effort."

That was reasonable enough. Ellie took in a breath. "Dr. Lukens—"

"I think at this point you can call me Georgia. You need to deal with this and you thought of me. Fine, I'm here to help. Help me back and tell me what exactly we're dealing with. Otherwise I am throwing darts at the walls."

Fair enough. "I just want a few insights."

"I've heard that one before, but in this case I believe it. So he's lying. Does *he* realize—after all in your profession you are naturally suspicious as you just said a moment ago—that you know he's lying?"

Ellie cast back . . . replayed the whole scene with her grandfather in her mind, and then nodded. "He knows."

"But is trusting that you won't probe too deeply? Good guess?"

"I suppose." Ellie stood and then walked to the single window. It looked out over the street. Her car was still there, and she'd parked it pretty well, considering parallel parking was not her forte. "He's counting on me to be polite and show respect and never ask the right questions."

"Father?"

Well, crap, that was way too close to the truth.

"Grandfather."

Dr. Lukens laughed softly. "Oh, how that complicates the situation. Let's face it, Detective, that is a lot of life experience. Grandparents are supposed to teach *us*. We are told that, and we believe it. Tell me about it."

That was the entire problem. She didn't want to tell anyone. "I'm having trouble just thinking about it—much less wanting to tell you. Can we approach this another way?"

"We can approach it however you wish to handle it, Ellie, but at the end of the day, I think what you are looking for requires some fairly brutal honesty. Am I wrong?"

She wasn't. Damn her.

Ellie took a moment and then turned around. "I have never understood how you went to school to just learn how to ask questions and not give answers."

"But yet you are here. And if we are making judgments, I suppose I could say I have never understood how you demand truths from people without ever offering them yourself." Dr. Lukens cocked her head. "How does that work? One-sided honesty? Come on, Detective. How can you possibly want my frank opinion when you refuse to give me more than just a vague scenario? It isn't fair. You would never put up with it. So, if you came here with a purpose, can you tell me what it is? There is one, right?"

That was a good question. Ellie stared at a painting on the wall. It was far too generic for her tastes, but then again, she certainly was not an interior decorator and once upon a time, Dr. Lukens had given her the piece of art that once hung there. "Fine, I will give you more details, but not everything."

"That's generous, considering *you* came *here*. I'm not asking for everything, just enough so that I can help."

"This is confidential."

"You know that is not an issue."

True. Ellie still had to weigh her words before she just sat back down. "A grave was found on my grandfather's property. He called me. I went. Of course I would."

Georgia waited and then said, "Okay, that's shocking, I admit. How did you feel about it?"

She held up her hand. "No, don't do that. I'm not here to talk about how I felt about it."

"I'm starting to get that impression, but you might want to reevaluate down the line. All right, I'll restate. Of course you would agree to go. What did you find?"

This was the hard part. She leveled her gaze. "I couldn't tell how old the skeleton might be. I just got the impression maybe he *did* know."

"Your grandfather knew the person?"

"I never said that. I said he just wasn't . . . . surprised enough in my opinion."

"Surprised enough? In *your opinion*."

It was always aggravating when someone assumed that tone, but because Ellie had been involved in a double homicide recently, it could be Lukens was sensitive to the subject. Ellie said evenly, "Look, police officers are just human beings, but we do have the dubious honor of being lied to more often than most. So, yes. In my somewhat expert opinion."

"No." Lukens exhaled, her smile a small twitch. "I think my profession can claim the dubious honor of being lied to the most. But I don't think that's the issue here. You got the *impression* he lied to you. I am not sure yet of the significance of the skeleton, but I do know already how you feel about his reaction. Did you tell him you thought he was not being truthful?"

"My grandfather?" Ellie looked at her incredulously. "Never. That is like a Catholic accusing the pope of lying to his face. If there is a one percent chance I'm wrong . . . well, let's just leave it there, shall we? I refuse to take a gamble on insulting him, even if it is that one percent."

Georgia nodded, her expression thoughtful. "Fine with me. Let's leave him out of this and address your fears."

"I don't have fears."

"Then congratulations, you are the only person on this planet without them, Detective MacIntosh."

That *had* come off all wrong. She readjusted the answer. "I meant the reason I am here isn't because of personal anxiety except to the extent that I needed to talk to someone about how to handle this. He isn't young and I don't want to upset him even more."

Georgia Lukens just looked at her. "I agree he isn't young but might argue you don't want to upset *you* more."

"If he does know who it is, that means he's culpable in some way because he denied it. How is that possible? He's the most honorable man I know."

"Ah, so there we go. *That's* what you're afraid of." Georgia's voice was quiet. "That this man you revere is going to topple from his pedestal."

Was it? *Shit.*

"No. I'm not afraid for me, but for him."

"You are sure about that?"

God help her, she wasn't.

Those forsaken bones had her in a tailspin and she was not sure she could survive the nosedive.

"Here's the crux of it," Ellie explained haltingly. "I could just walk away. I'm fairly sure there will be no huge investigation into this case if the bones are really old. The county always does its best with cold cases, but the budget is tight and there is plenty to do, trust me." She splayed her hands on the table. "Am I doing more harm than good if I push it?"

Dr. Lukens laughed, but there was no mirth involved. "Oh, for God's sake . . . you're a detective. Just accept that about yourself."

"What does *that* mean?"

"You're scared of what you might find. That seems reasonable to me. I think if you feel you can live with brushing it off, do that. If, from what you just said, you don't think you can live with it, investigate. Have you ever seen the movie *A Few Good Men*? Great flick. There is a classic line in there that I think everyone who is involved in the law in any way needs to remember. I don't think I'm quoting it word for word, but the gist is that a jury trial is not about the truth, it is about assigning blame. Are we having a discussion about this right now? So a person is dead, buried without ceremony, and you want to blame someone but you do not want to blame your grandfather, right?"

That was being simplistic, but it was pretty close to the truth. "We are having this discussion because I'd like your professional opinion on how it would affect him if I pursue this."

"Let me sum it up. In short, will it bother you more to let it go, or if you can't let it go? I think we both know letting it go is not an option for you. I also think you are wasting a great deal of energy on something that might be resolved without any more effort on your part. Perhaps the investigation will be straightforward and expedient and all your anxiety is unnecessary. Or can I venture to say maybe something else is bothering you and this allows you to think about what we are discussing instead. Possible?"

Ellie leaned back in her chair. It was possible, of course. Her relationship with Bryce was coming to a crossroads of sorts, or at least that was how she thought of it. She'd signed a lease on her condo when she moved down from Lincoln County and it was time to decide if she should keep it.

Maybe there was some benefit to therapy after all.

"I have a personal life, of course," she admitted. "It's a little complicated right now."

"Personal life. Complicated? Hmm, what are the odds?" Mildly, Dr. Lukens said, "Maybe we can talk about that next time."

Chapter 7

The letter sat on the table. She'd labored over it, starting, stopping, tearing up the paper into bits and starting fresh again.

It needed to be perfect.

Poignant but firm. And final. So final that there were no questions, no suspicions . . . no search. The problem was the date. It had to be exactly right, all contingencies considered, no possible mistakes allowed. The bus schedule was taken care of, the suitcase hidden, the other little details tidied and straight.

Or so she hoped. Make sure you aren't forgetting anything, her mother had always told her.

But it was doubtful she was referring to murder.

Jason thought that there was nothing worse than a cop funeral. It didn't improve the situation that the skies had clouded over and a thin mist began to fall about noon, so that everything was wet and bleak and dismal.

Ranks of uniformed officers stood in lines and the various wreaths of flowers held glistening drops of moisture. It was just as well it was raining for that could account for the dampness on Danni Crawford's face.

The instant that Chad was in the ground—the flags and the crying relatives aside—she would never see him again.

Not his face, she'd sobbed. Not his kind of quirky smile that turned up at one corner, and his hands would never again slide over her body . . .

She told him that, more personal than maybe Jason was comfortable with, but grief was an interesting emotion. Their relationship was, in a word, obliterated. Chad hadn't passed on her. Hadn't found her lacking, hadn't disliked that her hips might be just a little too curvy and maybe could even be classified as fat, hadn't decided to move on for any reason than someone had decided to just take him out.

They had loved each other.

Jason had let her talk. He wasn't good at sympathy, but he did stand with her, and . . . listened. There was nothing he could do about what had happened, but at least he could listen.

Chad's family stood in a small circle, his mother's face as gray and drawn as the weeping skies. She'd cried quietly during the service and Danni had wept with her, spine straight, eyes ahead, and her grief put a knot in the pit of Jason's stomach like a clenched fist.

Whoever had done this would pay.

It smelled like a contract hit, just like the killing the

week before. Everyone in the department was talking about it and homicide was all over both cases, but the murders had been so clean and fast there was virtually no evidence. Even Fielding's wife couldn't give a description.

Fielding's wife.

That had been an interesting interview, or so Danni had told Jason. Looking back, he now wondered if the woman's shell-shocked statement had been just incoherent babbling as she'd thought at the time, or if it meant something.

She'd said over and over: *Garrison. He shouldn't have called. He shouldn't have called.*

Chad had wondered too, Danni had stated in a small, wavering voice. They'd talked about it later, about how both of them assumed at the time it was the name of her child, a mother's frantic worry even though she'd been reassured time and again he was safe. Covered in blood spatter, understandably hysterical, she had been a useless witness.

But it wasn't the name of Joanne Fielding's son, Danni had found out.

The last message she had from Chad was that he thought he knew what it meant but he needed to check with the chief before he gave the information to the detectives assigned to the case.

And now he was dead.

Carl left the cemetery and turned his phone back on, seeing he had a text.

Missed you at the party. Lindsey.

Call her back? He might have except Ellie called him even as he was contemplating the question. "Lieutenant, I'm going to be out of town for the weekend. Considering everything, I wanted to let you know. Family matter,"

The brusque, businesslike tone of her voice made him wonder just what had her so . . . maybe unsettled was the word.

In his opinion, she didn't unsettle all that easily.

Carl had seen her at the funeral, serene outwardly anyway, standing in the rain with Grantham with a shared umbrella, and she'd briefly exchanged words with Santiago, but left quickly.

No one had really wanted to stay. Wet earth and dripping branches and tears.

He hadn't stayed either.

"Cell on?" he asked.

"Pretty much always."

"Not 24/7. Take some time for yourself."

"Excuse me?" She sounded surprised.

"You have a job, Detective, but it isn't everything. What I am saying is that if you need to take your weekend actually *off*, go ahead. We don't have a handle on what is going on, but we will. If something comes up I'll call you."

When they hung up he sat and thought about what he knew.

Not a lot. Two officers dead. No real witnesses. No idea of motive either.

No suspects.

Maybe, like MacIntosh he should take some time for himself and call Lindsey back.

* * *

When his phone beeped, Jason was taking a shower, always a mixed bag. The feel of the warm water helped the soreness in muscles that were healing in ways that tightened them with scar tissue. He also had two broken ribs from when he'd gone down after the second bullet pierced his chest, so the relief was appreciated. But doing something simple, like washing his hair, caused some interesting twinges.

So he gritted his teeth, rinsed out the shampoo, and reached for a towel.

The scars weren't pretty either, he thought as he dried off, staring in the mirror. In theory women supposedly found them sexy. In truth, they were rubbery patches of red skin that marred his chest, and though he'd been assured they would whiten and fade, at the moment he still looked like a victim in a horror film.

Worth it, though, at the end of the day. They'd gotten the bastard, even if Jason had taken a few bullets in the process, and hey, he was still alive and the other guy was dead.

Speaking of which . . . MacIntosh had texted him. Surprising, actually. She'd come to the hospital a couple of times, but otherwise his partner hadn't called before last night when she had visited with Grasso. He wasn't bitter about it because it wasn't like they were longtime friends or anything, but it would have been nice to have her visit.

This whole shooting had given him a somewhat adjusted view of his life.

It wasn't like he was a stranger to having bouts of loneliness, but he wasn't a slave to it either. He slipped on some boxers and a pair of jeans and ran a comb through his wet hair. Bare-chested, he wandered into the living room and contemplated her message.

You were riding along with Officer Crawford just for fun? Want to do something else with your free time?

What did that mean? The answer was hell yes, he was bored to tears, but he really didn't have any idea what she was asking.

He texted back. *Like?*

It won't be exciting, but can you help me investigate old unsolved missing-person cases in Oneida County?

What?

He stared at the display on his phone. He could, but why would he? That wasn't a lot better than watching reruns of *Gilligan*.

Except he really couldn't imagine Ellie asking anything of him and that alone made him read it a second time.

Well . . . interesting. Not what she wanted him to do; that would be tedious probably, but that she asked him for a favor. Twice now in as many days.

He hesitated, his phone in his hand, and then swiftly pushed a few keys. *Fuck yes.*

There was no question he liked messing with her. It was no secret she did not appreciate his colorful approach to the English language.

Very funny. Once I have a better idea of what we are looking for, I'll let you know. Thanks.

Last he knew, he thought, setting aside the phone on the counter and opening the refrigerator to peer in, she didn't work for a county sheriff's department any longer.

Cross-jurisdiction? Seemed unlikely, and asking for his help even more so, especially since he was still on leave.

He found he had two withered carrots and a quart of milk that had a date that made even his eyebrows elevate.

That was okay, he had the pizza place on speed dial and things were looking up.

Chapter 8

The diner did not go quiet as she walked in.

A good sign.

In fact it looked just the same, with the dishes stacked on shelves above the wash sink and the waitresses bustling behind the counter as usual. She picked a table and sat down, placing her pocketbook on the scratched surface.

"The usual?" Amy sauntered up and smiled, reaching over to turn her cup upright in the saucer.

It was almost difficult to nod because she was shaking. It was one thing, she was discovering, to commit murder, and another to get away with it. No one thought she looked different, was different, had burned blood-soaked clothing not all that long ago . . . buried a body . . .

The monster in their midst.

And none of the people sitting at the plain little

tables, eating their eggs and pancakes drenched in syrup, and rashers of bacon, had any idea.

By the time her coffee arrived she was calm, smiling, and the tension between her shoulder blades had eased.

Outside cars cruised by . . . everything was perfectly normal. Her plate arrived and she picked up her fork and murmured her thanks and ate with relish for the first time since she'd made the decision. . . .

Ellie stirred, rolled over, and encountered a warm, muscular male body, and she muttered a halfhearted objection when the man next to her pulled her close.

Very close.

Naked skin to naked skin . . . What time was it?

His hand smoothed her bare hip as she squinted at the clock and groaned. "It's six o'clock."

"Ellie, it's Saturday." Bryce kissed her neck and he did that very, very well. "You're off duty today."

It was tempting to pretend that she had the luxury of staying in bed—especially when his hands were doing some very interesting things to certain susceptible parts of her anatomy, but even if she *was* off, it was a little early for a romantic interlude and she'd promised herself she'd leave by seven at the latest. . . .

"Bryce." She meant to protest, but it wasn't sincere. She needed this. The connection. Someone was killing cops and there was a pile of bones in her grandfather's backyard. Not to mention the unsigned lease for another six months for the condo on her computer in a file waiting to be downloaded while she tried to make up her mind.

"Hmm?" He licked a path along her collarbone, and then lower, pushing down the sheet. "Bryce yes, or Bryce no?"

"I have to leave by seven."

"I have a whole hour . . . perfect."

She laughed, but it was a little breathless and she knew he heard that slight catch. In direct contradiction to what she'd just said, she ran her fingers through his dark hair. "I need to shower."

He adjusted their position in one smooth move, and his lips curved in a slow smile. "If we do this right, you certainly will."

They had a few problems in their relationship, mostly due to her hesitation to commit, but none of them were in bed. She murmured against his mouth, "That sounds very promising."

It was 7:18 when she pulled out of the driveway, but definitely worth the delay. Ellie slid a CD into the player and glanced over. "You don't have to come with me."

"I like your grandfather." Bryce picked up a travel cup and took a sip of coffee as they drove down the street. "I am not one hundred percent sure he likes me, but I do know we have one of those purely male understanding things going where if I never mention I am sleeping with his granddaughter—and this morning comes to mind—he and I will get along fine."

She blew out a short breath. "That I can believe. He rarely fails to make his feelings clear."

"True enough. Old Lutherans usually do."

Taking the turn for the freeway, Ellie said dryly, "I hardly think that is unique to the Lutheran faith."

"Okay, I'll concede that men his age have usually decided they dislike tiptoeing around subjects that they worry will upset other people. So, have you thought of asking him what you should do?"

"About?"

Mildly, he expounded, "Does he think we should get married and have babies?"

Put that way, she was slightly shocked. Bryce was not usually so blunt. It was one of the things she liked about him.

Eventually, she found her voice. "We haven't discussed it."

"And if the subject comes up?"

She'd meant she and Bryce hadn't discussed marriage, but she was more than willing to pretend they were talking about her grandfather. "Do you think for some reason it will?" She negotiated a turn toward the freeway exit. This time on a Saturday morning the roads were at least quiet.

"The single time I met him he did ask about my intentions."

"Old-fashioned." That sounded exactly like the pragmatic man she knew.

"Your father is gone. He's protective. He feels it is his role."

"This stupid male tendency toward—"

"Ellie," Bryce interrupted on a low laugh, but his

dark eyes held a serious glint. "You aren't a homicide detective to him. You are his granddaughter and he cares. I suppose it might be best if I knew what to say."

As much as she'd wanted and yet dreaded this conversation, she knew she was never going to feel the timing was exactly right. The ramp was clear and she gunned the car so they slid onto the freeway right at the speed limit. "What do you *want* to say?"

"To marriage or babies?"

"Come on, Bryce, have mercy. Let's approach this one hurdle at a time."

"Our role reversal never fails to astound me." He flipped open his cup and then shut it without taking a drink. Then he looked her with disconcerting directness. "Fine. I'll start with the foremost question on my mind. Small steps. What are you going to do about your lease? We aren't talking about it. Why? Each time I want to bring it up, I feel like you just don't want me to ask. If I'm not reading the signals correctly, tell me so."

And she'd wondered if he had been paying attention. She should have known better. A few puffy clouds haunted the horizon and she stared at them. "The real question, please."

"Do you want to move in? Live together all the time, night and day, and give this relationship a real shot, not the half-time wavering from one camp to the other?"

"My condo isn't camping." She immediately raised a hand in apology. "Fine, yes, sorry, I know we aren't joking. I think I've been waiting for you to say that is what you want."

"Even when you know it is *exactly* what I want." He theatrically checked his watch. "You *were* there not even an hour ago when I made love to you, correct?"

Her shoulders lifted just a little because he had a point. "Bryce, I needed to hear it. Besides, can I correct you? I think we made love together."

"You wanted to hear me ask? A clue to that would have been helpful. All right." He nodded, his long legs outstretched, his expression about as neutral as possible. "Detective MacIntosh, will you *please* move in with me?"

That was definitive enough.

But it required an answer. She responded tentatively, "I am thinking we should try it."

"Okay. I agree. Is that a yes?"

"And you should tell my grandfather that we are seriously dating, but nothing about the new living arrangements."

"I agree with that, too. Is it a yes?"

It was just plain time to change the subject. "Santiago is going to help me sift through all the missing-person reports, but my first stop today is the medical examiner's office."

He let her get away with the evasion. "Open on Saturday?"

"Someone is always available," she said as they passed the first exit for Oshkosh. "There's a deputy examiner or a tech always on call. Believe it or not, death has its own agenda."

"That's a lovely poetic observation."

"That is the reality. We aren't all writers, Bryce. I wasn't trying to be poetic."

"Maybe so, but since this isn't actually something you are assigned to investigate, can you do this?" His gaze was inquiring.

It was probably skirting the edge of protocol, but then again, so was Metzger's request for her and Grasso to poke around the department with regard to the two killings.

Ellie stared at the road and then equivocated. "There is no rule to say I can't go talk to my grandfather again about that grave."

"No." Bryce sounded as reasonable as always. "But obviously that is not all we are doing unless he is at the medical examiner's office."

Good point. She muttered darkly, "I sure as hell hope he's *not* there."

"I didn't mean it that way God, Ellie."

"I know. Sorry, bad attempt at humor." She was silent for a minute or so. "This is really bothering me, Bryce."

"I've gotten that impression."

"It's a big deal, not a small one, to have a body turn up on your property."

"It would definitely ruin *my* day. Wait, I believe when it happened to me last fall, it tore that day into tiny little shreds."

She signaled to pass a van. "I hate to say this, but I wonder if that kid hadn't been the one to find it, if he wouldn't have just covered it back up and not reported it."

"Why? Your grandfather seems to be the epitome of the upright American citizen."

Softly she murmured, "You know, I think that is what throws me the most."

The call came in mid-morning on a Saturday, and had Carl any other kind of life, he might have ignored it. Instead he registered the number and answered. "This is Grasso."

Short and to the point.

"Officer Crawford. You know who I mean, right?"

"Who is this?"

"I'm talking about Crawford."

He leaned an elbow on the glass-topped table in the sunroom that overlooked flagstone terrace and the pool. It was a nice day and he was enjoying a cup of coffee. He'd bought a new flavor: southern pecan. It was pretty good but maybe not a favorite. In the evening though, he'd decided right before the phone rang, it might be perfect with a splash of whiskey. "I know her."

"She was sleeping with Chad Brown."

The call ended, and in frustration he punched up a screen to show the number but had the feeling it was a generic burner phone since there was no name.

Immediately he got up to go inside. In the kitchen there was a computer nook he'd had built in a few years ago, and he powered up his laptop and made a few notes while the call was still fresh. *Voice: female. Accent: not heavily Wisconsin but definitely Midwestern. Soft vowels. Chicago? Information: a cop allegedly sleeping with another cop, the latter now dead.*

Connection: none I can really see, but check on first victim and see if Crawford might tie somehow back to him too. Caller: has my personal cell number.

More disturbingly, Carl thought as he wandered back to the sun porch, dropped into his chair, and stared out at the pool which this time of year was covered and already had a few withered leaves that had drifted on top of it, the caller had to know he and MacIntosh were looking at the case. Unless his partner had told someone else and the word had spread, as far as he knew, only Metzger and Santiago were aware.

That made the call even more interesting. He decided to make a call of his own.

Ellie answered on the second ring. "Lieutenant?"

"Good morning."

She laughed on a brief exhale. "Don't continue to confuse me by being polite. I'm so used to Santiago. Good morning to you also. What can I do for you, Lieutenant?"

"I have a quick question. Did you by any chance tell anyone about what Metzger wants us to do?"

"No. No one but Santiago, and you were there for that conversation." Swift and sure. She asked sharply, "Why? What's happened?"

"I got a call just a few minutes ago telling me that Brown had been involved with another officer. I can't see the significance of the information."

"I can't say as I don't agree with you on that score. They didn't identify themselves?"

"No, and no name came up. I have the number, but it could be untraceable."

"Who is the officer?"

"Danni Crawford."

"I don't think I know her."

"It's a big department and you haven't worked here long. She's on the street."

"Is this a good lead?"

Carl watched a robin in the landscaped part of the terrace as it hopped around in a flower bed full of dying plants he was hard-pressed to identify since he paid someone else to take care of the landscaping. "I don't have the slightest idea if it is solid or not. I've never heard a word against her."

"It might be worth looking into, I suppose, though surely if she knew something, she would have come forward already."

"I was thinking the same thing." He watched as the robin took off in the correct direction and wished it a safe journey. "I'm wondering how this person got my cell number."

Someone spoke in the background and he realized at that moment Ellie wasn't alone. "Good question, but it could be something as simple as just calling the station and saying they needed to get in touch with you. Easy enough to check on that." MacIntosh sounded brisk and businesslike, but she usually did. "Maybe we can both give it some thought and regroup tomorrow afternoon."

"No problem." He thought about the rest of his day. Wide open. "I might ask a few questions around so we actually have something to talk about. Right now, unless you know something I don't, we have nothing."

There was just the slightest pause before MacIntosh said, "If you'll keep me up to speed, I'd appreciate it. You're right. You know everyone and I am just getting my feet wet."

"Yes, like by catching the Burner?" He was quietly amused. He'd been on the force at least ten years longer so the competitive spirit was not exactly a new entity; in fact, most good cops had it. Only a few months on the job and she'd solved a very high profile case. "That is not tickling your toes in the water. That is taking a plunge in the pool. And in answer to the question, I will let you know if I find out anything."

"Thanks."

After he hung up he thought about what he did know about Officer Danielle "Danni" Crawford.

Let's see. Same age as MacIntosh probably. Early thirties. A little chunky but pretty in the face, with a reputation for being steady and reliable.

She'd been at the funeral—but they'd all gone. Despite what the public might believe, not that many officers were killed in the line of duty. She had cried, but so had pretty much every woman there, and quite a few of the men too. It wasn't like mourning for a colleague, a psychologist who had come to address the department once said. It was more like mourning in advance for yourself.

In case that was you one day. In that coffin.

That was cheerful.

He wasn't a mental health professional, but he understood the tears. Both murders had been senseless, and the lack of a suspect somehow made it all worse. If an officer was shot trying to apprehend a fleeing criminal, the dynamic was obviously volatile. If the person was peacefully sleeping in his bed or pulling someone over for a routine traffic violation, the danger level was usually quite low.

Two down so close together? Was Crawford the connection?

He had to wonder.

So, since it was a nice morning and he had nothing else to do, Carl decided, still gazing absently out the windows, maybe he'd check up a little on Officer Crawford. It sure couldn't hurt.

Chapter 9

She waited.

It seemed like that was the pattern. The ticking clock, the anxious nights, the cold mornings.

Why had she thought it would all change?

Maybe she was a dreamer. Her grandmother had always said so, and she was starting to believe it.

But the risk . . . God help her, the risk . . .

Life was unpredictable. It was true. There was no denial on that point. That was how it had all started. That awkward moment outside the post office, the dropped package, the proverbial meeting of the eyes. She'd known then. He had known too, but it was more complicated on his end, she'd understood that.

Death hovered. Tomorrow there could be the speeding car, the icy steps, the pain in your chest that didn't ease. . . .

And then it was all over.

But physical death was not same as emotional trauma. She hoped it wasn't over for her.

It was like a gruesome jigsaw puzzle. She recognized most of the parts, but this was not a fun game.

Ellie looked into the drawer and declined to have the deputy ME drag out the skeleton.

"There are the notes," he said, indicating a computer screen at a table in the back. "I'll print off the file. I'm afraid we don't have much. I guess I didn't realize Milwaukee PD was in on this one."

"I'm interested, that's all. More on a personal level than official department business." The reply was only a little evasive she told herself, staring down at the bits of humanity, trying once again to make sense of it. "Any of the local PD ventured yet to make an identification or ask for dental records? Anything like that?"

"They do their jobs pretty well up here, as you know." He handed her a sheaf of paper. "We haven't identified the victim but this is a short summary of the notations on the autopsy. Whatever happened to her wasn't yesterday."

"I was afraid of that." She took it and frowned.

Undetermined age. Female. Postpuberty but good bone density at time of death. Some teeth missing but more likely postmortem. Late twenties or early thirties maybe. Time period is difficult to define since there is no clothing or other artifacts. Speculation the skeletal remains are at least twenty years old, but possibly, dependent on the condition of the burial site, even a hundred or more. More tests needed.

"So our victim is an adult woman," she said slowly. "Cause of death?"

The deputy medical examiner was middle-aged, at least in his mid-forties, and his slight smile held a great deal of cynicism. His five o'clock shadow held a slight dark brown with just a hint of gray. He closed the drawer and brushed back his surgical cap. "We have two problems."

"Only two? That sounds promising. Go on."

His smile was ironic. "I love you guys, you know? Always so upbeat. Anyway, I can test a lot of things, but the absence of clothing or anything else makes this difficult to date. For instance, no wedding ring, no zippers, no buttons, nothing. You're the detective, but I am going to say she was buried nude, or buried somewhere else first and the bones moved later."

Ellie was well aware of that possibility. "What else can you tell me?"

He nodded and closed the drawer. "There are some interesting striations on the rib bones. Quite a lot of them. Normally I would say this is a stabbing victim, but if so, it was quite an event, and the evidence is difficult to pin down. The marks are so faded it is hard to tell, but it is possible this is a mauling. Bear maybe? The only thing that makes me discount that is that almost always in those cases the hands and arms take the brunt of it as the victim tries to defend himself. If attacked, we reflexively throw up our arms. Those bones are not damaged like I would expect."

He demonstrated and Ellie wished away the image. Being mauled by a bear would not be her choice when it came to making an exit from this world.

"The black bears around here don't often attack and kill people."

"True enough. Almost never. But there are plenty of creatures out there that don't mind eating us after the fact. Why were coffins invented? Not to keep the person in—they aren't leaving, remember? Why six feet under? To keep the smell of decay deep enough that nothing wants to dig us up for a little snack."

Ellie was not squeamish—in her job, she couldn't be—but that statement got to her a little.

"Nice mental picture. Thanks, Doctor."

"It is possible, and maybe even probable, she died of natural causes and was simply buried poorly and dug up by animals and therefore we have the marks. In my professional opinion, at least some of the damage is the result of a predator or scavengers."

"So no official cause of death or manner of death?"

He shook his head. "Usually the bones really talk to me, but this victim was buried in wet soil on the shore of a lake, she was only loosely covered, and there is a lot of damage. The television shows exaggerate. We can glean a bit, but soft tissue is the magic wand. I think your biggest clue is the lack of clothing or anything else."

Ellie wasn't the greatest fan of the morgue. At least the day was bright and sunny outside. It helped her to constantly remind herself of that. "But," she said with challenge in her gaze, "take a stab at a cause of death off the record." She leaned and looked at the tag clipped to his scrubs. "Dr. Logan."

He laughed softly and shook his head again. "Look, Detective, I want to help. But though I did this autopsy, this isn't your case. Until you ride off into the sunset, especially after what happened down in Milwaukee not that long ago, the ME's office will especially cooperate, but we are not obligated to give you information since we don't serve your department."

If he thought she didn't understand *that* . . .

"I know it. However this has a certain personal immediacy considering where the bones were found."

To her surprise he remained silent for a moment. Then he said slowly, "I'm trying to decide if something I discovered means anything. I left it out of the report because I wasn't sure it was pertinent. It smacks of speculation, actually. The last thing I want is to appear unprofessional, but there are always degrees of separation. I work with detectives from quite a few counties and I learn from you, just as you learn from me."

"Go on. Please."

"I have no idea if this will be helpful."

"I'm okay with deciding that for you. My philosophy is just toss out all the information you have, I'll take a look, and I will really thank you at the end of the day if any of it counts. Sound good? You have nothing to lose and I have everything to gain."

Logan nodded. "I get it, Detective. Fine. I think the person who buried her could not do a better job. It was physically impossible for them to dig a deeper hole, or haul the body elsewhere. When the grave was disturbed, I assume they used some means to cover it because I would present the hypothesis that most of the damage was done almost as soon as the body started to decompose. Once the body had decayed, they probably just removed the cover and tidied up the site. Therefore, your killer, if there was one, was keeping an eye on it."

"Or she died of natural causes and was improperly buried maybe because the family couldn't afford it."

"That is an excellent theory also, Detective Mac-Intosh, but I still think she would have been buried more deeply if there had been someone able to do it."

He had a very valid—and most interesting—point.

"Going through the missing-persons files is going to be pretty tedious already. If she was killed elsewhere, that makes it worse." Ellie thought about Santiago and the boxes she meant to foist on him with only a twinge of guilt. She had no illusions, he really *was* bored to death as he recovered, which was why he agreed to help. Not a secret. "I wish we had a better idea of how old that skeleton is."

"I do as well."

Ellie glanced around at the cold stainless steel tables and then focused on the tile floor.

White. Everything was white . . . generic.

She. Such a generic word for those abandoned bones. Once *she* had been a person. And they didn't know her name.

Ellie thanked him and went to sign out. She'd visited the facility before in her capacity as a detective with the county sheriff's department and the officer on duty nodded in recognition. Automatically, she smiled back and pushed open the glass doors to the outside.

Bryce had stayed in a café across the street, more than happy to sit with his laptop. She slid into the booth as he pressed a button to save his work, and she essayed a serene expression.

Not a good job apparently. He said, "Lunch? You pick the place, and I'll buy. Deal?"

"I don't like it when you are too ridiculously nice."

Mildly, he said in return, "Fine, you buy."

"I dragged you up here."

"You didn't. I think I lobbied to go. I could have sworn you argued with me over it."

She had. A little.

"Hmm. Just the same, *I* should buy. We have to go see my grandfather. We'll stop along the way."

"Oh, if we are going to see your family, you should *definitely* buy." Bryce grinned and snapped closed his computer before he slipped it into a case.

"We are hardly more dysfunctional than anyone else." She still liked that the mood had lightened, and truthfully, was pretty happy he'd come along.

Bryce rose and waited politely for her. "That needs to be debated over a hamburger and some hash browns." He walked to the door of the shop and opened it, holding it open. The air outside was cool and crisp and the sidewalk clean. Across the street Dr. Logan was getting into his car, a dark sedan, and she avoided eye contact. The interview gave her a lot to think about.

She'd left her car unlocked, so when she pressed the button, it locked instead. Old habits were hard to put aside. She did miss the freedom of small towns.

Bryce took the keys from her hand and remedied the situation. "Let me drive. You relax. Have I ever mentioned that one of things I like about living in Wisconsin, other than freezing half to death in winter, which is always a perk, is that pretty much everywhere hash browns are offered? Why would anyone not want to live in the tundra existence we all seem to tolerate if they could have hash browns with every single meal? Forget cheese. We should be known as the Hash Brown State."

So the tension was obvious, and he was trying to ease it. With an inward sigh she acknowledged it probably was. "I can see your point. Throw on some ketchup and all is right in this world."

When they were both in the car and he carefully stowed his laptop in the back, at least she was able to get beyond her self-absorption to ask, "How is the book going?"

Bryce tended to be reticent about his work so she didn't ask often, but now and then she was curious. He started the vehicle. "I actually have an agent in New York who is interested in the manuscript."

She stopped in the act of fastening her seat belt and stared over at him. "What?"

He hadn't mentioned that before. His dark eyes were amused. "Don't act so surprised."

"I'm not . . . I'm not. More curious than anything. When did this happen?"

"Last week."

"You didn't say anything."

"I've been working on the proposal she wants before she starts to shop the book."

Shop the book. That sounded quite official but she knew absolutely nothing about publishing. "That's wonderful."

The truth was, she *might* be a little surprised, she

thought as they pulled out onto the street. He was extremely successful at what he did as a programmer. Until this very moment it hadn't struck home she hadn't quite realized he was so serious about the book. The writing, in her mind, was more a hobby. Bryce murmured, "To me it was an affirmation it wasn't a bunch of crappy words on the screen when she said she thought she'd represent it. Now, once again, where the heck are we going to eat between here and the wilds of Oneida County? I'm starving."

It was so much like him to deprecate the moment—and so much like her to not know the right thing to say. He had to be elated over this news.

"Let's wing it and just pick somewhere."

"Fine by me."

No, she couldn't let it go without more. "The agent in New York. It's *really* wonderful."

He said simply, "Thanks."

Ellie would have gone on, but he said, as if to deflect further comment, "Tell me which way to go, will you? Or should I use the GPS?"

Kate.

Jason had walked down the block to his favorite tavern and saw her instantly, the swing of her dark hair unmistakable around her shoulders. She wore jeans and a red sweater tight enough it emphasized those full breasts he remembered so well, and when she glanced up as he walked in, their gazes caught for a telling second.

Well, shit. Not surprised to see him at all.

His reaction was a bit more visceral. Kind of like taking an unexpected jab to the gut.

A person would think he could grab a burger with impunity.

So . . . his ex-girlfriend was there and not by accident. No way. They used to eat at this place twice a week. On the other hand, maybe she just missed it and there was no law that said she couldn't have a drink with whomever she wanted, wherever she wanted.

Even if it was with some young guy with overlong hair and a pretense of a mustache. They were in a booth in the corner and Jason had to resist the urge to walk over and say something to his ex—the one who hadn't bothered to visit when he was in the hospital with tubes sticking out of his chest everywhere. Actually, other than other police officers, no one had come to visit him. It stung a little.

Kate had just broken up with him before the shooting happened, so maybe she didn't owe him anything.

He'd always felt she should have at least stopped by. It wasn't like the media hadn't been all over the case. The resentment was fluid; he felt the wash and then immediately the ebb because the former wasn't reasonable, and then he went to sit at the bar and ordered a draft. What did he care?

Some, an inner voice chided. *It matters some or you wouldn't be ticked off at her about it.*

Some. That was the problem. He hadn't ever cared enough, not so much that he had even tried to talk her out of it when she'd decided to move out, but now, seeing her—

It sliced deeper than he imagined.

Goddamn it.

"The infamous Santiago."

He glanced up and laughed on a short breath, the interruption actually welcome. "Lieutenant."

Grasso sat down. "Local place. You mentioned you could walk here. When you weren't at home, I thought I'd give it a try. I must have just missed you."

Jason lifted his glass. "Beer and painkillers. I really recommend the combination."

It was a lie. He hadn't taken so much as an aspirin.

"I want to talk about Fielding."

Yeah, Grasso wasn't one for pulling punches.

Jason contemplated his beer and shook his head. "I'd like to, but I really didn't know him."

"That's perfect. Tell me what you didn't know."

At his quick inquiring glance, Grasso just looked bland. "He's clean. I can't find anything on him, or on Chad Brown. But it's there, I just *can't* find it. They were murdered. That means there's something we don't see, and I don't like the creatures lurking in the dark."

"That's a descriptive way to put it." Jason took a drink, but he had to admit he was thinking about the case quite a bit too. The questions Grasso and MacIntosh raised were a welcome distraction in his life. That was why he was here, not sitting in his apartment staring at the walls. Silence was just not this thing.

"There has to be a link." Grasso shook his head when the bartender asked if he wanted a beer, ordered a bottled water instead, and pushed a small business card across the bar. "Who is this?"

Jason picked it up and squinted at it. "Lieman? Don't know him."

"DEA."

He really wished he couldn't see Kate lean forward out of the corner of his eye, the brush of her dark hair swinging against her cheek as she laughed at something her companion said. He could remember how those silky strands felt under his fingers, and that was an unwelcome recollection at the moment.

His attention returned to the conversation. "DEA? What the fuck? You just said neither Fielding nor Brown were dirty, which I'd told you already about Chad."

"I said I couldn't find anything, so you're probably right. But, for some reason, Fielding communicated lately with this Lieman, and now Fielding is dead and Brown is dead as well. The two of them were pretty tight, and you were friends with both Brown, too. Metzger is worried because both shootings were pretty smooth and spoke of a well-trained marksman, but maybe it is drug related."

Jason forgot about Kate sitting only about thirty feet away. Which, she would probably tell him, was part of the reason she'd left him. He frowned, his beer halfway to his mouth. "Once again, these are patrol officers. They aren't involved usually in big drug busts. I get what you're saying—opportunities are everywhere, but I don't see they are worth a hit. How did you get the tip on Lieman?"

"Lieman came to see the chief when he heard about Fielding's murder. I was at loose ends today and was just thinking about it."

Loose ends? Of course he was. The guy must have his reasons, but he spent a lot of his time at the station. "The next logical question is, what the hell did Fielding want?"

"Lieman has no idea. He just called and left a number for him to call back. Lieman was working a case undercover and didn't get the message for a few days, and by then, Fielding was dead."

It was a lead—maybe. "He could have gotten a tip off the street."

"You'd think Fielding would just tell Metzger or the lead detective, which is Fergusson, and they'd make the contact. And why Lieman? The guy claims they've never met. If it was a tip, is there some reason he didn't use the chain of command to pass it along?"

A valid question, for sure. Jason stared at his half-empty glass, the froth now subsided to a thin white layer on top of the golden liquid. "Obviously you need to go talk to the guy's wife."

Grasso leaned his elbows on the bar and shook his head. "We aren't part of the official investigation. I believe we pointed that out." He stopped and seemed to hesitate. "Look, I got a tip that Brown was involved with Danni Crawford. An angle is being played. Why?"

Jason had to agree. Good question. Not everyone had been aware of the relationship, but the significance escaped him. "I don't know. It is somewhat of a leap from DEA to a romance that is none of our business. I can't see what connection there can be. Not everyone in the department knew about Danni and Chad, but some did. They tried to keep it under the radar."

"She answered both 911 calls."

He meant for two murdered cops. Jason didn't like that either.

"I was with her for one. She gets my vote as unlucky cop of the year. How did you get this tip anyway?"

"Anonymous phone call."

That wasn't good. Jason lifted a hand. "Before you ask, no, I haven't said anything to anyone. If someone knows you and MacIntosh are sniffing around on the side, it did *not* come from me."

"Okay." Grasso put a ten on the bar. "I believe you. But I want you to talk to Danni Crawford for me. One friend to another. She obviously knows you're not even on duty right now. If she can tell you something, anything, about Brown's connection with Fielding, or a link to an event that might interest the DEA, then I'd like to know about it, and I think she'd talk to you way before me."

It was probably true. Jason knew he had a reputation for being a little too much of a cowboy now and then—he didn't even deny it. He'd been reprimanded once or twice, and the only reason MacIntosh had been assigned his partner was to tone him down a little, though no one had ever said it to him out loud. On the flip side, he'd worked his way up through the ranks and he'd earned detective. No one had ever handed him anything on a silver platter, and pretty much everyone recognized that fact. Grasso, in his expensive suits, was not the average cop.

"Sure, I'll talk to Danni." Jason smiled without

humor. "Between you and MacIntosh, I'm feeling like I'm back on the job."

The lieutenant slipped his money clip back into his pocket. "MacIntosh? How so?"

"Wants me to look into an old missing-person case."

"She does?" Grasso seemed interested. "Who?"

If she hadn't said anything to her current partner, Jason wasn't about to go there. They didn't always get along perfectly, but in this last case, he'd saved her ass, and she'd done the same for him. He shrugged. "I don't even know. I think she's out of town right now."

That seemed to satisfy her new partner, for he nodded. "She is. Let me know what Crawford says."

"I will."

After Grasso left, he sat there and thought about drugs and dirty cops and love affairs that ended because someone was killed, and wondered about his choices in life, which happened now and then.

"Jase."

His head came up and the familiar tone cut right through him.

Oh crap.

He turned with a very fake smile. "Kate. Yeah right. I thought that was you over there."

There was a problem in his life. He didn't do fake well at all. All up front was more his style.

Kate lifted one hip and slid onto the stool Grasso had just left. "*Thought* it was me? Please. You've said a lot of stupid things in your lifetime—there's a list miles long—but that might be the most ridiculous yet. We lived together for months. You've been doing your best to not as much as glance over since the minute you saw I was here. But you saw me, and I saw you. Can we be honest here?"

"Sure." He was just going to walk home, so maybe another beer was in order. He lifted a finger at the bartender. "Fine. It is a little awkward to see you have drinks at our old place with another guy, but you've moved on. Hi. There it is. We've said hi."

She gazed at him. "You are angry with me and I think I know why."

He'd always loved her eyes. They were really gorgeous. And her tits. He couldn't deny his affection for that part of her anatomy. Fantastic breasts.

And he was more pissed than he realized, or let himself realize, that she'd not come to the hospital after the shooting. It stirred in him as they looked at each other. Casually, he fingered his beer. The music faded into the background. "About you leaving? I'm a fan of self-preservation myself, so no, I get why you moved out. You wanted more dark and brooding. I'm not exactly the esoteric type. Who's the boyfriend?"

"I want you to know, I *couldn't* visit you."

The trouble was, she was in earnest. Did they really have to fucking talk about this? It was over. Staying home and playing solitaire on his computer might have been a better idea. He still tried to deflect. "Visit me?"

"You just can't play stupid well, so don't try." Kate, the soon-to-be doctor of psychology, shook her head. "God, you have so many issues I should have stayed and used you as a case study." She sighed and rubbed her cheek. "Jason, I wouldn't have moved in with you if I didn't have feelings for you, and just because you are impossible to live with doesn't mean they all vanished. Your job scared me from the beginning, and when I heard you'd been shot by a serial killer that was an affirmation of my fears."

What was he supposed to do? Apologize? He hadn't enjoyed the particular exchange of gunfire either. It must have been those two bullets that hurt like hell and nearly killed him. Maybe her tender feelings had been vindicated, but he'd nearly died.

He was making progress because he didn't actually ask that question out loud, but he still couldn't quite handle it the right way. "I exist to affirm your fears about bad decisions, Katie. If you didn't know that, you would not have left."

Her face tightened a fraction, but then she looked away. "I'm sorry."

"For?"

Her hand rested on the bar, and her eyes were soft as she turned to look at him again. "That you never fell in love with me. Or that I ever fell in love with you. I can't figure out even now which is worse. That was a great deal of the problem. I couldn't decide which one of us I felt sorrier for."

"Is that good English? Sorrier for? Doesn't sound right to me."

The minute he said it, he regretted it, but the flippancy was a knee-jerk reaction he couldn't help. Had he loved her? He was afraid he hadn't. Here he was, in his middle thirties and he'd never been in love. Ouch. Loser.

"I need to get back to the university. Take care of yourself, okay?" She slid off the stool and left, the man she'd been sitting with giving him a look of open curiosity as he held the door for her.

It didn't help when the bartender set his beer before him, and said, "You know, I think from the look on your face I'll just give you this one on the house, Detective."

Chapter 10

He came home to an empty house.

No *warmth*. The woodstove was cold, the furnace off

He said her name and it echoed through the hallway in an eerie repetition, as if someone whispered it back to him. The chill that touched his skin wasn't just the unmoving air.

Methodically he took off his shoes, his stocking feet freezing as he moved through the silent rooms.

She was gone.

Nothing. No one. Every bedroom deserted, the quiet unnatural, darkness and panic growing.

He'd wondered what she would do. There were rumors circulating . . . of course there were. Secrets were very rarely kept. Only a fool counted on someone else keeping their mouth firmly shut.

That was, of course, the problem. He hadn't counted

on anyone, anything, he'd just been a human being, and human beings were extremely fallible.

He should have just talked to her. Face to face. Addressed it.

At the end of it all he went to the kitchen, took out a bottle of milk that had seen better days, and drank a glass, staring off into space.

So it had happened.

The milk was really sour.

How long had she been gone?

The station was busy, but then again it usually was, and tourist season wasn't quite over either, so the county still had extra residents and more people always meant more trouble.

An inevitable equation.

Ellie weaved her way through the building with the ease of some familiarity and finally found the desk of Detective Jared Carson, a slight smile hovering on her lips when he glanced up and saw her, his expression going from distracted to welcoming.

She liked him. He was younger than she was, probably only late twenties. Tall, a little lanky, with blond hair already thinning a little and lashes as fair as his hair. She wasn't surprised he was stuck with this very old cold case, if it was even a case at all, since he was pretty young to be in his position. His tie was a little askew, but his handshake was all business. "Detective MacIntosh. I haven't seen you since this spring. What brings you here?"

She took the chair he indicated and smiled with as

much warmth as she could summon. "I suspect you know. The body found on my grandfather's property. Any progress?"

"You've been to see the medical examiner. What did he have to say?"

"I see there is open communication between your offices."

"Some." His grin was easy but conciliatory. "Look, I'm not going to give you false promises. Truthfully, the old records are a pain and the ME's office is giving me kind of a large window on those bones."

"And you have other cases."

"I do." He folded his hands together.

"So not a lot of urgency."

"Should there be, Detective?"

Well, now, that was the problem. Why the hell was she pushing on this case anyway? Obviously her grandfather just wanted it to go away, and in truth so did she.

"No." Ellie exhaled and pushed her hair behind her ear. "I'm just puzzled. Since there isn't an age assigned to the bones yet, I am wondering who could possibly be interred in an unmarked grave. That should make us all curious, shouldn't it?"

Carson nodded. "We are, but there's no specific indication of murder."

"And if there was, it would have been years ago."

"Pretty much."

"Those striations on the bones?"

"Inconclusive, I'm told, at least in labeling it a homicide."

And they'd given the case to a new detective who

was too busy to look into it. In his defense, they were probably overworked.

"I'm wasting your time." Her tone was apologetic.

"No." The words were gracious. "If you have a helpful lead we'd appreciate that, but otherwise, we'll just keep you informed if you like."

"What if I could offer some free help in the form of a colleague of mine from Milwaukee who is out on medical leave? He's already agreed to look over missing-persons files. He wants something to do."

"Free is good. I'll ask the sheriff, but I'm sure you'll get a thumbs-up. We like free around here, especially from MPD."

"Thanks."

Outside it had started to thicken with the dusk. Bryce had, as usual, opted out of entering the county offices, no doubt a reaction to his previous experiences with Wisconsin law enforcement. He was leaning against the car, his cell phone to his ear, and when she approached, she heard him say, "We'll be back in Milwaukee tomorrow. I'll ask Ellie."

They'd driven her car up and she looked at him inquiringly before she slid into the driver's seat. "Ask me what?"

"Dinner with my parents."

He came from a close-knit family, which she liked, but her schedule was sometimes erratic. Half the time she canceled, and while the Granthams had been very nice about it, it seemed like at the moment there was potential for another fall from grace. "Tomorrow? I don't know."

"How about we plan it at our house? I'll cook. If

you get a call, you don't have to apologize. Just take off."

In the act of starting the car, she faltered. *Our house.* How easily he moved ahead, when she was not nearly quite so confident.

And he caught it.

"Fine, I'll tell them we will do it some other time." He settled into the passenger seat.

"I haven't even answered yet."

"Body language is pretty effective."

The car started smoothly. She thought about bones on hillsides and dead cops. "I'm a little preoccupied, but I love your parents and don't want to make them think I don't appreciate the invitation. Feel free to go without me."

"Maybe I'll suggest next weekend."

She backed up, wished the slanting sunlight wasn't in exactly the angle that made it impossible to see behind her, and cleared the parking space enough to pull forward "Things could be better by then," she agreed neutrally. "Or worse, of course."

"Goes without saying."

"I don't want you to hate my job."

"I don't actually." His voice was mild, his expression reflecting pragmatic contemplation. "I've wondered often enough why I am intrigued by driven women, but the answer escapes me. Maybe in this universe, some things just *are*. Quite frankly, you worry about it a lot more than I do."

It could be true. She glanced over at his tall, relaxed body and wondered herself about the intricate and often inexplicable dynamics of sexual attraction.

Even though she was a detective, there were some mysteries she just could not solve.

"Let's go see my grandfather and talk about this later."

Danni answered the call on her personal cell with perceptible irritation. "This is Crawford."

"You on duty?"

For a second she seemed puzzled, but then the voice apparently registered. As did the lack of a polite greeting. "Santiago?"

"At the moment, no. I'm just Jason. I wondered if you might want to meet and talk."

"Meet?"

She sounded dazed still. Grief, he'd discovered, could bury a person more effectively than a load of sand. Maybe if she and Chad had been married or even engaged she would have gotten some time off. He still thought maybe Metzger should consider giving her some leave.

One look at the clock said it was almost six. "Can we? Hey, I'll buy you dinner."

"I'm hungry," she admitted. "It's kind of a surprise if you want the truth. I haven't felt much like eating. I keep thinking about it, but never get around to it. This isn't how I wanted to go on a diet."

He agreed, thinking about his encounter with Kate. "Actually, I went out for lunch and ended up just drinking beer instead. I'm kind of hungry myself."

"I have to work later."

"We can go right now, if you want. I'm pretty flexible these days. You know that."

"Where?" she asked simply.

He gave her the name and address and walked into the restaurant exactly half an hour later—and though he had one of those brief moments when he wondered why he was doing someone else's investigation while on leave, it passed pretty quick.

The apartment. Those close walls. It was a relief to be out of there for a little while. He wasn't anything apparently without the detective part of Jason Santiago. Maybe Kate was right, maybe he was a case study someone could get a Ph.D. analyzing if they wanted to bother with it, but he wasn't positive he was that complicated.

His job was the machine that drove the man. Hmm. Sounded like a bad movie.

He'd chosen a steak place that had the advantage of not being so noisy a person had to shout across the table, but wasn't dressy either. Good thing, as Danni arrived wearing shapeless slacks that he was sure she thought hid those few extra pounds, and a summer blouse over a camisole top.

There was decent atmosphere. Low lights, nice booths, vague piped-in music. There was also a bar with a polished top and racks of bottles. Nice but not expensive. Waiters in tuxedos were not his thing, no matter how good the food they served might be.

"Hi," she said, sitting down. "I'm . . . here. I guess that's it, I'm here . . . thanks for asking me out. I mean, I know you aren't asking me out . . ."

The first sentence sputtered to an end and he got the sentiment right away from the gloss of tears in her eyes.

Problem one: he was not the world's most sensitive guy, but he tried. "Hey, we're friends, right? I tell you what, let's catch up on what's going on in the department and order our food, and after we eat, we'll talk about more serious stuff. Sound reasonable?"

Her tremulous smile spoke volumes. "Sure. I've had enough serious to last a lifetime."

Normally he would have thought to himself that Grasso owed him, but this was as much about friendship as anything he could do for the lieutenant. She ordered a rib eye—medium—cottage fries, and a salad with oil and vinegar—on the side—and he got basically the same thing, except he opted for blue cheese dressing. He also asked for a glass of Merlot. Hey, he was taking a cab. Next week he saw the doctor and should be cleared for driving, especially when he told his physician he wasn't taking the pain meds any longer.

Having his autonomy taken away had been probably the most difficult thing about his recovery. Besides, he drove a sweet vintage Mustang, fully restored, and that of itself was a pleasure, pure and simple, he'd been denied for weeks.

"You come here much?" She asked it as if she was actually interested in the answer and he appreciated the effort, since he doubted she was.

"No." He and Kate had, once or twice, but this wasn't the time to think about that. "The food is good, you don't have to wear a tie, and it isn't a chain. I have no idea why I have such a problem with that."

"Meaning?"

"I don't enjoy knowing I am going to be served the exact same thing each time."

"It's the job. Different every single day." Her amber eyes filled with tears again. "You just don't know what to expect when you get up in the morning."

No doubt she was referring to Chad's death and the call they'd answered. Thank God, the salads came in time so he didn't have to respond.

Jason speared a leaf. "You doing okay?"

"Not so much." She ate a grape tomato. "I'm trying. The shootings and two cop funerals sort of trump everything else."

"I'm not officially on the case and won't ever be as I understand it, but I have a lot of time on my hands right now. I might poke around a little. I'm pretty pissed about Chad."

He'd debated whether or not to tell her about the phone call to Grasso, but decided against it.

Call it a personal flaw, but he didn't trust a lot of people. Maybe it was his crappy childhood. That could, Kate had pointed out with the wisdom of someone studying earnestly the human psyche, give a person trust issues.

Or, he'd countered, it could prepare them to be self-sufficient by instilling a healthy knowledge of survival of the fittest.

She never really did agree with him on that point.

But he had to acknowledge that the result was he was suspicious and not a fan of the integrity levels of some of his fellow human beings. Danni Crawford, who had just finished every scrap of her undoubtedly tasteless salad except for those lonely croutons, was probably like she seemed. A pretty, nice young woman with a job where she served her community by risking her life—no one would argue that in light of recent events—by helping to control crime and keep the peace.

Their steaks arrived and he asked a few general questions as they ate. Jason was just glad he wasn't sitting in front of the television with a plate balanced on his knees at least one night this week.

He was taking his last bite when she set down her fork and gazed somberly at him across the table. In the low lighting her eyes looked gold. "It's possible I know who killed David Fielding and Chad."

Grabbing his glass of wine, he washed down that last piece of steak and said, "If you are serious, start talking."

She knew nothing.

He'd asked, sitting on the sofa in the front room, pointing out they were friends, weren't they? If something had been said . . . could she please tell him?

She couldn't tell him anything, unfortunately.

All along he'd never really been quite handsome. Wide shouldered, no doubt of that, and with a slightly rugged air, but maybe that was just his occupation. He was very physical. It was what a woman noticed first about him.

What just about every woman in town had noticed.

But he'd chosen Vivian.

Lucky girl.

Or maybe, as it all turned out, not so lucky.

The house smelled like old cedar with a faint overtone of coffee. In Ellie's memory there was almost always a pot brewing in an old electric pot, the kind with the clear top that showed the water and grounds shooting up and had a red light that went green when it was done.

Ellie poured the coffee, took two cups out onto the screened porch, handed one to her grandfather and the other to Bryce, and then went back to get hers. They were at least talking in an offhand way—she could hear the murmur of their voices—and when she joined them, they were both looking out over the lake, discussing the fishing. Through the screen showed a picture of water with woods on the shores around, and the hint of autumn color in the sheen of the reflection of the water.

For two men without much else in common, it was a good thing that fish appeared to be so fascinating.

". . . some decent largemouth." Her grandfather pointed. "Right in that little cove. I used to go out there with night crawlers. Right as the sun was coming up, I could almost always take at least a four-pound fish."

The view was really scenic, Ellie thought as she settled into a handmade wooden chair, the screens a buffer against the notorious Wisconsin mosquito, affectionately named the state bird. The sunset reflected in a scarlet haze above the tree line, the pines in dark formations and the birches ghostly shadows.

Bryce nodded, looking out over the water. "Eighty feet deep? I bet you've got lake trout in there."

"DNR stocked it years ago, but no one catches them. I have a neighbor who claims he's seen 'em, though. However, he can be a bit of a blowhard."

"Is that right? I wonder if—"

Ellie cut in. "As fascinating as lake trout can be, I wouldn't mind talking about why we're here. The skeleton is of an indeterminate age." She hadn't really meant to interrupt Bryce midsentence, but the neutral avoidance of the subject was starting to irritate her. "The medical examiner was not able to give me any specific information. A female, most certainly, and not a child. They can carbon date, but it takes time and I'm not sure they'll spend the money on it."

The breeze was a light sigh. Her grandfather just looked resigned. "She's been there a long while then?"

"It depends on the definition of a long while. Right now we have no idea."

"At my age, that seems to be defined by the generation. What I think is long, Eleanor, and what you think is long, is probably not exactly the same thing."

Bryce coughed a little into his coffee, no doubt because she'd told him once that if he ever called her Eleanor, she'd strangle him. He hadn't either, so the threat was effective, but her grandfather was another story.

Even when she was a child, he'd never called her Ellie. That had been her grandmother's nickname for her. "We are going to try and match old records of people being reported missing."

No reaction except a contemplative look from her grandfather. "I've heard that works."

It did if given a fairly specific time period. Otherwise it was just damn tedious.

Whatever happened next, she noted, as she finished her coffee, the reaction she'd picked up on that morning when he'd showed her the grave was utterly gone. He was no longer that shaken man.

What has changed?

She was overanalyzing this. It felt that way on the serene porch with the view of the water, the birds making soft calls as the dusk thickened. Wisps of chimney smoke floated by like tired ghosts. Robert MacIntosh had simply been an old man startled by finding a skeleton on his property and she'd maybe seen too much in it thanks to a jaded knowledge of how human beings sometimes dealt with one another.

That conclusion lasted until she got into the car to drive them to her house, only about thirty miles south, still unsold though she'd moved months ago, and Bryce said succinctly, "He *is* lying to you."

Startled, she looked over, the vehicle straying for a moment on the county road before she jerked it back across the line. "What?"

Bryce, his dark hair casual and probably a little too long for her grandfather's taste—she'd caught the look—just lifted his shoulders. "I am not a detective, but it seemed to me that maybe he's had a chance to think about it all since he called you when the burial site was found and has come to the conclusion you are not going to be able to unravel this particular mystery."

That could be absolutely true. She wasn't sure she could unravel it either. "What makes you think so?"

"Ellie, how *are* you going to solve it? As far as I can tell, it isn't going to happen, or at least the chances are low. He is no longer the panicked man you described to me, but he has settled."

"Settled? What the hell does that mean?" She guided

the car past a logging truck, picked up speed, and headed for 51.

"Settled down. Considered what might happen next and come to the realization that you are faced with an almost impossible crime to solve, if there was even a crime at all."

"How can you possibly know that?"

"He was watching you the entire time."

She blew out a breath of frustration. "Bryce . . . watching me? What the hell is that? He's my grandfather and we were visiting. If he looked at me now and then, I should hope so. That's polite. Just like you sitting out there talking about good fishing spots."

"I actually care about good fishing spots."

"Don't even try and dare to be funny right now." There was a definite edge to her voice.

He reached over and lightly touched her arm. "I'm not. And maybe I'm entirely wrong, but it just seemed like, from an outside point of view, as you began to describe your interview with the medical examiner I thought he relaxed. I am not giving you anything but an impression."

And one hell of an impression it was.

"That body could have been there for decades. Long before our family bought the property."

"But you don't think so." His voice was mild, non-confrontational, but he was not often interested in an argument.

She stared at the road. Yes, some of the trees were really turning. It was almost full dark and she could still see the changing color, flashing red and deepening amber. It took a moment, but she admitted, "I don't like that she was buried nude. That's . . . not how people do things. Even poor people who decide to dump someone at the bottom of a hill in an unmarked grave. No clothes. Why? Even decades ago when forensics was just a baby science, criminals understood that what might not decay, might betray."

"Might not decay, might betray? Fabulous motto to live by," he said dryly.

"Depends on who you are."

"I suppose it does."

She shot him a sidelong glance. "Do you really think he was lying?"

"Tonight, no. You didn't ask him a direct question that he responded to with less than honesty, but I think he was *relieved*. He seemed not nervous exactly—a man that stoic could never seem nervous—but I think he might have been afraid of what you might say. And whatever it was, you didn't say it."

God how she wished she didn't agree.

Carl wasn't a stranger to the seedier sides of the city. He'd done his time on patrol what felt like a lifetime ago. It really was an invaluable experience.

It actually sucked him in a little.

Not strip bars . . . no. He wasn't that man. He didn't like them loud either, or those smoky honky-tonks with half-naked girls in jeans and leather vests.

But a man didn't have to slap down a bill on the bar and order a Bud Light to cross the line. Not hardly.

Neither did he pay for sex. He didn't have to. Usually women took one look at the house, the car, the rest of it, which was not a measure of him as a man but just stuff . . . and they were interested.

It said a lot about how mankind worked in general. He was never sure whether or not to blame the male of the species, or the female. At the moment, he blamed his gender but decided to unashamedly exploit it.

He saw Lena's long, sleek legs first as she slipped into the car. Walking around in heels gave her some excellent calf muscles and she knew it. Carl nodded. "Is it okay if I pull away right now, or should we seem to haggle for a minute or two?"

"This isn't a street corner in New York. Pull away." The woman next to him smoothed her skirt, if it could be called a skirt it was that short, and crossed her ankles. "Besides, if you think you weren't made as a cop, you can think again. It amazes me how naive you all are." She had long blond hair, which wasn't natural if the much darker color of her finely plucked brows was an indication, and her blouse was unbuttoned enough to show a hint of a lacy black bra. Carl actually liked her, and they had an informal deal where he used his influence to cut the charges if she was brought in, which had only happened once or twice. She was very pretty and tended to work privately for some very high profile clients, but now and then she was on the street. If she didn't dabble a little too often with recreational drugs, she could probably pull herself out of the life.

"*We* are babes in the woods?" he asked with sardonic amusement.

"In comparison, yes."

"And here I thought we were considered hardened bastards."

"Aren't you cute. Try sleeping with a drug dealer."

"No thanks."

"Good call." Lena Wasson studied his profile. "So what is this?"

"I have a tip about Fielding, the cop who was shot in his bed."

"And you thought you'd share it with me. Thanks. Last I checked, I didn't give a rat's ass about Fielding." She pulled down the passenger-side visor and checked her makeup in the lighted mirror.

"Such language from a lady. Word has it that Fielding was a zealous guy, right? I've been with vice for five years and he was pretty much hell on prostitution. Very high arrest record. Since we are on the subject of drug dealers, any of the girls that use complain about him confiscating their stashes during an arrest?"

"What stashes?" Lena blinked her eyes in mock innocence.

"Come on. I know he never brought you in, but have you heard anything?"

Patience tended to be a true virtue when dealing with the less than virtuous. It was an odd benefit of his notoriety that having crossed the line himself and been under an internal affairs investigation gained him some respect on the street. He wasn't afraid to take matters a little too far . . . stretch the law a little, and it put him at least a little on the other side.

Fine, he'd roll with that if it helped him get information. Most of his informants were at least a little afraid of him.

"Are you going to beat me if I say I do but won't tell?" Lena gave him another flash of leg. "Please say yes."

"Have you?" He liked the show, but needed the answer a lot more. Besides, she was just kidding. Even in her tight-fitting clothes, he suspected she was armed.

"Like what specifically?" Her tone was sulky, her spiky lashes lowered. "I know you're paying, but I only have an hour. You're going to need to drop me off downtown at the Marriott. There's a convention this week there and I have a date."

"Is that the new term for it? I'm so behind the times."

"Call it what you want. I'm calling it a date in front of a cop, okay?"

He braked for a light and glanced over. Without the drugs and a profession that was not conducive to a healthy lifestyle, she might even have been beautiful. Some things in life were just a damned pity. "I'm not asking about you, Lena, so relax. If you want put your hard-earned money up your nose, I am not going to say a word about it. All I want is to find out if there is any connection between Fielding and drugs. Was he pushing any pimp about supplying his girls?"

"I haven't heard anything."

He caught it, the slight hesitation. "Anything? You sure?"

The lift of her shoulders in a shrug was belied by the sudden tension in her body. "I'm sure that I don't have any definite information that can help you."

"Indefinite information is okay. Believe it or not, I can follow a lead." The light changed and he pulled out into the intersection, signaling for a street that would take them close to the hotel she wanted, but he had no intention of dropping her off until he had at least something. He could ask a lot of questions in an hour, and she was right, he was paying for her time out of his own pocket.

"I can't have anything leading back to me."

"Goes without saying." His tone was absolutely neutral. "Obviously you've made some sort of connection. Talk to me. Have we made a leap from pimp to dealer now? I'm not trying to get you in trouble, Lena. Quite the opposite. When I am doing my job effectively, I keep people alive by taking killers off the streets."

"Why can't you just ask for a blow job instead," she muttered darkly, tapping a long red fingernail on her thigh. "Those guys are a lot easier to deal with."

He muffled a laugh, because he was fairly sure that was true in a way he didn't even want to imagine. "I need a name."

"These are not understanding people. Come on. Just let me out anywhere. It's a pretty nice night. I can walk." Her hand moved to the door.

There wasn't a chance in hell he was pulling over right now. Carl said in measured tones, "I am not all that understanding myself. A name?"

She blew out a breath. "I don't want to do this. Usually you're just shaking down the small guys. Everyone thinks you're just a regular of mine. This—*this*—could be serious shit."

"On the street people think I pay you for sex? I'm offended."

"Hey, I'm expensive. But I mean it, serious shit."

"Murder usually is. I want a name."

Maybe it was the implacable tone of his voice, but she caved. "Angelo Terrance. He works for a certain family."

It rang a bell . . . vaguely. "What certain family?"

"The Henleys. When you mentioned drugs and the dead cop, I made a connection. But who knows."

"He's killed a cop?"

"I never said that. There's a bit of a rumor he's being looked at by the DEA."

The DEA. And Fielding had called an undercover DEA agent. Okay. A link.

"For what?"

"I don't know exactly. Some questions are better left unasked IMHO."

"IMHO?"

"In my humble opinion. Jesus, Lieutenant, don't you play on the Internet?"

The answer was easy. "I don't play at anything."

"Yeah," she said in response, sarcasm evident, "I get that impression. Maybe you should give me a call sometime and I can teach you how to do it. Just pull in right out front. I always enjoy my grand entrance. Everyone stares when I walk into a nice hotel, but I am pretty sure the advertising gets me new customers."

There was a well.

An old hole with crumbling rocks around it, lichen on the surface, and at one time there had been a winch for the bucket but it was long gone.

She could be there.

That was where he'd put the body.

He'd waited to look. Of course he had. It was the worst suspicion that anyone could possibly have of another human being, so he'd avoided it, shrank from it, and treated it like it was an unwelcome guest by giving it only the slightest bit of attention.

However, there was nothing a man could hide from forever.

A flashlight did no good. So on a crispy morning, with frost on the fallen leaves and the lake quiet, he'd taken a lantern and tied it to a long rope. He'd bought the piece at the hardware store, but it wasn't expensive, and if it fell, he was not going to mourn the loss.

Down, down, down.

The walls were slimy, so there had to be water at the bottom, and he caught the glimmer just before the light hit the water.

Holding fast, he jerked a little, but the wick stayed lit.

Throat tightening, he bent to look . . .

Ellie loved her house. River stone fireplace, hardwood floors, different levels . . . she'd never find anything in Milwaukee like it for even close to the price.

Not that it mattered, since she was moving in with Bryce.

A good decision? It seemed as if her mind was not quite made up when she walked through the door of her house, but then again, weighty matters in life were always a giant leap off a cliff. Or at least for her. Some people seemed to race to the finish line with a lot more ease.

The place had a faint odor of disuse, as if the air was slightly stale, and there was a thin layer of dust on the coffee table. The refrigerator was unplugged with the door propped open, and a sense of nostalgia hit her as she looked around. "I'm wondering if I should take it off the market."

Bryce switched on a lamp. "Hedging your bets?"

The words were said too softly for the remark to be entirely a joke. She slipped her sweater off and tossed it over the back of a chair. "It would make a nice place to get away from the city now and then for us both. Nothing but woods around. Peace and quiet."

"It's a thought." His voice was carefully neutral.

"Not too far from your parents' cabin either. Might be nice to come up and not have to actually stay with them. Like what we are doing now with my grandfather even though he wanted us to stay. If we had I can guarantee I'd have the guest room and you'd have been sleeping on the couch."

"I agree wholeheartedly that this is better then." His smile was a flash of white teeth. "I still remember the first night I spent here. There are worse things than being stuck in a raging storm with a beautiful woman."

A woman who just happened to be investigating him as the prime suspect in a series of disappearances at the time. Ellie still looked back on that night and mentally shook her head at herself. It had seemed like the right course, and she certainly had not intended on sleeping with him, but it had happened anyway. She'd been almost 100 percent sure he was innocent, but that meant there was a glimmer of a doubt.

Quite a leap of faith.

There was a pretty potent physical attraction between them. There had been from the first time they'd met, and she wondered often enough—maybe too often—if it didn't skew her perception of their relationship.

Maybe staying at the house was not the best idea after all. It brought back the indecision of that first night and she really didn't need that right after she'd agreed to move in with him. Oh, now she knew he wasn't a murderer. He could be one of the most decent men she had ever met, but then again that also had always applied, in her mind, to her grandfather.

So she said lightly, "That really was quite a storm. Want to open that bottle of wine we bought? I'll get the glasses. I think I left a few here because I don't have as much space at the condo." Ellie moved casually into the kitchen and opened a cabinet. "Will a juice glass work?"

"Fine with me." Bryce took out a pocketknife that included a corkscrew and went to work on the cork in the bottle.

Moment passed. Except she wasn't convinced—and here she was the cop—that he hadn't caught subtle nuances of the exchange. Maybe that was what she couldn't get used to. That he could see it and not insist they talk about it.

In her world, the strict world of fact and enforced rules, when there was an issue, two people *talked* about it. Detective. Suspect. Investigator. Criminal. Witness. *All must talk*.

His world was kind of inviting. The let's-pretend-it-isn't-important world . . .

But no. She just couldn't seem to not sweat the important stuff, however small or large it might be.

"Our relationship is freaking me out," she admitted, picking up the bottle he'd set down on the counter and dashing Merlot into both glasses. "I like you. I really like you, I might even love you . . . don't try and pin me down on that one, and yet, Bryce, I am terrified."

"Might even love me? Let's not have that." His voice was tenderly amused.

"Shut up. Don't tease me. I carry a weapon." She sent him a lethal look.

He sat down on a bar stool next to the kitchen counter and looked unfazed. "I know. Detective MacIntosh: serial killers, no problem; long-term commitment, not so brave."

"How can you be so . . . understanding?" She truly didn't get it, which might be something she needed to discuss with Dr. Lukens at some point.

"Don't sound annoyed. This entire argument is ridiculous."

"I am just . . . mystified. There you go. A good word for it. Mystified."

"Ellie, do I have a choice except to be understanding?"

He had a point. To a certain extent anyway. "You can always walk away."

"Yeah, but I get hung up there. I don't *want* to walk away."

Were they really arguing over the issue of his patience? She inhaled through her nose, let it out slowly through her mouth, and then laughed. Then she deliberately put her elbows on the counter, facing him. "Here's part of the issue. No matter how this all shakes out, I'm the bad guy. If it works it is because you tried hard enough for the both of us, and if it fails it is because I can't claim the same thing."

"Someone has said this to you, or is it your perception?"

"Jody," she confessed before taking a drink of wine. Her older sister was ridiculously opinionated.

Bryce laughed. "I don't want to accuse your sister of meddling, but sweetheart, your sister *meddles* with your life. You decide. If you want more time, that's fine. Continue your lease. However, keep in mind that just because she has the suburban dream of two point something kids and a husband who is an insurance adjustor, it doesn't mean you aren't meant to travel a different path."

He was right. Hands down.

"This is complicated," she muttered before taking a drink from her glass, the thick rim not exactly ideal, but the wine tasted good.

"Love?" he said in reply, his gaze locked on hers. "Sometimes it really is. It's when you think it is simple that you find yourself in real trouble."

Jason was in the middle of a dream. A prisoner in the moment, the roof seething with flames, his breath caught in his chest, his limbs immobile.

Been there. Done that.

Then he was free, there were swirling lights, and he could see Ellie's face, pale and concerned, and suddenly someone pushed her away and sunk a needle into his arm.

He woke sweating, disoriented, and it took a few minutes before he realized that he was twisted awkwardly in the sheets and that was part of the reason he couldn't breathe.

"Fuck." He sat up and swept a hand through his hair.

The lights outside his window into the pool courtyard were comforting at least, illuminating the room. He rolled over and imagined the kids, splashing in the pool, and wondered how that would have felt when he was five or six. He would have loved to have a pool.

When he'd looked at the apartment, it had been because the rent in the listing was in line with what he could afford, and it actually boasted a laundry hookup in the unit. It was a testament to how much he hated to have to go out to do laundry that it was a must-have on his list, but in the end, that wasn't what made him sign the lease.

It was when he pulled up. The first thing he'd seen was a boy about ten years old, walking a puppy in a grassy pet-designated area. Then he noticed the parking lot was full of minivans and realized it was a family oriented complex, and as a bachelor, you'd think he would have just turned around and left, but instead he found he kind of liked the idea of all the happy families, even if the place was kind of a zoo at times.

Go figure.

His upbringing had been much more about being painfully quiet. If his old man noticed him it was never good, and like any very self-reliant creature, he'd learned early to stay still and in the corners.

Wood mouse.

That was him.

They were stealthy little animals, striving to live in an environment where virtually everyone wanted to kill them one way or another. On that note, he knew exactly how to survive.

Dreams were for the damned.

It wasn't so much a dream as a memory of that night when he was shot. He knew it was a result of not being able to remember exactly in a conscious stream because of the trauma, but it was all there, locked away in his brain.

Ellie MacIntosh had taken off her shirt when those two bullets pierced his chest. Lying there, gasping, blood pouring from potentially fatal wounds in his torso, he'd still noticed the little lacy black bra she wore under her conservative blouse. She'd whipped the garment off over her head and crouched there over him, pressed the fabric to those bullet holes to staunch the bleeding, her commentary a profane litany of how he should just hang the hell on, not give the fuck up, and what the shit had he thought, walking into two bullets that way . . .

Even dying, he'd wheezed out a laugh.

When he woke and discovered he was still alive, he laughed even harder, though it had really hurt.

If there was one thing he could say for himself, he could be a bad influence on anybody.

Without looking at the clock, he called her. "MacIntosh."

She sputtered. In books he'd always thought they made it up, but not so; she actually sputtered. "What . . . when . . . have you . . . you lost your mind? Do you know what time it is?"

"Danni Crawford says this could be related to organized crime. Not directly, but her idea caught my attention."

"It's three in the morning."

"I have trouble sleeping."

"Apparently so do I since you entered my life." She exhaled and he could picture her up on one elbow, hair tousled and her eyes sleepy . . . wearing a T-shirt or a thin-strapped negligee . . . no she wouldn't go for that. Nothing too girlie. Maybe just *nothing*.

Jason liked that image best.

MacIntosh. Wearing nothing. Nice picture in his brain.

He'd been off work for a little too long if he was indulging in phone fantasies about his partner. Or maybe just celibate a little too long.

"Danni's got a theory, and since she was involved with Chad, it might be what you are looking for."

"Have you been drinking?"

He had, but not for a few hours. He wandered out onto the balcony off his apartment even though it wasn't exactly warm out, but it wasn't too cold either. The fresh air cleared his mind a little. "Not much."

That wasn't exactly the truth. In general he'd been drinking too much since going off the pain meds, but it was more boredom than anything else.

"Jesus, Santiago, go to bed. I'm interested in what you have to say, but I'll be a lot more interested after a cup of coffee in at least four hours."

"I thought we were supposed to be on the cop angle of this investigation."

"We are, but—"

"I had dinner with Danni and we talked about Chad and she has an interesting angle on maybe why both he and Fielding were targeted. Grasso called me and said he'd gotten a similar tip, but a different name."

"Like what name?"

Someone said something in the background. Male voice, a low rumble of sound. Grantham, no doubt.

They were in bed.

Of course they were.

She was right, it was late.

Damn.

Jason ended the call. Churlish of him maybe to not at least say good-bye, but formalities weren't his thing.

In his boxers, he went back inside to the kitchen. The entire contents of his refrigerator still consisted of an outdated quart of milk, two jars of pickled peppers—though why he'd opened the second one before the first was finished he had no clue—a few condiments, and one lonely hot dog swimming with nitrates and nitrites.

He eschewed the milk, chose the hot dog, and threw it into the microwave, tossed a couple of peppers on top, and ate it in about three bites, standing by the sink. Then he got a glass of water and went out to the balcony again. Sleep was probably not going to be an option for the rest of the night . . . he knew the signs. He'd seen the shrink that the department provided for officers shot in the line of duty, but besides "the dream" he was pretty sure he didn't carry around a lot of baggage from that experience.

The killer shot him, he shot the killer. End of story.

The trouble sleeping was not a product of that event. He'd had that going on pretty much his whole life.

Settling into a chair, he propped his feet on the railing and brooded at the empty courtyard. Having insomnia had its advantages; he did his best thinking at times like this, when the world was dark.

So Danni thought maybe Chad had stumbled across something that was linked to Fielding's murder. Garrison Henley.

Cops linked to corruption? It wasn't a new story. The temptation was always there. Drug dealers made a ridiculous amount of money and police officers were paid pennies in comparison. Equal danger and unequal pay. The Henley name was pretty prominent, but Chad had apparently gotten some sort of information that implied organized crime might have contributed a bit to the family fortunes.

Were the two killings blackmail gone bad?

Fielding and Brown, however, were not that kind of law enforcement. There were officers Jason trusted and those he didn't, just like any other facet of life. If asked, he would have said he trusted them.

But someone had tipped off Grasso. Which meant they knew Metzger asked them to keep an eye on the investigation.

Who? Jason thought as he slouched down. It was a damn good question.

The moon was a crescent in the sky and he stared at it, thinking, wide awake, the rail cold under his bare ankles.

Chapter 13

The porch swing moved and her skirt flowed across the weathered boards. The morning was clear and pleasant, though she gathered her sweater around her as she slowly pushed with her foot.

The rings screwed into the rafters creaked a little.

Murder.

The word really hadn't come up.

Was that good or wasn't it? She wasn't sure.

He was back, and they weren't talking. He suspected. She knew he did. A part of her had wanted him to know, to realize the lengths she would go to, the sacrifices she was willing to make.

But he said . . . nothing.

Maybe paybacks *were* hell.

Jason rolled over and searched for his phone, finally finding it on the side of the bed with a groping hand, his mind not quite functioning properly. Finally, he must have fallen asleep.

"What?" His voice sounded like he'd ingested a pail of rocks, so he cleared his throat and tried again. "Santiago."

The sound he heard was a rush of breath and then . . . nothing.

Like absolutely nothing.

He didn't understand as he looked at the display, but that was definitely Danni Crawford's number according to his phone.

"Hey, Danni? You there?"

Maybe she'd dialed him accidentally. God knew he'd done it before. He was awake now, sitting on the side of the bed. He ended the call and when he dialed her again, it went straight to voice mail. Leaving a message for her to call him back, he set aside his cell and contemplated the chances of falling back to sleep.

Slim to none at a guess.

Forget it. He stared out the window. The sun was coming up anyway, the low glow giving shape to the building across the street.

But he couldn't forget it.

It was probably a misdial, but she'd looked pretty shaky when they'd had dinner, and considering what she'd told him, he just had a bad feeling.

Cleared for it or not, he tugged on his jeans, pulled on a T-shirt, and picked up his keys. A few minutes later he was out the door and headed down to his car.

He'd find nothing, he told himself as he slid into the familiar cradle of the seat for the first time in two months and slipped in the key. Danni would be as annoyed with him as MacIntosh had been earlier if he just showed up at this hour of the morning, and so what? She worked the night shift. No harm, no foul.

Right? He was worried about her.

When he pulled up at her house, he saw her patrol car in the driveway. Nothing unusual. It was still pretty early but people were up, getting their kids ready for school, and the lights on around were reassuring until he realized that as he walked up the neat sidewalk, the front door to her house wasn't quite closed.

Maybe she'd not quite gotten it shut. He knew firsthand she'd been tired and distraught. In fact, he'd urged her during dinner to think about a little vacation. Someplace tropical. But she'd just smiled sadly and said she and Chad were both saving for a trip to the Bahamas. Or had been.

There was no doubt he had a knack for putting his foot in it sometimes, but it really seemed like there was no subject that didn't bounce back to her lover's murder.

"Danni?" He knocked first, seemed the right thing to do, but that damn feeling that something was wrong hung on and he pushed the door open a crack.

It was the rug. There was only the slightest rumple, but it was there; like someone stepped on it and slid a little.

And someone who smoked had been in her house.

But Danni didn't smoke.

It always amazed Jason that people who had a cigarette habit didn't realize it was pretty evident to others and this was not just a hint of it. Someone had smoked a cigarette in her house, and recently.

He reached into his coat and settled his hand over the handle of his service weapon and widened the doorway with his foot. "Hello?"

Nothing. There was a curious knot in the pit of his stomach.

Burglary?

No. It didn't look too much like anything had been disturbed. The television was still mounted to the wall in the tiny living room, and at a glance her computer seemed to still be in the case where she'd left it on the coffee table.

Normal.

Or was it?

That metallic smell . . . the bunched carpet . . .

The dead body.

Like a bad dream, Jason found nothing seemed to work as he went around the corner into the little kitchen. Knees—pure rubber. She wasn't holding her gun any longer, the weapon next to her sprawled body.

She was without a doubt dead, eyes open, mouth slightly parted, her eyes glazed.

This cannot be happening.

Someone had a giant hand around his heart, squeezing it.

Ironically, he felt . . . alone.

So damn alone. She sure wasn't there with him. Not her, just what remained of her physical presence on this earth.

But fuck him. Was there anything worse than dying alone?

Wait a minute. Is there anything worse than dying?

Phone. Pocket. Concentrate. You are a homicide detective.

Crouching down, he studied the scene with a practical, impartial eye.

Why hadn't she fired? Broken arm? Could have happened when she fell . . . it was possible. It was galling, he remembered it too well. The uncooperative muscles, the increasing weakness, and the smell of blood cloying and a distraction.

Use the other hand.

Awkward . . . impossible, at least in this case.

It was easier actually to reach across, and her fingers had found the right pocket, probably slipping on her blood-soaked clothing, but the object in her hand was her phone. She somehow had managed to get it out.

It was eerie to see his number in the display.

He hung his head and took in a deep, shuddering breath.

Carl was drinking a cup of coffee and toasting a bagel when the call came in. It was a nice fall morning, a Sunday with crystalline blue skies and he was off duty, which should be a good thing, but he was wondering just what the hell he was going to do with his day . . .

He glanced at his phone, saw the name, and answered, his cup slapping down on the counter so fast dark liquid sloshed out. Metzger didn't call personally unless it was something weighty. "Chief?"

"We've got another officer down."

What? "Line of duty?"

"No."

"Who?"

"Crawford."

Okay. This is starting to get interesting.

"She was killed at her home. Let's play a game now, okay?"

When Metzger took that tone, it was always better to just agree. "Okay."

"It is called: Guess Who Found Her."

Carl took a second. "Santiago."

"What the hell was he doing there? I'm not sure what's going on, but it isn't good. Dammit, Carl, the timing is always too perfect. No witnesses."

Grasso gazed out the French doors toward the sunny backyard. He wished he hadn't closed the pool up so soon because it always made it seem like winter was hovering. He asked, "I take it this call means you are more convinced than ever it might be professionals, and more specifically, maybe we trained them."

"I don't know." Metzger's voice was testy. "In fast, out fast, quiet, good shots . . . it narrows the field. The crime scene unit said not one bullet in a wall. She was hit with every shot. Quite frankly, it could be organized crime or a drug cartel, but these are uniformed cops, not detectives. Crawford didn't even work the same beat as Fielding. Why would anyone hit her?"

Danni Crawford.

There was a blink of a moment. Carl thought about the general reluctance of criminals to bring about the full force of the law. "I got a call. A tip she was sleeping with Brown. It draws it in."

"Oh, shit, seriously?" Metzger exhaled heavily. "I guess I don't get the water fountain gossip. You need to follow up on that."

"Does MacIntosh know about the killing?"

"She didn't answer when I called. I got the impression she was heading north yesterday, so it might be a signal issue. Carl, the last person Crawford called was Jason Santiago. Do you have any idea what that means? His story is he got nervous when he couldn't reach her back. I hope everyone realizes he isn't officially on duty right now."

Was this the time to confess they'd asked Santiago to help even though it hadn't been authorized and he was technically on leave?

No, not until he asked MacIntosh. If she agreed to reveal that to the chief, fine with him. Usually he might just go ahead, but he was being cautious, playing the perfect partner. He had too much at stake to even allow the possibility she would complain about him.

On the way to the scene, he called Santiago instead of Ellie. She was four hours away and a murder victim hadn't called her, so first things first.

Jason picked up on the second ring and his raspy voice was thick. "What the fuck is goin' on?"

"You tell me." Grasso negotiated into a center lane. "I just heard that Danni Crawford called you this morning and you went to her place and found her dead."

"Not my finest morning. They booted me out as soon as they got on scene."

"The call . . . what did she say?"

"Nothing. Like . . . nothing. The phone rang but she

wasn't there. That's what made me uneasy. I tried to call back but no luck. It made me nervous. Mind filling me in on the investigation? Metzger called and drilled me a few minutes ago and asked me the exact same question."

"If I can."

"You'd better." It was not a usual day when Jason Santiago sounded shaken. "Call me back, okay? I fucking just had dinner with her last night . . . something is up, man. This is nuts."

Something *was* up. It wasn't good either. Santiago was right. Carl was doing the math and he was coming up with quite a startling figure when it came to cops who'd been targeted in the past few months. The department was not doing all that well.

Just as he pulled up, Ellie called him. "Okay, what's going on? I've got messages from you, Metzger, and as we speak, Santiago is beeping in. My phone was dead but I didn't realize it. I'm on my way back, by the way. About an hour out."

"Someone killed Officer Danni Crawford."

Silence. It took a second and then in an altered voice, she said, "Like the others?"

"Pretty much."

"Can you give me the address? Or does Metzger not want us on the scene."

"This is getting big enough I think he might give this homicide to us, pass it off as too many cases for one team. Hamish and Rays are pretty overworked as it is. We might just all have to pitch in if we can connect the cases."

She didn't argue. "That would make it easier. I never did like the idea of creeping around someone else's investigation just because Metzger is worried the department will get more mud on its face."

"I couldn't agree more." He did. "Crawford had just gotten off her shift. Went home and walked into an ambush blind, or so I'm told. I'm just getting here. She tried to call Santiago instead of 911. Maybe it was the advantage of speed dial and she was already getting weak. I'm not sure."

"Are you kidding?" It was a mutter.

"I wish I was." Carl slid out of the car, extended his badge to a waiting officer controlling the perimeter, and walked up the front steps with the phone still to his ear.

"Why Crawford?"

"I've been having this conversation with myself."

"Did you happen to answer yourself by any chance?"

"So far, I don't seem to know. But, as she and Chad Brown were in a relationship, at least we have a link there. Santiago might know more. They had dinner together last night before her shift. I have another name . . . Lieman, the DEA guy. This is all over the place."

"Santiago called me in the middle of the night. He sounded kind of wired up."

"When is he not wired up? You should have talked to him two minutes ago. I'm here now. I'll text the address."

He shut off his phone, ducked under the crime scene tape, and entered the house. A deputy medical examiner was dictating notes into a handheld recorder, and the crime scene techs were everywhere, dusting and searching.

Crawford was still in uniform, on her back, one arm extended, the other lax against her chest. They must have already bagged the phone, but her service weapon was on the floor next to her.

The medical examiner was fairly new, but they had worked together on a case involving a double homicide and high-profile actress recently, and she glanced up and recognized him. "Detective."

"Dr. Hammet." He pulled on a glove and knelt down, avoiding a pool of congealing blood. "We meet again, but I certainly wish it wasn't quite this way. What do we have?"

"You know I can't be conclusive until after the autopsy, but she was shot six times." Hammet's voice was somber. "I think from first glance that there were two different weapons involved. I'm going to guess she was still alive when her assailants left, since she was able to move and take out her phone, but she was bleeding out. I won't know until I get her on the table if they hit any vital organs, but definitely nicked an artery or two from all the blood. Looks like one of the bullets shattered her femur so she was really losing blood fast. I'm going to speculate that killed her."

There was something about a dead cop in uniform . . . brought it all home, Carl thought. Not the world's most dangerous job, but up there.

"She get off any shots?"

Hammet shook her head. "I'm bagging her hands and I'll let you know." She said it with pragmatic analysis. "Some scenes are a little harder to sum up at a glance. The gun is lying in her blood as you can see. Time of death? I'm guessing two to three hours ago from body temperature, but by the time she was found she was already dead. Obviously, she walked in and someone was waiting for her. At that time of the morning, most people are sound asleep."

"Still . . . that much gunfire?" He stared at the body, at the vacant eyes, the pale dead color of Danni Crawford's face. "How could no one hear?"

"You are the detective, Lieutenant Grasso."

He was. Just thinking out loud, he murmured, "Silencers." They worked. Forensics might be able to tell the story. In any case, it was all overkill, no pun intended. He straightened. "At a guess, she didn't have a chance to return fire."

"The lab will let you know."

True, but in the meantime, evidence was like melting ice. It deteriorated fast. He said, "I'm going to look around until my partner gets here."

Though it had never been his strong point, it was always good to at least seem like a team player.

Chapter 14

The ax cut into the wood with a clear, sharp sound. He picked up another log, arranged it, and then brought the blade down.

Two pieces successfully fell apart and he repeated the motion.

There was something cathartic about chopping wood.

What amazed him was the utter ease of it. Not what he was doing at the moment—he was sweating under his shirt—but the deflection of suspicion.

No one really was asking questions . . . no, they were sympathetic, afraid to look him in the eye, avoiding the topic.

To his shame, he wanted to avoid it too.

No one wanted to ask him about his wife and that was just as well, since he didn't know the answer.

* * *

"Sorry," Ellie said shortly as they pulled to the curb "This will be a zoo. I'm not sure how long . . ."

"I have my laptop," Bryce said agreeably, "and trust me, I would rather not go inside even if I was invited to this party. You go have fun."

She would have taken him home first but this was pretty urgent, and still she hesitated before she shut the door of the car. "It could be awhile."

"I'll hang with my manuscript."

"Keep the car keys. You can go home whenever. I'll call if I need a ride. Grasso can always drop me off."

"Sounds fair enough."

He truly seemed fine with it, which was a relief. By the time Ellie got out of the car and went up the steps of a small brick house with a trim yard, the neighborhood midwestern suburban, maybe even the type of house she might have chosen for herself If she was in the market, his dark head was bent and his eyes focused on the screen.

The scene inside was disturbing, no doubt of that.

The body was being bagged as she walked in, her credentials in hand, edging past obviously angry cops, the aura antagonistic all around.

It was one thing if a cop fell in the line of duty. Another if they were targeted. It made all of them feel vulnerable and no one liked that.

Danni Crawford exited via a stretcher and ME personnel, and all that was left was a house covered in fingerprint dust and a few more crime tech team members peering into corners. Dr. Hammet nodded as she went by, and Ellie nodded back, but her gaze was focused on the significant blood pool on the beige carpet and then whipped up to where Grasso stood talking on his cell phone.

This was a mess.

He caught sight of her and said something before he flicked off his phone.

"Santiago?" It was a guess. When he didn't get her—and she hadn't called him back because she preferred to actually have some information before they talked—he'd pester Grasso. She could picture her partner in that generic apartment, pacing around, using his phone to bridge the gap between boredom and helplessness and anger. . . .

She thought about the tricycle in the hallway, and the laughter in the pool, and the smiling moms getting into their cars every afternoon in his apartment complex, and it was simply the oddest realization to come to, but of all people on this green earth, Jason Santiago didn't do alone well.

Go figure.

Grasso, on the other hand, did alone extremely well. He just looked distant, all emotion wiped from his face. "It was my idea he try to pick her brain. Not that he's blaming me, but he's flipping out over this murder even more than Brown being killed." His expression might be bland but his tone was grim. "Must be the correlation of them getting together and her getting dead. Let's keep in mind he was also with her when she answered the call about Brown. That makes two dead cops for him recently, and considering why he's on leave, almost three if he includes himself. He's jumping out of his skin."

"I don't really blame him." Ellie looked around at the small living room. "I am not going to go so far as to say he's a sensitive guy, but I have been surprised before by his reaction to certain situations. In the first case we worked together he spent quite a bit of time finding the victim's dog so he could return it to the widow."

"Did he? You'd think I'd be surprised, but actually, I'm not."

"Santiago aside, what happened? Do we have any witnesses?"

"We don't, as usual." Grasso wore gray pinstripe silk, and he wore it well, his silver eyes as intense as ever. "As far as we can tell, she walked in, they were waiting, and then started shooting. She drew her weapon, but so far there is no evidence she even got off a shot. It seems there were two of them, or that was what the ME speculates. It was probably over in less than a minute."

"How did they get in?"

"Bedroom window. It was pried open. Out through the back door because they were in a hurry is my guess. They knew she was dying . . . beyond rescue." He stared at the bloodstain on the carpet. "But they left a little too soon. She tried to call Santiago. I think they'd have just taken care of it if she'd moved."

"Why didn't she call 911?"

"How do I know? If I had to call it, I'd say since they talked to each other last night, maybe she just pressed redial because that was easier. She was confused, dying, and beyond a doubt in shock."

Ellie scanned the room. The couch was floral and

feminine, the beige carpet ruined now, but it looked like it was fairly new and suited the decor, the walls a neutral ivory color. The kitchen had a minimum of clutter, with three pretty canisters on little iron pedestals, and an embroidered hand towel hanging on the oven door.

A woman's kitchen, Ellie thought with a twinge of genuine sorrow. The softness at home Crawford couldn't get from climbing into that patrol car every single time she wore the badge.

An hour later, everything was done, the scene processed, the neighbors interviewed. Bryce had left, but only because she'd gone and told him she'd call later. She said to Grasso, "Can I hitch a ride?"

"Absolutely if you don't mind a slight detour. I thought we might go see Santiago."

"I was thinking the same thing."

They walked out together. It was a peaceful day, the street quiet now, the ambulance gone, the leaves whispering in a light breeze. Rows of pleasant houses, mowed lawns; not a scene for murder, Ellie thought bleakly. There were two patrol cars left, the officers standing by, both of them with cell phones pressed to their ears. They nodded as she and Grasso walked past, but this was not a casual crime, not by a long shot, and their expressions showed it.

"I have mixed feelings over Metzger passing this to us." Carl pressed a button and his expensive car beeped. "Being in the background is one thing, but this is all over the department, especially now."

He started to the passenger side as if he was going to open her door, but she beat him to it. She appreciated the polite thought, but this wasn't a courtship. "I thought you wanted back on homicide for good."

"This isn't the best case for it." He got into the car, his face set. "This is exactly the kind of case that gets you fired. Cops do not like cops dying."

Ellie thought about those lonely bones in a drawer up north as she fastened her seat belt. "Cops don't like anyone dying, Lieutenant."

Jason was sitting on the balcony, sipping a beer, when he saw the BMW pull in. Maybe he would get some answers. He needed them. He needed to know about the details, though at the end of it, Danni would still be dead, and dammit, he was really pissed . . .

. . . and sad. He wasn't quite willing to admit it yet, but he was sad. This needed to be resolved and she was a very interesting casualty to this informal war.

Whoever started it might just be sorry as hell.

No. Correction. As he rose, he vowed that whoever started it *would* be sorry as hell. He might have not known Fielding very well, but he'd lost two friends in Chad and Danni, and the truth was, he didn't have that many to begin with anyway.

He opened the door, stepping back with an exaggerated flourish. "Another visit? I'm starting to feel pretty important here."

MacIntosh was with Grasso, dressed casually, her hair caught back in a careless ponytail, but he was still guilty of a flashback to his erotic image of her from that middle-of-the-night phone call, and he grinned, though it wasn't all that funny.

"I would put out the duck liver pâté but it turns

out I'm out, wouldn't you know. Same with the champagne and caviar. Can't ever keep enough on hand with my social schedule. I hope chips and a light beer is okay."

"Um, usually it's goose liver, and no, I think we're good," Ellie said, her expression clearly saying she didn't think he was funny at all. "You know why we're here. Let's talk about Danni Crawford. We just left the scene."

"Seems to me I called and tried to talk to you about her and you were kind of pissy about the whole thing."

"It was three in the morning." Exasperation edged her voice. "And you hung up on me."

"But my heart was in the right place." He raised his brows, but then sobered and shook his head. "I've been sitting here thinking about it. I sure as hell hope having dinner with a homicide detective didn't play a part in what happened to her. Want to have a seat and tell me what went down?"

MacIntosh chose his couch again and Grasso pulled out one of the bar stools from the counter.

"You tell us, since you were first on the scene."

"I followed perfect protocol and called it in right away."

"That wasn't the question."

No, it hadn't been. Jason sighed and ran his hand through already rumpled hair. "I was asleep when I got the call. It is bugging me that she might have been alive when I answered, but just couldn't talk. She didn't say anything. I decided to go to her house because it was strange, and let's face it, some strange shit is going down. I wish I could offer more, but I can't. Now, it's your turn."

Grasso said, "Six shots. We don't think she fired her weapon but she'd pulled it. They came in through a window and went out the back door in a hurry, leaving it open. No one heard anything. We think there were two because it looked to the MF like there were two different caliber weapons."

"Wham bam, huh?" Jason pictured Danni's good-natured face, the careful amount of dressing on her salad, and his throat tightened a little. Her last night on earth . . . she should have had the blue cheese. Worth every damn calorie. "The front door was also open, but probably because she sensed something was up. Those bastards. So we have a team of killers again it sounds like. The real question is: are they acting on their own, or are they sent by someone? Taking one hell of a chance, killing cops. Not everyone does that."

"What did she tell you last night when you had dinner?" Ellie leaned forward, her hazel eyes intent. "I want to know exactly what she had to say about Fielding and Brown."

Chapter 15

The sex was hot, sweaty, almost ferocious, pleasure crossing a line toward violence almost but not quite. The bed creaked and then stilled when it was over, and suddenly there was nothing but the sound of the insects in the trees through the open window.

They didn't talk anymore.

Afterward he stared at the ceiling, unspeaking, his face shuttered, almost cold.

In her opinion, he went away at these moments. Exited the intimacy in the aftermath of what should be tender and shared and just emotionally removed himself.

Was she afraid? No, but she wasn't unafraid either. The difference? She wasn't sure.

"Can I do something?" She set her hand on his bare chest.

"No."

She hesitated, not sure how to start the conversation, how to continue, especially when he was so visibly distant.

She loved the shape of his chin, of all things. It was very square and male, and suited the somewhat melancholy lines of his face. Her Brontë hero, she thought sometimes, but she was a little fanciful now and again, especially on a night like this, when they were together and he'd come to her . . .

Softly, she began, "If you want to talk about it—"

"I don't," he interrupted curtly. "I just don't. Leave it."

Carl sat there at his desk, picked up the phone, set it back down, reminded himself it wasn't his first canoe trip, and picked it back up to return the call.

"Lindsey?"

"Yes." She sounded quiet and hushed, like she might be buried in a library somewhere and couldn't speak any louder, which could be true. "I don't recognize this number, who is calling?"

Why did he get the feeling she was lying?

"The lieutenant. How was the party?"

It took a second but then she said with evident warmth, "The cheese guy?"

That brought back a picture of her sparkling brown eyes. "I'm not sure if I love the nickname, but all right, yes, the cheese guy."

"It was boring," she told him, still keeping her voice low. "We could get together and I'd tell you about what you missed, but you'd fall asleep in five seconds. Or we could get together and have a big fat margarita and talk about something else."

This was entirely not him. He didn't call college students, but graduate school wasn't quite the same as being a wide-eyed freshman and . . .

Carl felt like he needed to step away for an hour or two. It worked sometimes if he thought about something else and then a case would come back into focus with more clarity.

He found himself saying, "That sounds fine to me."

"Address or meet?"

"I'm a little old-fashioned. I can pick you up. Are you at the library?"

Silence. "I'm going to have to get used to this detective thing."

It was his turn to laugh. After the day he'd had, that was a miracle. "You're whispering. You are a student. It isn't actually a brilliant deduction."

"Okay . . . I'll give you that one. How about we just walk over to the local place, okay? That way you can still drink."

"You think of everything."

Her response was playful. "What an understatement."

"When?"

"How about now? I've studied torts until my eyes have started to bleed."

He groaned theatrically. "You're a law student?"

"That a problem, Lieutenant?"

No, but he found it interesting. "Be there in just a few minutes."

"I'm ready."

Lindsey was true to her word, standing just inside the glassed doors of the law library, her smile genuine as she walked out when he pulled up, getting into the car. Her hair looked liquid in the lamplight when she leaned back to fasten her seat belt. This evening she wore a sweater over a T-shirt and sandals with her jeans. Her toenails were painted a pretty light pink and she had a backpack.

"Best margaritas in town just around the corner. You might want to just park here and we can walk."

Once upon a time, he'd gone to Harvard. It felt like it all had happened to someone else: the Ivy League school, not the interest in law enforcement . . . he'd known *that* from the beginning. But being the student, the one with the backpack, the urgent campus walk that signaled class was going to start and it was getting late . . .

He missed that young man sometimes. Wondered who he might have been if everything was different.

"Fine with me. Nice night."

"Great." She gave him a sidelong approving look as he pulled out of the parking lot. "Despite this really expensive car, you aren't so fancy you can't walk a little. You look like you're in pretty good shape, so you must work out. What do I *not* know about Lieutenant Grasso?"

"I'm too old for you."

"No, I know that already. I need new information."
Her laugh was light and mischievous. "We don't agree
on that, by the way. The young, hungry types drive me
nuts."

"Young hungry types?"

She didn't directly respond to the inquiry in his question. "Shall we go rub elbows with the future of America's judicial system? It's kind of a popular place for
law students, but like I said, they make a killer margarita there. You are entirely overdressed, by the way,
but I don't care if you don't."

"How about if I lose the tie?" He smiled and tugged
at it.

"And the jacket maybe."

She gazed at him with open approval when he tossed
his jacket over the top of his seat and held the door for
her. "I might have competition. Hadn't thought about
that. Some of the professors go there occasionally. You
are pretty noticeable."

Flirtation was a lost art to him. Actually, he was
never sure he'd possessed any skill at it in the first
place. He tended to be too analytical. Some women
liked it, and some didn't like it at all. He hoped he
wasn't too old to learn.

There was no doubt he over thought things, but it
had saved his life once or twice.

She was right about the margaritas, he discovered
once they'd walked the few blocks and seated themselves in a place that screamed college bar. His was
suspiciously brown in color and one sip told him driving was not going to be an option for a few hours if

he drank the whole thing. Lindsey laughed at his expression and the spontaneous sound cut through the music and general hum of the crowded place. "I told you. Killer."

The televisions mostly were tuned to sports channels, but the news flashed on, and just his luck, Danni Crawford's murder was a headliner on a set above the bar. Killer took on a different meaning and he watched the broadcast, his fingers idly smoothing the condensation on his glass, his attention so focused that Lindsey turned to see what he was watching.

"Sorry. My case," he said in response to her inquiring look, his smile humorless. "It helps to know what the press is saying. Not that they know more than we do, but so that they don't make sure whoever did it is in the loop. Leaking information needs to be done carefully."

"I couldn't agree more." She settled her elbows on the tabletop and looked at him in challenge. "Be careful, you are talking to an almost-lawyer, Detective. Have you ever done that?"

"Talked to an almost-lawyer? Sure." He took another sip. "I'm talking to one now, right?"

"Funny. I meant carefully leaked to the press."

He had in the Burner case, but he usually kept his secrets pretty close, and though Lindsey was undeniably attractive, articulate, and bright, he didn't know her. "It can be a useful strategy if used properly. I try to follow the rules of protocol. Why do you ask?"

"I'm definitely trying to get the hang of how all this works, and not just from dry professors who tell you about it. *Try?* Hmm, interesting choice of words. What case are you working now?"

"Someone is murdering cops, remember?"

"I do. Any progress?" She took a sip from her drink and gazed at him with inquiring eyes.

"Nothing I can talk about. But I'm pretty curious. Is that why you said yes to the invitation?"

She shook her head convincingly. "No, just a perk. Do you like guacamole?"

"I do."

"A man after my own heart. Let's order some, shall we?"

"Good redirect, almost-counselor." Then he said without inflection, "Tell me, Lindsey, why did you call me about Chad Brown and Danni Crawford, and more important, why are they both dead?"

"Oh shit," she answered, licking salt off the rim of her glass. "You know who I am, don't you?"

Ellie typed in two words and hit the search button just as Metzger walked up to her desk. He looked tired, drawn even, which was hard to imagine since his rugged features were designed to hide emotion as far as she could tell.

"Do you know how happy I am Jason Santiago is alive?"

Her fingers stilled on the keyboard. "I have to admit, sir, as a conversation opener, that one gets my attention."

"I am referring to the recent rash of homicides involving this particular branch of civil service. At least he survived the shooting back in July. I have lost far too many officers." He pulled out a chair and straddled it, looking pointedly at the half-eaten sandwich sitting on a wrapper by her keyboard. "I expected Grasso to still be at his desk this time of evening because I could swear he lives here, but not you. It's been a long day. Why don't you go home?"

"Just wrapping up the report from this morning."

"The scene at Crawford's house was a wash, I hear. No real evidence."

"Used gloves, came in through a window, left out the back door, no one saw anything. She must have heard something since she never really shut the front door, but her neighbors weren't helpful. Not because they are scared, more because they are bewildered."

"Is there anything? One single lead?"

"One lead." Cautiously, she said, "Santiago had dinner with her last night."

The chief of the metropolitan police department of Milwaukee registered that with due equanimity. After a second, he said, "If this is a club, I decline the invitation. I suppose that explains why he found her. Why the hell would he do that? I've been told she was dating Brown."

"Good friends with both her and Brown, sir." Her screen flashed the answer she'd been looking for but she concentrated on the conversation instead. "You know Santiago is going crazy being trapped at home. Why else was he riding along with Crawford that night? I'm going to venture to say that it is his idea of entertainment."

"I'm going to venture to agree that as crazy as that sounds, you might be right."

"I gathered she thought it might be a link back to

drug trafficking, which supports something Grasso found out as well."

"The two detectives I have assigned to the case tell me they think it is revenge motivated, not a conspiracy. Both Hamish and Rays have leads on possible suspects who Fielding and Brown both arrested. I want you and Grasso to check and see if Crawford is also a common denominator."

"We will. I've already started on it." She didn't flinch, looking him back in the eye. "But, as odd as it sounds, I really am starting to trust Grasso and also Santiago. They have some interesting . . . er . . . methods at times, but they both think this might connect back to the Henley family business and their instincts seem pretty spot on."

"MacIntosh, if I didn't think they were talented detectives, I would not employ them, and tell me nothing about these interesting methods. Feel free to follow that angle, but keep in mind, defaming a prominent family—and Ely Henley could easily be our next mayor, or even our next governor—without the evidence to back it up, could just get us sued, or even cost me, and you, of course, your job."

She flushed a little. "I don't even know if we have an angle, but I do know that it seems like no one really agrees on why this is happening. There is no finger pointed anywhere, and Danni Crawford died simply because someone broke into her home and wanted her dead. From what I understand of her dedication to the job, if she had known something obvious, she would have come forward."

"So it isn't something obvious. She called me and

asked for a meeting but I have no idea what she wanted."

Her thoughts exactly. "And now she isn't around for us to ask."

"Which could be the killer's intention." He shoved himself to his feet. "I suggest you and Santiago go put your heads together. Let me know how it all goes. If he wants back that bad that he's riding around in squad cars for kicks, I'll approve it now, but for desk duty only. Tell him if he does anything stupid, he's just on his own."

"He's bound to do something stupid, sir."

For the first time since she'd met him, the chief actually laughed. "That," he said with precise inflection, "is the absolute truth, Detective MacIntosh. Good luck."

After he left, she touched the pad and brought her screen back up.

Needle in a haystack applied. The list of missing women from northern counties in Wisconsin could be pertinent, or it could not, and without dating on the skeleton, maybe she'd asked Santiago for an impossible favor. It was nice of Carson to send the file he had the computer, but sifting through those paper files would be even more cumbersome.

The medical examiner had sent an e-mail to the department and Detective Carson had kindly forwarded it to her as well.

Jared:

This might be of interest. The skeleton from Oneida County had what had first appeared to be a postmortem fracture, but due to Detective Mac-Intosh's personal interest in the case, I decided to give it another look. The only thing I think I didn't mention to her, but it is in the report, is that our unfortunate young woman had at one time broken her right wrist, probably as a child. Hardly pertinent to her death, but perhaps to identification.

Perhaps. Ellie stared at the screen, trying to remember how many friends she'd had who had fallen from their bikes or jumped from the monkey bars on the playground and broken their arm in some way. Offhand she knew quite a few.

Not much help.

She logged off and noticed the time.

It was getting late. As always, she was juggling the job and her personal life.

The job usually won.

Chapter 16

Into the darkness.

He'd named it that, when he had these moments of doubt. His mind wandered, and then there was nothing but black.

Cold and bleak.

He sat on the side of the bed, shivering, head in hands, his shirt clammy against his skin, his legs weak, feet on the cold floor.

The damn nightmares.

They just didn't stop. Invading his mind, ruining his sleep, blocking out the past.

It was easy to forget what was real and what might just be the worst dream his imagination had ever spun . . .

And no proof. He had no proof.

A blessing and a curse.

* * *

Jason woke up on the couch. He registered that someone had just knocked and managed to squint at the clock.

Okay, so it was only eight-thirty in the evening, kind of early to go to sleep, but then again, he didn't have a lot of deadlines at the moment and had drifted off during a sitcom, wearing his boxers and nothing else.

Luckily his jeans and shirt were on the floor and he jerked them on as the person knocked again. He said irritably, "Coming."

Three steps forward and he was almost there before he thought of Danni, and before her Brown and Fielding, and stepped sideways from the door in case a bullet came through it. "Who is it?"

"Me."

Okay. Definitely the voice of one Ellie MacIntosh, he thought sardonically, detective extraordinaire from northern Wisconsin. Her third visit in just a few days.

"That narrows it down." He flipped the lock and swung open the front door. "But I do at least recognize your voice. What?"

"Please don't try to bowl me over with your enthusiastic welcome. Can I come in?"

She stood, wearing a light jacket because it was a cool evening, her hair straight and natural, and her hazel eyes challenging but clearly meeting his without apology.

"Sure."

She walked past, set her keys on the coffee table, and turned around. "Your dinner with Danni Crawford . . . we need to talk again."

"Where's your sidekick?"

"Believe it or not, I think Grasso had something to do tonight."

"Yeah, I kinda don't believe that." He shut the door. "Beer?"

"Coffee?"

"That's boring, MacIntosh. I've got instant, that's all."

"No to instant coffee, but thanks for the offer." She sat down, slipping off her jacket. Her arms were slender and smooth but her expression was about as relenting as slate. "I've talked to them up north and you can look over the records."

"Wait a minute. Are we talking about the cold case? I am sure it will be my pleasure to have them laughing at me as I bust my ass going over decades of dusty files. Do we even have the slightest clue as to who she could be?"

"Do we have the slightest clue who might have killed Danni Crawford?"

Jason lifted his hands in a gesture of impatience. "What direction are we going? I'm starting to get a little confused here. We are investigating both, right? What is it you want from me you didn't get on your previous visit?"

"Metzger wants you back, but desk only."

It stopped him cold. That *was* good news. He'd been hoping. His throat actually tightened.

"Music to my ears." He sat down suddenly and said in a weak moment, "I've been struggling with all this; the down time, the—"

Too much information. He *never* had weak moments, he reminded himself, and sure as hell was not going to admit he'd been starting to worry he was suffering from some mild depression.

The emptiness. God, he didn't even want to say it out loud, much less say it to her.

With an equanimity that surprised him, she responded evenly, "I get it. There's always stress related to an injury like what you've experienced."

"Now you're talking like the psychologist they made me see."

"Now I'm talking like someone who has been through it. I shot a serial killer and was shot myself. Let's face it, it can't be defined by someone who has not walked the path. The professionals mean well, I'm sure." Her smile was brief and ironic. "But surely even they realize as they dig into it and try to figure out how we feel that it is impossible to know exactly how to react to an experience a person has never had."

He liked her. Maybe that was the pull of attraction. Ellie had a lovely body he'd like to explore, but more important, an agile mind. He *liked* her.

"I agree. Ever thought about climbing Everest?" he asked, raking his hand through his hair. "Me? God, no. I realize I live where I live, but I hate to be cold. I can't get past the cold. I would stand there on the top of the world's highest mountain and ask how soon we could be back down at the bottom. The entire idea anyone ever wanted to do it—and they still do— flips me out. I just think they are all fucking nuts."

"I get what you are saying. When you climb Everest you must come down with a sense of accomplishment that cannot be achieved without actually *doing* it, right?"

"Right. Most people don't have a deep-seated desire to put their lives in danger by chasing bad guys either. I'm starting to think I can't be happy if I don't chase bad guys. Some people stare at the mountain and want to climb it. I watch the news and wonder how to catch killers. Unless you have the passion, you can't understand it."

Was he really discussing philosophy with Ellie Mac-Intosh?

Not at all his style, but maybe he was.

"Bryce is writing a novel." She shook her head, her hair softly swinging. "I love to read, but it stops right there for me. He spends pretty much all his free time doing it with no promise it will ever get published. I don't quite understand that either, but it seems to be a very real need for him, so I say go for it."

Grantham. Mr. Brilliant, successful, and good-looking. Now he was bound to write the great American novel too. "It figures," Jason muttered.

"What?" Ellie gazed at him, obviously mystified. "It figures he wants to write a book?"

"Jesus, tell me he snores or something. Sits down to pee. Talks with his mouth full. Better yet, his favorite breed of dog is a Maltese." He tossed his empty can with remarkable accuracy toward the trash can. Two points as it went home. Bet Grantham couldn't do that.

Ellie considered him with her unsettling brand of directness. She could look right through a person like no other. "You don't even know him, but if you are inferring he has the big house and some sort of fairy-tale life, think again. Subject closed. Ever consider you are drinking too much since you were injured?"

He has you.

Christ. Where the hell did that thought come from?
Jason said flippantly, "I was drinking too much before that for your information. Look, I need to know
more about the missing-person case, but let's talk about
three dead cops first. The real question is, did Danni
tell her theory to anyone but me?"

"You didn't tell us about this theory. You walked
around it and only said she intimated that she might
be able to link Fielding to Brown and was looking
into it."

"Maybe she said a little more than that."

It wasn't her fault, Ellie thought irritably, she didn't
understand Jason Santiago. She doubted anyone could.
"Why didn't you say so?"

"Can we trust Grasso?" He sat there in what was
obviously his favorite chair since he chose it every
single time, careless in his worn jeans and T-shirt, and
stared back at her, slightly defiant. The combative air
was an annoyance. "He moves in some circles we
don't."

"What? *You* were the one who trusted him on our
last case. I have to admit I'm in the dark here now."

"But *you* didn't trust him."

No, she hadn't. As a matter of fact, she'd considered Carl Grasso a suspect for a while in the Burner
case, but it turned out she was wrong. "Well, he isn't
here now. Did she name names? I'm still waiting to
hear about this conversation."

"If she had, I would have contacted Metzger on the

spot. She didn't *know* names. She just had an idea of what could tie the two murders together."

"Like?"

"I don't know if I believe it, but I believe it a hell of a lot more now that she's dead too."

"For God's sake, just tell me what she said. Did she think there was a cop connection?"

Jason flicked at a piece of fabric on his torn jeans, his face suddenly abstract, his long fingers restless. "She definitely thought there was a connection. Now, I can't argue that point. Can you? Grasso thinks it could be drugs tying into organized crime, and I understand there are a few other ideas floating around out there that link both murders to some sort of message to street cops to back off a little. She didn't agree."

Ellie clasped her hands and wished he had regular coffee. "What *did* she agree with?"

"She thinks this has something to do with Fielding's wife. It is kind of a long story. She was going to call the chief and tell him about it, one on one, and I told her she should." He added quietly, "Now she can't."

It was her turn to blink. "Um, yeah, fine . . . maybe I will take that beer while you explain. Go on."

"Good, I could use another one." He got up with alacrity, coming back to set a bottle in front of her on the coffee table. He sat back down, popping his open with theatric enjoyment. "It's like this: Fielding busted a guy a couple of years ago. That's how he met his wife. A drunk and disorderly at a very nice club. A *very* nice club, if you get me. She doesn't come from money, but her boyfriend at the time does. He spends the night in jail. No big deal, right? He pays the fine because the family really, really can afford it, and at the end of it, goes on his merry way."

Ellie didn't really like beer but it was certainly preferable to instant coffee so she took a drink. "All right."

"Then Fielding marries her. Apparently they hit it off during the arrest."

"Marries the girlfriend? Apparently so, but this doesn't sound all that sinister to me."

"But what if that kid she had isn't his."

Now maybe it was a little more interesting, but still . . .

"That is why God invented the paternity test."

"The kicked-to-the-curb boyfriend agrees to one according to Danni. His father says no to the test on his behalf through a dozen lawyers. No dice, no thank you. Go fuck yourself. Someone is delusional, this is not his baby."

"But the son wouldn't have agreed if he didn't know there was a possibility."

"That's my take on it too. Very few men, no matter how responsible they might be, are anxious to claim the kid that belongs to another guy, especially if the woman is married. She'd slept with him and there's obviously a chance it is his."

Uneasy now, Ellie shook her head. "Can we define just what family we might be talking about here?" There was some big money in Milwaukee. There was big money in any city of its size.

"Henley."

Ellie took in a breath. "All right. Wow. Henley. Grasso's source said something about drug money filtering through their corporation."

Santiago grinned in that cocky way he had, like life was one big joke and they weren't talking about murder. "This isn't my investigation, or even my guess, but it is kind of intriguing, right? I feel positive in the great United States of America no one has used liquor stores as money laundering to further a criminal cause."

Ellie held up her hands palm forward, all ten fingers spread. "Give me a minute. Okay. So Danni Crawford thought that Fielding's wife had an association with . . . what's his name?"

"Garrison."

"Garrison Henley. She's pregnant with his child when she marries Officer Fielding, and *he* thinks the baby is his, but Garrison also thinks he might be the father and at first agrees to have a test, then says no. Then he has her husband killed? I'm pretty confused on that point. What does that accomplish?"

"Close, but no cigar, Detective."

He needed to work on his happy face. It just made her want to kick him.

Testily, she said, "I'm sitting right here if you'd care to clarify."

"It sure could be why Fielding, if he was feeling some pressure, called the DEA. He was trying to get Garrison Henley to keep his word. What if that backfired and just ticked the Henleys off?"

Okay, she could buy that . . . though she actually had never heard of a link between the Henley family and organized crime and wasn't positive Grasso's one source was pure gold, but it wasn't her area of expertise either.

"Please tie it to Chad Brown and Danni Crawford, and I'm in."

Her partner smiled again in a lazy way, but there was nothing casual about the look in his azure eyes. "Chad confided Fielding had told him that the Henley fortune was not solely based on fine whiskey and wine coolers. Suddenly the name Henley is tied to two deaths, and it looks like they went after her too."

"That is weak."

"But it is a connection, right?"

He had a point. Fielding and Henley, Brown and the Henley family business, Crawford and Brown. She admitted, "It's interesting. Any facts to back this up? Proof is always so nice when you try to run an investigation."

He shook his head, his blond curls as disheveled as usual. "We have hearsay, and that's it. So now what do we do? Share with the detectives assigned to the first two murders? This is a sort of buyer beware situation. If Hamish and Rays start poking around . . ."

". . . three cops have already been killed," she finished for him, her voice somber. "The alternative is to poke around ourselves, and that sounds a little dangerous if we have no idea what we are really dealing with—"

The sound of the explosion ripped through the building.

It was startlingly loud, and before Ellie could even react, her partner had jumped from his chair and knocked her not too gently off the couch, covering her body with his. He said through his teeth, his face inches away, "What the fuck was that?"

"I don't know," she responded curtly, at the last minute remembering his injuries before she shoved him off, hearing car alarms going off *everywhere*. "I'm fine. Let's go."

"Sorry." He stood up and one hand went to his chest. In the hallway outside, people were shouting, and she didn't know about him, but her ears were ringing.

She scrambled to her feet, her hand going reflexively to her Glock, pulling it out. "I'll go look. You sit down. You've gone pretty pale."

He was definitely white under what was left of a decent summer tan but he shook his head.

"I'll go with you. For all I know someone is about to come through that door. The last person I had dinner with is dead."

He had a point there.

For punch, he added, "The Henleys live about two doors down from Grasso, just in case you are still wondering why I kept my mouth shut in front of him."

Chapter 17

*N*o one knew.

    That was the hardest thing to accept.

    Human life reduced to a simple equation of loss and acceptance.

    But life wasn't simple. He understood that so very well; more than most. So he mourned, not with others, but with her.

    Because so few questioned her absence and he wondered about himself.

    Were he gone, would they believe just any story?

    It was all too easy.

"Police officers."

    He and MacIntosh edged by some confused people in the hallway, all of them alarmed by the sight of their drawn weapons. Fire trucks were on the way already, he could hear the sirens.

It took about two seconds to figure it out once they burst out the doors into the parking lot.

His car.

The spots weren't assigned but out of habit he always parked in the same place, and other people in the building fell into the same routine, so that there was a natural ebb and flow of those who went to office jobs, took kids to school, and worked other schedules . . .

But hell . . . his *car.*

That cherry Mustang he'd sunk a lot of money into, and really was about all he owned that mattered to him, and . . . *fuck.*

The driver-side door was on the sidewalk right in front of them, so in case he hadn't known exactly where it was parked, he would still be aware that he was the one targeted.

For the first time since he'd signed the lease, he was sorry he'd decided to move into a family friendly building. It wasn't as if he didn't know he didn't exactly fit in, but at this particular moment, it hit home how much he *didn't* fit in. His presence had put everyone in danger.

"Better stay inside," he said grimly to a few people who had followed them out and were staring in horrified fascination at the smoldering shell of his vehicle. "I feel confident we are going to have officers and the bomb squad swarming all over this parking lot in minutes." He turned to Ellie, who stood silent, weapon now lowered. "I think someone did hear I had dinner with Danni Crawford. How about you?"

"I'm sorry . . . your car." It sounded like she understood his sense of loss and violation.

"Yeah, I'm sorry too, those sons of bitches." With an inner fury he surveyed the blasted bits littering the parking lot, the shell still smoking. The acrid smell of burned plastic hung like a pall. "I wonder how insurance companies deal with car bombs. Maybe I should call Ireland and find out."

"At least you weren't in it."

"If you tell me there's a bright side to everything, I might say something very ungentlemanly, MacIntosh."

Her delicate eyebrows went up. "No. You? I'm still waiting for you to *say* something gentlemanly in the first place."

Her phone started to ring and she answered it before he could reply, which could be just as well.

The cars next to his were both badly damaged and the light pole was slightly bent, like a drunken person trying to stay upright, which told him something about the blast.

The first rescue vehicle pulled into the parking lot a minute later, the tires loud on the pavement. MacIntosh was still talking, her weapon holstered, blond head bent. The fire trucks were right behind, three of them, screaming in, and all he could think as he stood there was *how the hell did this happen?*

She echoed it exactly as she ended the call. "How the hell did this happen?"

"Look, I don't want to scare the shit out of you or anything, but you just read my mind." Jason took her elbow and pulled her down the sidewalk. "I'm trying to process and analyze this as we stand here, vulnerable and in the open, and it makes me uneasy. Is it just a warning, or did someone want me to come out of the building? Maybe you should go stand about fifty feet away from me and watch what everyone else does."

"Maybe you should—"

Testily, he pointed to a spot on the sidewalk near the edge of the parking lot. "Go stand and fucking watch. I am about to be cornered by all kinds of law enforcement because someone toasted my car. Do me a favor and just watch the crowd, okay? Someone has me on their radar, Ellie, and three cops are dead. Just get away from me."

He never called her by her first name, so maybe his point got through. Her lips compressed mutinously, but then she did turn and walk toward where the fence for the pool began, her phone in her hand again.

He was sweating. He could feel the cling of his shirt to his chest and shoulders.

It had to be bigger than drugs. Yes, people got killed over drugs, by drugs, and because of drugs, all the time. Bad news all around. But this wasn't the same scenario.

This just smelled bad, and it wasn't just the fried odor of his expensive seats that he'd paid a fortune to have replicated to original condition.

Jason walked toward the fire truck that was currently putting out the few remaining flames and was immediately stopped. He flashed his badge. "I'm Detective Santiago . . . and that"—he pointed—"is my car."

The young man who was holding the perimeter was maybe twenty-two, in full gear, and his eyes were alight like he was a five-year-old on Christmas morning. "Holy shit. Really? Too bad. Nice ride."

"It was. I'd cry but it might give the bad guys the edge. We have a bomb squad on the way?"

"I think, sir, this is going to be an interesting scene. I answer to only my command and don't know, but my guess is there are going to be lots of folks arriving soon."

That was probably accurate.

He really wished he hadn't left his favorite pairs of flip-flops in the back of the Mustang, but compared to the cost of the car, it wasn't too much of a loss. Still, for whatever reason he was pretty ticked off by the flip-flops.

He slowly walked around the perimeter of the scene, aware of everything. Aware his ribs ached, aware of the chaos in general when something like this needed to be contained, aware that he had really gotten the message, loud and clear.

Worried this was like a disease . . . Fielding had been infected and he'd spread it to Chad, who had given in to Danni . . . it looked now like he had it.

This very morning he'd still been bored and dissatisfied with life.

He wasn't bored now.

Taking out his phone he called a private number he had but had never, ever used.

"Yes?"

"I think," Jason said to the person who answered, looking at the smoking remains of his car. "Chief, we have a really big problem."

"A timer." Metzger paced up the sidewalk like he visited a scene every day—which he didn't, not any longer.

Just the really bad ones, so his presence really meant something. "That means they didn't care who might be nearby. Our guys are trying to see if it is a signature piece they can finger to someone they know, but they said at first glance it was just a simple bomb set to go off at a certain time."

"I'm not cleared yet to drive," Santiago said, looking remarkably calm in Ellie's opinion. She was still a little in shock he was taking it all so well.

"Then how the hell did you get to Crawford's house?" Metzger immediately shook his head. "Let's pretend I don't know that, okay? Let me rephrase. Then why would someone blow up your car? Which either means that the person who did it is your best friend and didn't try to kill you, just sent a message, or that he blew up your car not caring if you were going to be in it or not, and is your worst enemy. Can't be both." The chief looked up at the apartment building. "Lots of kids in this building, right? That's a tragedy we barely avoided."

That part of it was really disturbing.

Metzger turned and looked out over the chaos. The colored lights slid across his face in blinking patterns. "Santiago, I think you two should disappear for a few days until we figure this out here. I have some calls to make and I want to talk to the FBI. MacIntosh will be point. Right now you are no more than a potential witness."

"What?" Ellie said the word out loud, but she'd really not meant to do so.

The chief of the Milwaukee Police Department gave her a level look. "That's an order. Get out of town.

Both of you. Obviously, Santiago can't drive off into the sunset for two reasons; no car and he isn't quite ready to assume full duty either. He's targeted, and he's your partner, and you were here. Consider yourself his protection detail. If they blew up his car because he was seen with Crawford, then I assume you were just seen with him."

No.

Ellie found her voice. "*You* were just seen with both of us, sir."

"I'll cover my ass, Detective, you can count on it." He hesitated and then shook his head. "This doesn't feel like organized crime to me. I once was a pretty damn good marine and if I can say so, a good detective. This is like guerrilla warfare. In and out fast, hit 'em when they don't know it's coming, always keep them afraid, looking over their shoulder. This isn't New York or Chicago, but wise guys make sure you get the message. Unless the message here is that they enjoy killing police officers, I'm not getting it. Are you? The real-deal criminals don't want the attention of law enforcement if possible, and this is not what is happening here."

It certainly wasn't.

She had no idea what *was* happening, but having to go sit somewhere with Santiago and his restless habits held absolutely no appeal.

Unless . . . maybe this would free her up—and him, since he'd promised to help—for a little on-the-side investigation.

Those missing-person cases that might link back to

the neglected grave. Jason had said he'd do it. If she had to babysit him, he'd better deliver on the promise.

"Yes, sir," she said with as little inflection as possible. "I think I know where we can go."

There was not a large presence of organized crime in Oneida County. If someone was intent on following them there they could, of course, but she doubted that was the priority. Or else Santiago would have a very valid point and they would have come through the front door like what had happened to Fielding and Danni Crawford.

"I want to talk to Fielding's wife," Santiago said, his normally bronzed face still pale. "Let us at least do that."

"Too late." Metzger shrugged. "She and the kid left for Florida right after the funeral. I can't say I blame her."

Ellie might have run for the hills—or the beach—if her husband had been murdered when she was lying right next to him. But Ellie was still frustrated. "I know you have officers on this case, but don't you think now *we* need to talk to her?"

"No. She's been interviewed." Metzger turned on his heel. He looked back as he walked toward the man in charge from the fire department. "MacIntosh, take your car, and the two of you just go. I'll be in touch tomorrow morning."

"Tomorrow morning? Sir, with all due respect—"

But he was already done with them, yards away and evidently not listening. As a brush-off it was effective.

"At least your car wasn't burned to a crispy-crisp." Her partner had his hands in his pockets, feigning indifference when his body language suggested anything but. She'd never seen a shirt quite as wrinkled as the one he was wearing. "The two vehicles next to mine didn't fare so well either."

The dispassionate tone of his voice didn't fool her. He was unnerved.

"You weren't in it."

To give him credit, he gave a small, muffled laugh. "All right, touché. And from the look on your face you aren't any happier being saddled with me than I am to have my car—which I might say was a mechanical work of art—blown into a million pieces."

"I don't know," she said succinctly, "if you can judge my level of unhappiness at this moment."

"Don't think you can evaluate mine either." His reply was sharp enough to make her turn her head. Jason Santiago took in a long, measured breath. "Once upon a time, Detective MacIntosh, I was called into the chief's office and he told me he was assigning to me a fairly green detective who had just made a splash in the media with a high-profile case but didn't have much experience. I told him no thanks. He didn't listen to me then, just like he didn't listen to you now, and I'm starting to think he wasn't completely nuts anyway. So, where are we going?"

A compliment from Jason Santiago? And he was right. There were times in this life when a person just had to adjust to the circumstances. This appeared to be one of those very instances.

"Northern Wisconsin is nice this time of year."

"Jesus, why did I know you were going to say that?" Santiago bent over, theatrically clutching his stomach, which alarmed some of the rescue workers, but she waved them away.

"Pack a bag and stop whining." She already had her phone out. Bryce was going to have to be told, and she knew he was not going to be jumping for joy either. "I'll wait right here."

"How could I possibly resist such an enthusiastic invitation?"

"Could you just hurry?"

He went, which was a relief because this hadn't been quite the stop she'd envisioned. Bryce answered on the second ring. "Ellie, I've been—"

"Worried, I know," she supplied. "Turn on the news. You'll be even more worried. That is Santiago's car."

She was pretty sure he said *shit* in the background. "Car?"

"I'll explain later."

"And when would that be?"

"Not tonight." Then she told him the bad part. "I'm wondering if you need to go somewhere."

"Excuse me? Me? Why?"

"The chief is acting like Santiago really has kicked a nest somewhere and someone has killed three police officers and planted a very effective bomb in his car. It doesn't look, in case you are wondering, nearly as nice as it used to."

"Why would *I* need to go anywhere?"

She stood there on the sidewalk, phone to her ear, and struggled to make sense of it herself. A bad feeling?

"Because there seems to be this crazy link from

Fielding to Brown to Crawford and now to Santiago and guess who is next in line? Metzger wants us out of town. We're going. But I won't be able to sleep if I don't know you're safe."

"Because you might love me?"

"Not now," she responded firmly. "We aren't going to discuss that now. What about your parents'? Can you go there?"

He took a moment and she wondered if it would always be like this. In a very Bryce-like way, he was weighing the pros and the cons . . . maybe even wondering if it was worth it to even be with her.

"Ellie," he said reasonably. "If they really wanted to get at me, my parents would be the first logical place to look if I wasn't at home. Not to mention I'd like to keep them out of the line of fire. Where are *you* going?"

Bryce and Santiago . . . that sounded like not so much of a great mix, but then again, she didn't want to lie awake all night worrying either. "I haven't decided, but north . . . if we are on ice for a few days he can help me with the other case."

"Your house?"

"No." She'd already decided on that. It was evident they had no idea what they might be dealing with. "We're trying to figure it out. What I'm saying is please pick a generic place for a couple of days, leave right away, maybe pay cash for it, and use your cell for personal correspondence."

"That sounds ominous."

"I'm going to say I'm being overcautious."

"I'm going to hope you are."

"Where are you going to go?"

"Is it safe for me to tell you over the phone or will some international satellite device pick it up?"

She took in a deep breath. "Look, I know you aren't happy about this, but the sarcasm is not needed at the moment."

It was easy to picture him, casual in jeans and a T-shirt, probably sitting at his desk. He said finally, "I'll just pick some place at random . . . Ellie, now I am going to worry about you all the time."

"Vice-versa, but tell me you'll do it."

"I'll do it."

She let out a small breath. "Thanks. I . . ."

He waited. "Yes?"

"I do love you," she said quietly and pressed a button.

The first time she'd ever said it to him. She wasn't sure how she felt . . . relieved, elated, scared, maybe even a little ridiculous. Over the phone? Really?

Santiago emerged from the building, carrying a small bag.

Time to go.

Chapter 18

It was the cup of coffee.

It spilled across the morning paper and soaked in, and she had to ineffectively swab at it, but at the end, it was just lost. The words blurred, the moment awkward.

And then he finally said it. "I want you to leave. It might be better for both of us."

No question, of course, of him leaving, she thought in silent shock now that he'd finally said it. No, his house, he was staying. He couldn't really leave when she thought about it, since all he had was tied to this place.

This dead place.

She could argue, or she could just accept.

She'd never been all that good at accepting. So she got up and began to spoon coffee grounds into the pot, turning up the stove. "We'll talk about it over a fresh cup. Why don't you go and buy another paper?"

* * *

Carl saw it on the news before his phone even rang once, but that might have been because he had absently turned his cell off and hadn't resurrected it until he realized what was going on.

Car bomb. The car of a cop.

The missed call from Metzger made him shake his head. *Try for once to have a nice date and all hell breaks loose . . .*

Except it hadn't been exactly a nice date.

If he had to place it in a category, he would say it was an interesting date.

"What happened?" he said by way of greeting when he called back. "I saw the video and that was Santiago's apartment complex, wasn't it? I was just there the other night and thought I recognized it."

Luckily the chief did not stand on much protocol. Solve the case and that was all that mattered. Metzger said in clipped tones, "They took out his car."

"Yeah . . ."

"Hit him below the belt but not between the eyes, so he should just consider himself lucky. I sent him off on a little vacation."

Carl digested that and crossed his ankles, a scotch in his hand, and his body, which had been relaxed, tensed. "Good call there. You think he's in the same kind of danger as the others?"

"I think he's not going to be sitting in that apartment waiting on it if I can help it. Someone is putting out a fire but we just can't see the flames."

No disagreement on his part. The rapid succession of the murders indicated that containment was an issue. "At least he's not on duty currently."

Metzger grumbled, "Dammit, Carl, you've met him. I am going to venture to say whoever blew up his car is going to pay. I don't need retaliation on the agenda."

He muttered, "He does love that car."

"*Did* love it. That affair is over because the car no longer exists. So, the game hasn't really changed, but ante has been upped. I don't think this is what we imagined at the beginning and I sure as hell am not convinced cops aren't involved somehow."

"Even now? When we have a possible link to laundered money and the Henleys?"

"God, Carl, give me a viable theory. You know, like the kind a prosecutor could take to a judge? I'm sure you're familiar with that part of our due process system."

He couldn't even really argue with the sarcasm. "A demolished car? That's not enough?"

"No." Unequivocal.

"Fine, MacIntosh and I will go tomorrow to—"

"She's gone."

He had to admit his hand froze as he ran it through his hair. "What do you mean?"

"She's with Santiago. And none too excited about it either. You are on your own for two days at least. Then I'm bringing them both back in as long as it seems safe enough. If you want a shot back at homicide, this is it. Show me brilliance and no more dead cops."

"Are you serious?"

"Single-handedly solve three homicides involving

police officers and you have a definite zip line back into homicide."

"Is that a carrot?"

"Oh, yeah. You might want to book a flight to Florida. Talk to Joanne Fielding."

He'd actually already done that, but he was curious. "Why?"

"MacIntosh thinks it is the key to the whole case."

"Actually, I think I have a lead."

"Call me when you *do* have one. 'Think' does nothing for me." The line went dead.

The night sky was clear, the stars gleaming as they pulled out of the parking lot.

"Where the hell are we going?"

"I'm thinking someplace small. There's a small town outside Fond du Lac."

Jason turned his head as if he thought she was insane, which he did a bit. "What? Is there a great Arby's there you haven't hit yet and feel life will not be complete until you do?"

She drove with the same competent assurance as she did everything else and took an exit off the freeway. "I just don't want us to be followed. You have something against Fond du Lac?"

He leaned back, body lax, but he was still buzzing from the events of the evening. He hated to acknowledge it, but his chest ached like hell now. "What's not to like? I am sure they have two stop signs. I can take some pictures for my scrapbook."

"Don't be so judgmental, city boy."

"Am I?"

She knew nothing about him. Or maybe a little. Jason knew it was no secret he'd had a bit of trouble before he'd joined the military and then settled on law enforcement.

"I'm going to guess, yes." Very quickly MacIntosh shot him a sidelong glance. "You *are* a city boy, right?"

His turn.

"I grew up in Milwaukee," he admitted. "Not a very ritzy part of it either. How about you?"

"I've lived in the city and the countryside. There are advantages to both, I guess. I like the quiet of the latter, but on the other hand, the convenience level drops considerably. It's pretty nice to be able to shop for groceries at a place that carries everything from fresh-baked scones to sea bass."

He could picture her in an apron. And preferably nothing else. *Damn, I need to get over this.* "I didn't know you liked to cook."

"Some. But Bryce does most of it." She shot him a look of warning. "No smart-ass comment, please. Lots of men like to cook."

He *had* been about to make a caustic observation that maybe Grantham also knit his own sweaters, but her tone was fairly uncompromising, so he just shrugged. "If there's one thing I miss about Kate . . . well, there's two things actually"—he grinned—"but we're talking about cooking right now, right? I did like having something to eat now and then that doesn't come out of a box, can, or from a take-out place. I'm sure I *could* cook, but my mind doesn't operate along those lines. When I'm hungry, I get something to eat. There isn't much preplanning involved. At that point, boxes and cans are pretty handy. The inside of my fridge has never seen sea bass."

"We think like cops." Ellie's profile was all clean lines in the illumination from the lights, her tone no-nonsense. "I'm not saying we have no imagination; just that it works differently. We can predict how criminals might behave, but have a bit of a time with other creativity because our focus is influenced by a more grim side of life."

"Given it some thought?"

She was actually right. The term "relax" didn't mean much to him, not when there were people out there doing bad things to other people. It wasn't a moral stand either—he sure as hell was not motivated by an urge to save the world, but it did offend his sense of humanity that some individuals felt empowered to break the rules and walk away.

He liked catching them. It was fairly simple in his mind.

"Some." Ellie smiled faintly, just a subtle curve of her mouth. "My current involvement requires some speculation on whether or not opposites really do attract."

Involvement? Interesting choice of word. He might have gone for relationship. Jason stared at the ribbon of road, which was fairly quiet this time of the evening. It was almost midnight now. Fatigue was settling in, something he'd never experienced often before the shooting. Sure, everyone got dog-tired now and again, but he understood fatigue for the first time in his life. Different entirely.

"Kate and I were pretty different." He briefly shut his eyes. "She didn't even come see me in the hospital."

"People handle things in different ways."

"Not that I cared. We'd broken up."

"Oh face it, you cared or you wouldn't have mentioned it. I don't blame you either." MacIntosh sounded pragmatic, but thankfully changed the subject. "That sign said there are a couple of motels up ahead and I don't know about you, but I've had a fairly eventful evening and a long day before that. If someone is following us, I haven't noticed, and I've been paying attention. Should we go ahead and stop?"

It wasn't much fun not being 100 percent. He'd been warned that bouncing back from two gunshot wounds would not be as easy as he imagined. At first he'd thought the doctors were exaggerating, but now he wasn't quite so sure. "I'm fine with that."

"Since we've been on the subject, you did eat dinner, right?"

"Christ, MacIntosh, you aren't my mother."

She signaled to take the exit. "Thank God for that. I'm asking if you want to swing through and get something, because, let's face it, you are having kind of a bad run in the luck department and starving yourself half to death won't help. If you are my only backup, I'd just as soon you weren't going to faint from hunger."

"You heard the chief. *You're* supposed to be protecting *me*."

"Yeah, whatever. I'd sleep with one eye open if I were you. *Have* you eaten?"

In the end they went through a fast-food place and she ordered the coffee he hadn't been able to provide, a burger for him, and then drove to a chain motel that at least had a pretty well-lit parking lot. While he ate, she checked them in.

"Here's your key card," she said when she slid back into the car. "The good news is there is no outside entrance to the rooms on an individual basis and you need the card to get through the inner doors as a guest."

"Separate rooms?" He gave a theatrical sigh.

"I'm afraid so. If I get reprimanded because it all goes south, I guess that will be *my* problem, right?" She started the car and pulled around to the back. At this hour the place was utterly quiet, the lights in the parking lot illuminating only deserted cars and asphalt. "Or yours if they kill you."

Actually, since he was the one who technically got her into this, he did feel a little guilty even if he wasn't really culpable. Neutrally, he said, "I'm good. It looks clear."

"I agree." Ellie got out, and before he could stop her she opened the rear door and took out his simple duffel bag. "And I don't know about you, but I'm tired."

The television didn't do too much for her.

Ellie lay in bed and watched the screen flicker, sorting the day out. She had a pen and paper out courtesy of the hotel, and made some notes by hand, her mind slowing as her body wound down.

This was what she had:

Fielding. 1. Wife was possibly involved with Garrison Henley. 2. Maybe his son is really Henley's child.
3. Called DEA. Murdered in his bed, but wife and
child not harmed.

Brown. 1. Knew Fielding. 2 Knew Santiago. 3.
Having an affair with Danni Crawford. Shot on a
major thoroughfare but no viable witnesses. 4. Possibly had a tip about the Henley family.

Crawford: Involved with Brown. Had dinner
with Santiago and told him about Fielding's wife
and Henley. Ambushed at home and didn't see it coming. Dead next morning.

Santiago. 1. Car blown up. Friends with both Brown
and Crawford.

It really didn't seem like much.

The links weren't very strong in her opinion but
Santiago was right. They existed. What did they
mean? She took a sip of water from a bottle she would
make sure the hotel charged the department for because the price was ridiculous, and rubbed her cheek.

It was too thin as it stood, she decided thirty minutes later. They didn't know enough and whatever was
happening was so loosely linked she couldn't follow
the thread.

Except one thing was consistent, and even as the
weight of exhaustion made her lie back and close her
eyes, she had to wonder if it meant something.

No matter what Metzger said, they needed to talk
to Fielding's wife.

Her phone beeped. She glanced at the screen and

sighed before answering. "I could swear you'd be asleep. For that matter, why would you think I *wasn't* asleep?"

Santiago said, "We need to talk to Fielding's wife."

"Could you stop doing that?"

"Doing what?"

Reading my mind.

She muttered, "It doesn't matter . . . what caused this epiphany for you?"

"The damn Henley thing. It doesn't feel quite right, but I can't discount it. So she screwed him and maybe he is the baby-daddy, but I can't see him murdering three cops over that. We are still in the dark about something *really* important."

Since that was a summary of her feelings, she really couldn't argue too much. "If you decide to go to Florida, go ahead."

"What if we both go?" Santiago said. "Aren't you babysitting me? Metzger wants us out of town. Let's just head south tomorrow."

"The case up north counts too."

"The missing-person case that could be decades old compared to exploding cars and cops splattered on sidewalks? Not to us, not really."

She snapped off the television. "I get the point, so you can stop."

"MacIntosh, do you mind telling me why this cold case is so important to you? I mean the truth of it, not the evasive bullshit."

"I've already told you," Ellie said. "The skeleton was found on my grandfather's property—"

"Your grandfather's property, right. Look, I'm just going to ask it. Do you think he did it?"

"What?"

"Put that body in the ground."

At that moment she really despised Jason Santiago. "No. Can I say no again? I'm just puzzled and understandably concerned."

"No?" he said with more directness than she wanted. "Man up. You think he did it but want to prove otherwise. I get it."

"You get nothing." The defensiveness was too much. She heard it in her own voice and toned it down. "I don't think he did anything. But I do think maybe he knows something. It puts me in a very tenuous position."

"Tenuous? It is kind of late to sling around big words."

"Good night."

She hung up, not in the mood for his caustic comments. Maybe he was right. Maybe she should just forget the whole thing, let Carson handle it, and do *her* job.

On the other hand, perhaps Georgia Lukens was right, and it wasn't in her to let it go.

The indecision did not bode well for a good night's sleep. Maybe in the morning she'd call Metzger and find out how he felt about the two of them flying down to Florida and let that decide what happened next.

It would be nice to be absolved of the responsibility, she thought dismally as she rolled over and looked a the patterned curtains blocking the view of the parking lot. Orange and black zigzags on the material. Who chose that?

If the chief said go, it would probably just postpone her decision, not make it for her.

Chapter 19

The flames grew, hungry and demonic, leaping and licking with a hissing sound.

Purge by fire.

He wasn't quite sure what possessed him. Anger. Frustration. Fear. Guilt.

All of those, probably.

Not a new concept to burn away the evidence . . . people had been doing it for ages, and he embraced the ritual of destruction.

Everything went. He spared not one beloved thing. Clothing, shoes, even the letters she'd saved so carefully, written by her father to her mother during the war. The faded blanket knitted by her grandmother . . .

Gone.

Afterward he'd been so sure he would feel better. Relieved. Absolved.

But in the end, after the last ember faded, he felt . . . empty.

* * *

Trees.

Jason had to admit there were a lot of trees.

He'd woken to the surreal realization that he was in a generic room by himself, a little disoriented and a lot unhappy as he remembered the destruction of his car, with nothing but a duffel bag with two shirts and some clean boxers—at least he'd put those in—a shaving kit, and his cell phone charger.

So he'd brewed coffee in the crappy little pot the hotel provided, tried to ignore the picture of a giant peach blossom on the wall—hell, this was Wisconsin, after all, where had the peach thing come from?—brushed his teeth, and took a long, hot shower. MacIntosh didn't call, and he didn't call her either. He'd been sitting on the bed, surfing the channels, when she'd finally knocked on his door.

"Ready?" She'd looked as if she slept maybe four hours, with slight circles under her eyes, and wore jeans and a light blue shirt.

In his mind, he knew that feeling bad about it was ridiculous because he certainly hadn't blown up his own car, but he still did for some reason. So he coped with it in his usual way and said with his best leer, "Whenever you are. Unless you want to stay for a bit. I thought I'd made that clear enough. We've got the room until eleven, right?"

Luckily, she just brushed it off, which was just as well, since sometimes he even embarrassed himself. "Let's go utilize our current banishment from Milwaukee to further the good of law enforcement, shall we?

I've a found a place on Highway 21 that is pretty good for lunch. Then we'll catch 39 and go straight north."

"That's how this is going to go? I still think we need to talk to Joanne Fielding, face to face."

She'd taken the time to look at him searchingly. "I called Metzger. He's sending Grasso to Florida. We're out of it for now. He made it painfully clear. I got an earful about us involving you in the first place, and another one about you having dinner with Crawford, which by the way, was not my idea."

"She's a friend." He stopped and briefly closed his eyes. "*Was* a friend. Dammit."

"I'm sorry."

So was he, remembering finding Danni, the ominously cracked door, all the blood . . .

"Me too." He'd gotten up from the bed with only a minor twinge that he hoped didn't really show. "Let's just not argue about it. I don't know if I've ever mentioned it, but I hate flying anyway. I much prefer skeletons. If we are banished from Milwaukee, let's dabble in the foibles of past sins."

"I can't believe you even know what foibles means." But MacIntosh had laughed, not with mirth particularly, but it had cracked the tension at least a little.

"Let's just go," he'd told her, picking up his bag.

Now, as they drove past towns with names like Wautoma, he ventured into shark-infested waters again. He was terrible about expressing regret. Kate would support him on that, but it was worth a try if it kept the conflict to a minimum. "I could have been out of line last night. I was pretty tired."

"Are you actually apologizing? Don't make me faint

while driving, please." Ellie's mouth curved slightly but he doubted it was a smile.

"That shit about your grandfather. I was kind of shooting from the hip."

"From foibles to shit. That's more you." She slowed down for a tow truck with an old International Harvester hitched to the back. He hadn't seen a truck like that in years. When did they stop making those? About a billion years ago.

He moderated his voice. "Just tell me what happened. One on one and nothing else."

"Define the question, please."

"What happened with the grave."

"If I knew what happened, you wouldn't need to be part of the conversation."

"We are in no-man's-land here. I wouldn't mind a purpose." He looked at a corner tavern called the Pike and Post as they drove by. A pretty little lake with a dock was right beside it, the water glassy in the late-morning sun. "Pike and Post? Who came up with that name? Do you fish and drop off your mail at the same time?"

"I haven't been in that particular bar," she said dryly.

"Well, let's definitely stop at one fairly soon. Leinenkugel is my current painkiller of choice. Anyway, could you give me a little more information on just what we might be looking for? No offense, but you've been kind of vague on this, and every time I ask, you clam up."

"I'm not withholding information, I just don't really have much. Carbon dating is actually really expensive, did you know that? If we could say with some burden of proof to substantiate the claim that we thought we could solve a possible crime and that this was so-and-so, the state might pick up the tab. For a random case like this, probably not."

Her voice was entirely neutral. He wasn't sure that was how she felt.

She went on. "That said, the ME was able to give a little information that is helpful. She had fillings in the teeth that were left, and the wear was minimal, so our victim probably wasn't that old when she died, and he is certainly thinking it was in this past century. A broken wrist that had healed but fractured again postmortem is another clue. Otherwise, nothing. Not a scrap of clothing, not one button, not a single indication of how she came to be there. Animal damage to the bones and scavengers might be responsible for the missing teeth because the body was obviously disturbed, but there were some suspicious striations that might indicate cause of death."

"Knife?"

"He thinks so but couldn't say for sure. It is possible to stab someone to death and avoid leaving much evidence of the homicide once the soft tissue has gone away."

He had to admit it stirred the detective in him. "So she's stabbed to death, stripped, and buried in a makeshift grave. That is someone not playing nice at all."

MacIntosh frowned. "Putting it mildly, in my opinion. She's been there awhile. This didn't happen last month or even last year, obviously. The ME is not a forensic anthropologist and doesn't claim to be. He took a guess and said between twenty and sixty years."

"Kind of a big window."

"I'm not going to disagree."

He walked the plank again. "You don't think the remains could be anyone in your family, do you?"

"No." Her eyes flashed as she shot him a lethal look. "I don't know what your family was like, but mine might have noticed if someone was missing."

"My mother left when I was five. My father checked out not long after he physically shoved me out the front door and told me to not come back. All I know are missing people. None of us would have noticed at all."

He'd shocked her. He could tell because her face went very still and she drove with a sudden concentration. A dairy farm flashed by, cows in the field, the sun warm on the bucolic scene, which was incongruous to the conversation. She finally murmured, "That's terrible."

God, that was the last thing he wanted. Her pity? No thanks. "Not as bad as you might think. I had it a lot better than some kids. Roof and food. *Much* better than some. What I am saying is that sometimes we do take at face value what people say when maybe it isn't the gospel we think it is."

"What does that mean?"

"Is there anyone else you can ask besides your grandfather?"

It was galling that Santiago was more intelligent than he seemed on the surface.

His observation took Ellie in a different direction. They'd been headed up to Oneida County so she could show him the spot where the bones were found, and then she could take him to the county sheriff's office for those files it looked like they would both be reviewing, but instead she turned off for Schofield, just south of Wausau.

Her great-aunt had a cell phone, which amused her, especially since she could actually use it pretty well even at close to eighty years of age. When Ellie called, Mae answered with a warm, "Hello, baby girl."

"Auntie Mae . . . hi." She hadn't been a baby for thirty-two years, but there were people in your life you allowed latitude.

"I haven't seen you since spring."

Okay, that was a fair complaint, but she also had a litany of good excuses. "I moved. We had that big case. One thing after another. Speaking of such things . . . what are you doing this afternoon?"

"Today?"

"Like in an hour or so."

"You're just in the neighborhood? This is pretty far up from Milwaukee."

"Is it okay? I have a . . ." She stopped not quite sure what to call Santiago as friend didn't really qualify, and substituted, ". . . fellow police officer with me."

"Of course, honey. I'd love to see you at any time."

When they pulled into the driveway bordered by trim flower beds, she turned to her companion. "I don't know if I even need to say this, but my great-aunt is a little old lady with an emphasis on that last word."

He unfastened his seat belt and looked remarkably agreeable, which didn't reassure her at all. "I really only swear in front of people it will annoy."

"Hmm. Shall we go in? Please wipe that smirk off your face."

"Smirk?" He opened his door and eased out in a manner that said he wasn't entirely healed yet despite claiming to be just fine. "I think I need a definition on that one, baby girl."

She'd kind of hoped he hadn't heard that.

"If you know foibles, you know smirk." She also got out and slammed her door.

She'd always loved her great-aunt's quaint home. It reminded her of a doll's house, with a gabled roof and painted siding, and a small comfortable porch with a swing. Out back there was a truly magnificent oak tree Ellie and her sister had climbed as children.

"Where is the picket fence?" Santiago asked, shoving his hands into his pockets. "And shouldn't there be twenty cats or so lurking around?"

"No cats, just one little dog."

"Let me guess. Poodle?" The smirk deepened.

"Some kind of terrier, I think. His name is Jack. He'll hate you, by the way. He hates all men."

She was worried about making this visit, but only a little. Santiago was the kind of man little old ladies wanted to reform. Smart but wounded, wary and distant, but with a little sliver of vulnerability now and then.

Auntie Mae opened the door and Jack came rushing out, barking furiously, but when Santiago crouched down and held out his hand, he quieted and came forward to at least sniff it, then lost interest and shamelessly dropped to the floor and offered his belly for a scratch.

Seriously? It figured. Just to spite her, the dog liked him.

Her great-aunt was slightly stout in a matronly sort of way, with wavy gray hair and surprisingly smooth skin despite her age. She never wore anything but a dress or for an informal event a blouse and skirt— she'd said firmly more than once that she would feel ridiculous in slacks—even when tending to her garden, in which case she wore a smock and a hat. The stereotype had always amused Ellie but also was in some way very comforting. Her grandmother had been much the same. They'd only been a year apart in age and their closeness might have been a mirror of Ellie's relationship with her own sister, even though they had been sisters-in-law and not actually blood relatives.

"Hi honey." Her aunt gave her a quick kiss and a hug, and then turned an inquiring gaze in a request for the requisite politeness to the man standing beside her.

"This is Detective Santiago. Can we ask you a few questions?"

"My, that sounds official. I watch my fair share of television. All those shows are so popular. I have to remind myself, my great-niece really *is* a police officer. So you all really do say that? My answer is yes, of course, but let's go into the kitchen. Coffee?"

Santiago laughed and shook his head. "I love you Scandinavians and your coffee. Morning, noon, and night. I'm fine, but thank you very much."

"How about iced tea?"

"That sounds great actually."

The house smelled as always like cinnamon with a hint of talcum powder in the background. Ellie sat at the old wooden table and accepted a cup of impossibly strong coffee she would only sip and said without preamble, "Is there any chance you can help us in the identification of those bones?"

Her great-aunt sat down opposite and gave her a puzzled look. "What bones?"

"The skeleton found on Grandpa's property."

"First I've heard of it." Her aunt's face tightened. "They found . . . a human skeleton?"

"He hasn't said anything?" Ellie prodded gently.

"No, but it's not surprising." Mae took a drink from her cup after a moment, her hands steady. "I guess I didn't realize such a thing had happened. Robert is my brother, but it isn't like we talk often. I doubt we've spoken since last spring. There isn't much of a need. Aside from you and Jody, there isn't a lot to talk about. We chat occasionally. Old people get a little boring. We tend to do the same thing every day."

"The medical examiner is a bit iffy on the age," Santiago explained. "It's a female, probably not that old when she died, but it was at least two decades ago, and maybe more. Understandably the sheriff's office is reluctant to pour a lot of time into it. I'm not sure I am either, but I don't have a lot else to do right now, so some help, if you can give it to us, would be appreciated."

That was pretty reasonable. His smile was actually close to charming. Who knew that was even possible. Ellie added, "No one seems to have a theory. I just wondered if there is a story or anything you recall from when the property was purchased."

"No, but then again, honey, your grandfather bought it years before he married Helen."

That was slightly confusing.

"I thought he built the house as a wedding present."

"He did." Mae nodded and smoothed her coffee cup with the tips of her fingers. "The original one burned down. That was right after his first wife left him."

It felt like the world stopped revolving for a moment. "His *what*?"

"Didn't you know your grandfather had been married before?"

She hadn't. That was . . . incredible. Was it significant? She wasn't sure, but as a detective, all information was significant until proved otherwise. "No," she said quietly.

"They divorced. It wasn't quite so usual back then."

Her voice was stuck somewhere in her throat. *Young woman, shallow grave, a secret never mentioned . . .* she didn't like it. "How come no one has ever told me?"

"I'm not sure, but does anyone celebrate a failed marriage? Besides, people just didn't talk about it so freely back when *we* were young. Now no one would think twice about it."

"Not to celebrate it, but it is a piece of family history." Ellie thought it over, conscious of Santiago across the table and now wishing she hadn't brought him along. "Does my mother know? She has never mentioned it. Neither did Dad either."

Not once.

"I'm not sure, actually," Auntie Mae said with some measure of surprise. "Is it important?"

It was Santiago who said agreeably, "Ma'am, we will be sure and let you know."

Chapter 20

There was fate and there was the kind of bad luck that just followed people around. She'd never really orchestrated anything. She'd just been a victim, in many ways, as much as anyone else.

Now, after weeks, here came someone asking questions, just when she thought it was behind her.

The sheriff . . . he had a job to do, she understood that.

"Any truth to it?" He'd been direct but polite.

How strange it was that she really hadn't balked much at murder but didn't like the lying. So she'd said, "I am really not sure what you are asking, Calvin."

"Sir," he'd corrected. "At this moment, I'm sir, understand?"

They were cousins. Life liked to play small jokes.

"I don't suppose anyone could misunderstand that statement." She could feel her jaw tighten. "Cal, what do you want from me?"

He rested his knuckles on the table and bent down to stare her in the eyes. "Did you have something to do with this? Because I'm going to tell you, there are a few people in this town that think you did."

"To do with what?"

"You are in a sexual relationship with her husband. Rumor has it you were after him all along."

The blunt declaration jarred her and her head snapped back. "Says who?"

"Everyone knows it. Jesus, Helen," he muttered as he straightened. "I cannot believe you put me in this position."

The corporate offices of Henley Enterprises were situated in a towering building downtown; a glass and steel building with a bank title on the marquee on the city skyline and an escalator, and for those who needed to go to the twentieth floor, elevators.

But Carl figured it was much easier to just walk a block or so and knock on the door.

He didn't know his neighbors. Not any of them really. He knew what kind of cars they drove, and out of habit noticed. Otherwise, no real contact. He really didn't belong and his occupation made most people cautious for some reason.

The house was unique, but all of them on this particular pricey drive were different, the neighborhood an old one, most of the places built in the 1920s, when opulence was a way of life if the money was there. He actually had no idea when the Henley family had bought theirs, but it was a huge, sprawling, two-story brick home, with two wings and three chimneys, set back a good way from the street by a shaded drive. No gate, but he didn't have one either. Gates were pretentious and real wealth required no pretention.

Hands in his pockets, he strolled up the drive, not quite sure what he was going to accomplish from this visit. He'd talked to both Hamish and Rays and been informed the family had not been interested at all in discussing their son's possible involvement with Fielding's wife, brushing it off as just a brief affair.

He was scheduled to fly out to Florida in just a few hours, so he needed some information quick, which was why he'd decided on this course of action.

Carl was a firm believer that people looked at the profession of detective in a different light if you wore a very nice designer suit and spoke perfect English. Maybe they'd talk to him. Hamish was a small, clever man with a tendency to let his New York accent slip through, and Rays looked like a cop, big and buff, with a flattop and a scar on the side of his neck that Carl had never asked about. They were both thorough and good at their jobs, but in this instance, he thought maybe he could be more effective.

The woman who answered the door was middle-aged and well kept, with carefully tinted hair and a draped scarlet cashmere sweater. Her perfectly plucked brows rose in inquiry. "Yes?"

He didn't hold out his badge, knowing in advance that would set the tone of the interview. "I'm Carl Grasso. I actually live just down the street. I'm also a detective with the Milwaukee Police Department. I would very much like to talk to Garrison. Is he home?"

She hesitated just enough. "My son does not live here."

"We know he has his own apartment. A few questions, that's all. You've already spoken to detectives, and we appreciate the cooperation. I'm just following up."

"My husband might not like him talking to you without our lawyer."

Her husband, poised to possibly make an impact on the political vista of the state of Wisconsin, would probably prefer Carl be shooed away politely.

"He's hardly under arrest or even close to it. I just have a few questions that were not asked the last time."

She bit her lower lip but didn't invite him in. "Everyone is sorry about that young police officer, but my son had nothing to do with it."

"We have no proof he did. Can I just have a word?" It might not be a reassuring statement, but was at least truthful enough that Mrs. Henley widened the door at his sincerity. Carl followed her into a massive foyer—much bigger than his—and the hollow echo of their footsteps resonated in his ears.

"Which house?" she asked him over her shoulder, her gaze cold and inquiring.

"Which house?"

"Do you live in?"

He wasn't a snob, or didn't think so, but he got the question with a certain ironic sense of amusement. "On the corner. The brick two-story."

"Apparently we pay our law enforcement too generously."

"Or else my father made a lot of money as a young entrepreneur and then married well."

"Oh." That made her step falter and she said nothing else until she gestured him to a seat in a room that looked like a study. He had doubts it was ever used as one if a person considered the immaculate desktop, and more important, the disused smell. It felt decorated, but not lived in, and though there were pictures on the walls of some of the liquor storefronts, he highly doubted the expensive leather chair behind the desk was for more than show.

It really wasn't Carl's concern if Mr. Henley wanted it to seem as if he worked out of his home. At the moment, what he wanted to know was if point A connected to point B. Fielding to Brown. He needed to get a measure of Garrison Henley.

It didn't take too long.

The man in question was young—it was hard to tell how young since his features were obscured by a ball cap, incongruous to his playboy image, and he entered not in a half-slouch that indicated belligerence, but tall and straight, his eyes direct. "My mother told me who you are. What do you want?"

"Are you Garrison Henley?"

"Would my mother send anyone else if you asked for me?"

Young, yes, hard, yes, and arrogant, *yes*.

Looking bland, Carl chose a leather chair without being offered a seat. "Can we talk about the wife of the police officer who was killed recently? The one who asked for a paternity test for the baby boy she had"—he flipped open a notebook he took from his pocket—"twenty-three months ago?"

"I've already talked to the police."

"Yes, but not to me."

"Lieutenant Grasso. Yeah, you know, I've heard of you, actually." Henley's gaze was assessing.

Once people heard his name, and looked into his past, they tended to pay attention, and so when Carl said Grasso, even if they didn't have all the facts, the notoriety was helpful.

Besides, he and this kid were talking kind to kind. On sight they had both recognized it. The privileged children of the elite. Henley's father was not just wealthy, but sat on the city council. Had breakfast with the mayor. There was some meat behind that fist.

"I don't know what I can tell you that I haven't said before." The young man walked over and dropped into the chair behind the desk, probably unconsciously mimicking his father. "I slept with Joanne, yes. Quite a few times. She worked in our corporate offices. I can't remember exactly the last time, so the kid could be mine, I suppose. In case you haven't noticed, my family has money. She swore she was on the pill, and I took her word for it."

Idiot. There is more than unwanted pregnancy to worry over . . . ever hear of venereal disease or AIDS?

Carl wasn't his parent, so he just asked, "You weren't afraid she'd blackmail you later?"

"Not until Fielding called. Obviously we'd broken it off. Shit, she was married then . . . like two years or so. He said something about the kid . . . I was kind of taken off guard, you know?"

"What *did* he say? I need to know specifically."

"I've already—"

"Tell *me*."

Henley looked at him. He didn't respond at once.

"The man was murdered," Carl reminded him in an inflexible tone.

"He said he wanted a paternity test. Asked me if I would agree. I was actually blindsided. I hadn't talked to her in a long time. I certainly didn't know about the baby."

Carl considered an armoire in the corner that probably cost thousands of dollars. He had a good eye and the mother-of-pearl inlay on the front was definitely custom. The family had money and it showed. "You weren't harassing her?"

"No. Absolutely not."

The vehemence of the answer fit with his perception of the situation, but not quite with the information provided in the file.

"So what made him call you after so long?"

"No idea. I guess she told him finally we'd been together."

Every single time Carl thought he might get a glimmer, it just got more complicated. "He knew that already from the arrest, correct? You were at the club with her."

Garrison Henley tilted his head a little to the side, his mouth tightening. "Oh, he did. Hitting on her while arresting me? I was unhappy in about a hundred ways that night, but that made me *very* unhappy. Is that how cops usually work?"

Against all odds, Carl kind of liked this young man. It reminded him of . . . well, he wasn't going to analyze it, but Henley wasn't what he expected. "No, that's how men and women usually work. You agreed to the test, right?"

Henley shrugged. "There was a chance, so I owned it. I wasn't the one all winched up about it, Fielding was. But when I told my father, he talked to our lawyers, and in the end, I was told to refuse."

It did give Henley a motive to kill Fielding, but it was still pretty thin. Money had to be the motivation for the request, but it didn't really fit. "What did she want?"

"I don't exactly know. I am not sure Joanne wanted anything. This seemed to be more about her husband."

"That really wasn't what I heard."

He said with a hint of ironic humor, "Detective, do you believe everything you hear?"

"No." There was no equivocation on that agreement. He was lied to so often he didn't believe the truth ninety percent of the time.

Of all things, Ellie had to be with Santiago when she found out such a personal thing as that her grandfather had been married before and she didn't know it. Really, with his lack of tact, she was getting tired of the conversation.

He repeated, "So he never said anything."

"No."

"Not a word about the first wife."

"No."

"Not even hinted about—"

"No!" She took a turn deliberately too fast and

inhaled deeply as she calmed down. "Okay, I admit he has not told me the complete truth apparently, but it is his life. It is a sin of omission. You won't get any argument here. I don't know everything about your life either, but you are not obligated to tell me just because we know one another."

Jason Santiago looked at her, and he had a way of doing so that made her distinctly uncomfortable. "Actually, I told you pretty much everything about my life this morning. So you are fine with this new development or are you just rationalizing?"

"Now you sound like my shrink."

"You have a shrink? No shit?" He looked genuinely surprised.

"I'll give you her card. No one could use one more than you. We are almost there."

"I don't need a shrink," he said.

"There are those of us who would beg to differ."

"MacIntosh, this isn't about me. Can you tell me what you walked away from that interview with your great-aunt with?"

She wasn't really ready to talk about it yet. "I walked away with a desire to talk to my sister. Just because I don't know about this story he hasn't seen fit to mention, doesn't mean Jody doesn't."

"So that is where we are going?"

"She lives here in Wausau. Sorry, it won't take long."

He shrugged. "My car aside, it beats sitting in my apartment, and as far as I can tell my other choice involves cases of files sitting in some courthouse basement. Tell me this, though. If your sister did know and you didn't, what difference does that make?"

It was actually a pretty good question, as little as she wanted to admit that. "It would mean it wasn't a deep, dark secret. Secrets bother me, especially when coupled with unmarked graves."

"Christ, I hope you do realize there could be a dozen reasons that body was buried where it was. Smallpox epidemic, a stranger dying on the side of the road, a body found floating in the lake no one could identify . . . it could be anything."

Of all people, Santiago sounded reasonable and reassuring? Ellie turned onto Jody's street, saw her sister's minivan in the drive, and pulled in behind it, putting the car in park. She unfastened her seat belt. "I'll be gone five minutes, tops."

"I don't get to hear this conversation?" He looked like he was enjoying himself, and since he didn't have a vested interest in the outcome of the case—if it was a case—she envied him.

"No."

"I'm hurt."

She slid out of the car, her shoes scraping the asphalt of the neat drive. "I'll be back. Why don't you play with your phone and find out from Grasso what's happening with the official case we are supposed to be investigating. You know, the one where they destroyed your car?"

"I seem to remember it." He gave her a sardonic look. "I'll try Grasso. You go talk about your family skeletons."

She would have told him that wasn't amusing, but it wasn't worth her while, so she instead closed the door with a satisfying slam and went up the walk. Jody answered the door before she even knocked, and said succinctly, "Auntie Mae just called me and I got your text. What's going on?"

Her sister might meddle, as Bryce put it, but of all the people in the world, Ellie did trust her. "Can *you* tell *me*? Did you know that our grandfather had been married before?"

"Before what?" Her sister looked perplexed, coming out onto the porch. "I'm kind of in the dark here."

"Before our grandmother, apparently."

Jody wrinkled her forehead. "Are you serious? No. I guess I didn't. But that would have been a very long time ago."

True. At least it gave them a time frame to work with. "I just wondered if you knew."

"Because of why?"

"Because I really want to make sense of the situation."

"Are you going to come in and tell me about this, because quite frankly, I'm not sure I know what you are talking about. You didn't even tell me you were coming up this way . . . and who is the guy in your car? Ellie, is something wrong?"

Yes, something is wrong. There were a couple of things wrong actually. Ellie lightly blew out a breath. "No to coming in. Sorry. I'll tell you why when I can give you some sort of solid information. I didn't call to say I was coming because I didn't know it, and the guy in the car is my partner, Jason Santiago."

"Looks kind of cute from here." Jody peered over her shoulder at the driveway.

"Until he opens his mouth," Ellie muttered. "Can you do me a favor?"

"Always."

"I'm busy with this triple-homicide case. Talk to Mom for me. Surely Dad told her about the previous marriage. What happened? Mae was vague, but it really was a long time ago."

"I suppose I can, but do I even know the right questions to ask?"

"At this point, you know as much as I do."

Chapter 21

The evening was cool and getting crisp, a hint of wood smoke in the air, and the world was slowly going silent this time of year, the insects dying, and the moon brighter in an obsidian sky. Soon Orion would be there with his vivid belt. Though he'd never been much for astronomy, he knew that much.

It was hard to be young. Not that he wanted to be old, but it seemed like the choices solidified and changed, became a little easier, were less defined by passion and impulse.

Impulse.

He read the letter again.

The message was clear enough.

But he wasn't sure he believed the words.

He set it aside and got up to stare out the window. Had he really been that wrong? Once he'd believed in a lot of things that didn't seem to apply to his life any longer.

He'd never believed in evil. That was abstract. . . .
But he might be coming to terms with it after all.

The woman next to him on the plane nursed her baby.

Carl couldn't decide if he was fascinated or appalled at being sat next to an infant, but he did have a definitive uncomfortable reaction, especially when the mother headed off to the bathroom, leaving the infant in the seat, ostensibly in the charge of her son, who might have been seven years old. True, it was a plane, no one was going to make away with the baby, and nature did call.

"Going to Disney?" he asked, taking some pity on the boy, who seemed to not know what to do except keep picking up the pacifier.

How the hell any human ever survived surprised him. The pacifier had landed on the seat about three times and God only knew who had sat there.

"Yes." The boy had a sprinkle of freckles and a candid smile. "You too?"

Disney? Not exactly. "Well, no."

The pacifier went south, to the floor this time, and Carl was no expert, but it was not something that needed to go back into a baby's mouth. He picked up the child, inexpert but by far better than a seven-year-old. "Your mother is going to want to wash that. Let me hold her for a minute. I'm a police officer. It's okay. What's her name?"

A baby. Really. He could have sworn he had no idea what to do with one, but he carefully held the child and she made some sound that inexplicably moved him. Wide blue eyes stared into his as she trustingly sat on his lap.

"Chloe." The boy shrugged.

"Chloe. I like that."

"A policeman? Really?"

The mother returned, wary at first at the sight of someone else holding her child, but then warming up and talkative. Very talkative. By the end of the flight Carl was relieved at the bustle of the airport. It was far better than excited children and screaming babies, though tiny Chloe, who did have a small little accident on his shirt but otherwise was actually rather engaging, was by far the best baby on the plane.

Who the hell takes infants to Disney? he wondered, holding on to the bar as the shuttle slid away.

Everyone, he decided a few minutes later, exiting the terminal. Not that he disliked children . . . one of his regrets was that he might never have a family, but traveling with small human beings seemed to be an excruciating experience after his afternoon.

At this moment, though, he was intent on getting out of the airport. He followed the crowd, skipped the baggage claim since he had his carry-on, ducked into the queue of taxis, and gave the address.

Joanne Fielding was expecting him and she opened the door at his light knock. His first impression was that she was an Italian beauty with a topaz hint to her skin, large dark eyes, though her lipstick was a little dramatic for his taste.

A decade older than Garrison Henley if he had to guess, but striking enough most men would not mind being seen out with her on their arm. Fielding had apparently agreed with that assessment. The house was nice, but definitely middle-class, with a stucco exterior and a cracked cement drive.

He needed some straightforward answers. Did they lie with her? He wasn't at all sure, but that was why he was there. He extended his credentials. "Mrs. Fielding?"

"Lieutenant." She stepped back and the skirt of the light yellow sundress she wore swung around her ankles. "I got your text when you landed. Would you like an iced tea?"

"No, but thank you."

Her composure was much better than tears, but he still noted that she didn't look directly at him. Her gaze slid past, and when he declined the offer of a drink, she gestured him to a chair by a glass-topped table in a room that overlooked a gracious backyard with several waving palm trees and then sat about as far away as possible without outright rudeness.

In a self-conscious movement, she clasped her knee. It was supposed to make her look comfortable and actually had the opposite effect. "You've come a long way. How can I help you?"

"You look a lot like your sister Lindsey."

"When she called me and asked if I would speak to you, I almost said no, but in light of what happened to my husband, it is better than having her investigating it. I never dreamed she'd do something so stupid."

"There have been three murders, so I couldn't agree more. I was the one talking to the press when the Greta

Garrison murders happened, and she recognized me in the grocery store. I think she took an opportunity to make a friend in the homicide division, just in case I had information she could use."

"Oh God." Joanne was pale under her tan. "David is dead. Doesn't she realize that?"

Carl had never been one to ease around difficult questions. It wasn't his style, though he still did it differently from Santiago's blunt approach. "I *am* assisting the department on these cases. I thought it over, and I am sure you will understand that I decided, in light of what is happening up north, maybe we should have this conversation face to face."

"I'm surprised they paid to have you fly down here."

In truth the department hadn't, but maybe they would eventually compensate him. If Metzger refused he didn't really care all that much. Carl just lightly lifted his shoulders. "I'm sure, if you've been paying attention at all, that you realize this seems to be getting pretty personal. Fingers are starting to point at the Henley family in all three shootings. Did you know the car of a homicide detective was destroyed last night? We'd like to contain this as soon as possible. Your assistance would be invaluable."

The breeze coming in the screen moved her hair but otherwise, she was utterly still, her body rigid. "I don't have any assistance to give beyond what I've already done. My husband was killed. I don't know what I would have to tell you that I haven't. Do you think I am indifferent to the fact he was murdered?"

She wasn't indifferent. She was scared. That told him something, but he wasn't sure what. She'd also left the state, though most people would think Florida preferable to Wisconsin just for the weather, but he doubted that was why.

Patiently, he explained, "I can tell you one thing you can do to help me. Can we have a candid conversation over the paternity test? I first heard Garrison Henley said yes, but he changed his mind."

Tight-lipped, she looked away.

"The Milwaukee Police Department doesn't care who you were sleeping with, Mrs. Fielding," he said. "Your involvement with the Henley family is not a secret."

"I dated Garrison. That's it. Involvement is a little bit of a stretch."

The flat sound of her tone made him wonder if the trip hadn't been worth it after all. "If you had his baby, I'm afraid some people might see that as involvement. You worked for the corporation they own. That's how you met, correct?"

"My son isn't his."

"If you are so sure, why wasn't your husband?"

"Jealousy, I guess. He started to get this crazy notion Garrison and I hadn't ended our relationship."

He really did not like how she refused to meet his eyes.

"Did he have some reason to think that?"

It was a shot, but he hit a nerve. The muscles in her throat rippled as she swallowed and color came up into her face.

When she didn't say anything, he added pragmatically, "If Garrison agreed when your husband wanted the paternity test, it follows that he acknowledged you might be already pregnant when you got married. I admit I'm not sure why your husband suddenly felt the need to know years after the fact, but you're right, guys can be touchy that way, raising someone else's child and all. So he asks, and Henley refuses in the end because his rich family apparently doesn't want to pay child support. That all makes sense to me. What I don't understand—and I mean *at all*—is how it could be worth it to kill three police officers over this situation. Lindsey doesn't either, or so she told me, but she seems to feel strongly that crossing the Henleys is a very bad idea, and I assume she got that information from you."

Joanne just shook her head and whispered, "I had no idea . . . she needs to stay away from them."

He couldn't agree more. That Lindsey had been able to connect Brown and Crawford spoke of how much she'd been poking around, but when he'd called to get her sister's location and number, she had at least trusted him enough to give it to him.

"Why did your husband call an undercover DEA agent? Leverage to get Henley to agree to the test?"

Joanne's lips parted and her response was a whisper. "No. I . . . I don't know."

But she did know.

It was not as if he hadn't seen that telltale shift in attitude before. "Mrs. Fielding, your husband was a police officer and a dedicated one. I've thought about this and I cannot come up with a single reason why he would not go through the proper channels, unless this was personal. He didn't, and now he is dead. Help me catch who killed him."

"I have a child. Do you even understand that, Lieutenant?"

Directly, no. But he knew quite a bit about the fear of loss and little Chloe came to mind, trusting enough to sit on his lap and play with his tie on the plane, vulnerable and innocent. That might be exactly why he had never married and *had* children. His job was dangerous . . . he didn't want to leave anyone bewildered and alone.

But he sensed something about the case was going to break. He asked urgently, "Have you been directly threatened?"

Joanne rose, her eyes pleading. "I'm not going to answer that question. Don't ask again."

"The government of the United States has a good witness-protection program. I was able to find you."

"Through my sister."

"That means someone else could do it too. She gave me the information voluntarily, but—"

"Don't say it." Her voice broke. "Please, come with me."

The place was generic, a rented condo in a beach-side community, ten minutes from the gulf side, the furniture brown and beige and the floor tile. Carl followed Joanne Fielding down a short hallway and into a small bedroom. A portable crib sat next to the bed.

The child was peacefully sleeping, his thumb in his mouth, a blanket patterned with bunnies tangled around his chubby legs.

She whispered, "I think you can understand why I can't talk to you. Thanks for stopping by, Detective. Have a nice flight back."

Jason listened shamelessly, and quite frankly, he was pretty good at deciphering a phone call on a one-sided basis. This wasn't a good one.

He actually thought it was kind of funny when Ellie pressed a button and looked at him with caustic accusation. "Got all that?"

"Grasso is in Florida and Fielding's wife cut him off without giving him a thing. Am I right?"

They were in a small supper club near some town called Merrill he'd never heard of, and he was having what he had to admit was some of the best walleye of his life, crisp and perfectly fried. While the bonhomie atmosphere was not his usual style because they were actually playing polka music in the background, the food was great and there was a spectacular view across a very pretty lake. They had checked in late afternoon to a motel on the same lake that had been at one time a summer resort obviously, made up of small cabins grouped around winding paths, with stairs down to several long docks and a boat-rental facility for canoes and rowboats, already closed for the season.

The person at the desk had recommended the restaurant, and as he polished off another piece of walleye, he had to admit he was really glad they had taken the advice.

It was a little cheesy, with deer heads and mounted bass on the walls, but these places had always appealed to him, like a glimpse into another life. Just the term "supper club" conjured images of rented cabins and evenings fishing off docks and campground fires.

He needed to vacation more, though having his car blown to smithereens as a catalyst to his current circumstances was not his preferred method of travel planning. In fact, losing his car made it more difficult than ever to travel anywhere.

Thinking about that was for another day. Staying alive took precedence.

"You're right." Detective MacIntosh took a bite of fish and looked deeply and thoroughly frustrated. "Grasso found her, though I am not sure just how he did it since she seems to be in hiding, and I can't blame her for that."

Why wouldn't she be frustrated? She wasn't able to be there with Grasso looking into the case, she was instead stuck with Jason, though that wasn't entirely one-sided.

But there were worse places to be on this earth than sitting at a lakeside table with Ellie MacIntosh, a rising moon glimmering illumination on the water, even with a polka band in the background. He picked up a forkful of coleslaw. "I'm right? I just don't hear that from you often enough and it gets sweeter each time. Let me bask in this moment. So, what now?"

"You are as much of a detective as I am."

"Ah, vindication." He ate the coleslaw and cocked a brow. He actually shared her unease. "I have no idea what it is Danni could have told me that would have caused anyone to take a preemptive strike at me. I keep sitting here and asking myself what I could know, and the answer is I have no idea."

"You don't have to know anything." MacIntosh set aside her fork. "They just need to think you know something. Therein lies the problem."

"Therein?" His derisive tone got to her, but he'd known it would.

"I read a lot of Poe, give me a break . . . So, as you said, what now?"

"Poe?"

"As in Edgar Allan. You've heard of him I hope."

"Jeesh, that'll keep you awake at night and—"

"I was joking." She glanced out over the moonlit lake. "I'm much more likely to read a romance novel. And fiction can't keep anyone awake as much as real life."

He didn't disagree. "Lots of pretty ruthless people out there. Gives me the creeps now and then what they are willing to do to each other."

"Just now and then?" She took a sip of water, considering him over the rim of her glass. "So I think I can now give you some approximate dates."

For searching those damn files in the cold case no one else but her cared about. He'd sensed the subject change by the reflective look on her face. "You know," he said, actually weighing his words before speaking, which was not natural to him so he hoped she appreciated the effort, "I'm having a pretty hard time trying to figure out what you hope to gain from all this. I get the concept of justice—I hope I do, since this seems to be the profession I've chosen—but whoever that woman was, you can't save her."

"I can find answers for her."

"Which she will never know," he pointed out with what he thought was inarguable logic. "You want answers for *you*, and we both know it. Don't get me wrong, I'll wade through a load of crappy files if you insist, but have you asked yourself if you really want to know the answer?"

"Are you shooting from the hip again? I'm not interested in a philosophical discussion with you about my motivation."

"That's a great attitude. And here I thought we were bonding at last. I had tea with your great-aunt. We *must* be best buds. I hate tea unless it is of the Long Island variety."

"You had tea only because she didn't have any beer."

"It *was* a disappointment."

Her hazel eyes were direct. "I admit I'm curious, and to answer the question, I think that yes, I want to know. I think most people would want to know the identity of a skeleton that might, or might not, be associated with their family."

Her aunt may not have offered him a beer, and to his credit he hadn't asked, but he had one now and he took a drink. Fine, he'd given her the choice of just dropping the whole thing. "I saw the expression on your face, by the way. So, like me, you think it is the first wife in that grave."

There, he'd said it. He was pretty good at being upfront.

His partner didn't like it. She stared at him across the table. "Hardly. They divorced."

"That will be easy enough to confirm."

"It *is* confirmed. My great-aunt told us. You met her. She wouldn't lie."

"I met her." He nodded. Mae had been one of those soft, sweet ladies who had a hint of steel underneath. "And I agree one hundred percent she would never on purpose tell us something she did not believe to be true. Not the same thing as lying."

Ellie hooked her hair around her ear. The mannerism always seemed to mean she was thinking hard, which he respected. Besides, he liked the feminine, graceful movement of her hand when she did it. Her eyes were shadowed, but that could just have been the supposedly romantic effect of the inadequate lighting. "Maybe you're right."

"Which would indicate missing-person records are useless. Let's find the record of the marriage instead, then the legal documentation of the divorce. This mysterious first wife might be alive and kicking somewhere, which will then take her off the table. At that point we can go back to missing persons."

"Unless it *is* her."

See, he'd known that was what she was worried about. "Unless it is her," he agreed.

Someone laughed loudly at a table behind them, but then again, they probably weren't discussing hidden graves.

"In which case, she was most likely the victim of a homicide."

"Odds are. I believe there is some protocol involved when a person dies of natural causes and it doesn't involve dumping them in an unmarked grave and saying they left and later divorced you."

All things she already knew and maybe he shouldn't have been so blunt. He softened it a little by adding, "But look, MacIntosh, you obviously think he's a good guy and not the type to murder his wife, and he was able to legally remarry, so he is probably telling you the truth."

But if he wasn't, he would be the main suspect in a homicide investigation. There was no statute of limitation on capital cases. So her difficult decision now was whether or not to tip the county sheriff's department on whom it might be. He didn't envy her that one. He didn't remember his grandparents on either side very well, but he would not want to carry around the burden of being the one to get one of them convicted of murder.

"Where is your family from?"

The question took him off-guard. They hadn't worked together long enough to read each other's minds so often. "I've mentioned my parents."

"Mentioned, yes, but no, I mean your family. Santiago? Not a super common Wisconsin name."

"Johnson is a super common Wisconsin name. Anything that doesn't end in a *berg* or a *son* is someone from outer space here."

"Not an answer."

"Exactly." He set his napkin on the table. With his upbringing she should be grateful he'd remembered to use the napkin at all. His father tended to use his sleeve. What good manners he had he learned in the military. With a flourish, he took out his wallet. "You ready to go? This one is on me."

MacIntosh didn't look disappointed, she just looked tired. "I should have known better than to ask you, of all people, but I am trying to decide how to figure it out and deal with this."

"Oh," he said with ironic inflection, "I am the perfect person to ask if you want to figure it out, but not the right one if you want to know how to feel about it."

Chapter 22

"**W**here are the letters coming from?"

She gazed at him steadily. "She doesn't want you to know."

It was like a nightmare. He wasn't an intellectual man in the sense that he enjoyed books and music, but more that nature had its own rhythm and beauty. He appreciated a sunrise through the trees with a kind of poetic wonder, and the glimpse of the sleek movement of a northern pike slipping through the weeds in a glassy lake, or the graceful swoop of a nighthawk across a thickening indigo sunset.

But he wasn't stupid either. Not at all.

The woman sitting there across the table was lying to him. "I know you always claimed to be Vivian's best friend, but this is not actually how a friend would act in my opinion. You and I both know I need to find her."

Softly, she said, "I don't think that's going to happen."

He didn't either and it scared the hell out of him.

Jody called around ten o'clock, which was unusual for a woman with children who participated in just about every activity known to mankind. Ellie had been half dozing, the book she'd taken the time to toss into her small bag sliding from her hand, when the ring jolted her awake. She was getting used to Santiago's nocturnal interruptions, so she answered abruptly without looking at her phone, "What?"

"And here I could swear I was your favorite older sister."

She levered herself more upright on the pillows of the hotel bed and brushed her hair back. "Sorry. I was half asleep and you are my only older sister, so don't get too full of yourself with that favorite thing. . . . What's going on?"

"After you left, I called Mom like you asked, but wasn't quite sure just what I was looking for. The result was interesting anyway. Maybe you aren't the only detective in the family."

"Okay." Ellie had to admit to a certain level of apprehension. "Did she know about the previous marriage?"

"Yes, but not until the two of us put the pieces together. I was on the phone with her for two hours."

"That is definitely taking one for the team." Ellie adored her mother in many ways, but there was a reason—Santiago listening aside—that she'd asked her sister to call their mutual parent. Apparently living in a beachside condo on the Florida coast afforded her lots of time to talk and Ellie didn't have time for that right now. "I owe you. What did she say?"

"Oh, you'll pay. Anyway, she at first was a little quiet. I mean, this is Dad's family, and though they were married for decades, I guess they hadn't ever talked about it. But, yes, he'd said something once or twice. I guess his grandmother had mentioned it when he was a young boy. No details. Dad had the general impression the ex-wife had just up and left. No real explanations as to why. It was way before he was born, obviously, since by then Grandpa had remarried, and as a boy and even a young man, he hadn't bothered to ask what exactly happened."

"But he *had* mentioned it to Mom."

"Anyone would be a little curious, don't you think? His father was married to another woman. As we get older, we tend to not be so self-absorbed and start to ask these sorts of questions."

Some people might be a lot curious. Ellie knew she was. "Mae acted just a little strange once she realized the direction I was going . . . swore she could not remember her former sister-in-law's name. I don't believe that for a minute, do you? She is way sharper than I am. Not that it matters, because I can access court records and find out, but I really need to know in what state they were divorced. Here in Wisconsin, or wherever she went? That many years ago not all records were kept the same. Here, no problem. An obscure county in New Mexico? I might never find that one. Did you know that New Mexico was not admitted as a state until 1912? With a per capita of about one person a square mile back then, and—"

"Just ask him."

The interruption was warranted and Ellie knew she was tired and torn in more than one direction, so she stopped talking.

Jody said again emphatically, "Ellie, I don't care about the history of the state of New Mexico right now, though I assume it is very fascinating. Just ask Grandpa these questions you want answered. I am not at all sure where you are going with this, or even why you are so concerned, but the truth is, you need to just go straight to him and *ask* him. Not Mom, not me, and not Mae. *Him*."

Trust her sister to get straight to the point.

"I did ask him. The day he called me and asked me to come up because the grave had been found, I asked him face to face. He denied knowing who those bones could belong to."

"Then I'd say he doesn't. But if you are so bound and determined to find out, ask him again."

"I'll think about it. This is not the only thing going on. I'll call soon."

When she pressed the end button, she stared at the popcorn ceiling of her motel room and contemplated the other case, putting this one out of her mind. Grasso had said, the hum of the airport in the background, their conversation interrupted by the announcements of flights going in and out, that Joanne Fielding had been an interesting interview.

She seemed afraid. Okay, Ellie would buy that. Her husband had been killed right next to her while she slept. She would be afraid too.

But Joanne had been spared and so had her son.

It gave her some measure of satisfaction to call Santiago at such a late hour, but to her disappointment, he was obviously still awake and answered on the second ring, irritatingly clear-voiced and alert. "Yeah?"

"Answer one question for me."

"MacIntosh, I'm in the room next door. Why are we talking on the phone? If you need me to come over and tuck you in, just say so."

"Thanks but no thanks." She was getting pretty good at ignoring his more irritating comments. "If Grasso thinks Joanne Fielding is scared, but she isn't particularly in hiding, what is up with that? Yes, she left the state, but he discovered where she is, so it follows the bad guys could find out too. She is not in the witness protection program, she never even asked apparently. If, through her, Fielding found out something about a drug cartel supposedly laundering money through the Henleys' chain of liquor stores, wouldn't she have been targeted too?"

His answer took a minute. "That's true. I guess I'm not sure either why she is comfortable enough with her situation to not ask for help. You can't have it both ways. Was the call to the DEA agent a strike back at the Henley family by Fielding that backfired? It sure looks like it on the surface, but it all doesn't fit together very neatly. I wish we knew more about Lieman and how Fielding even got his number."

"I know they keep the operations involving under-cover agents close to protect them, but we are also law enforcement. I say we ask Metzger to try and get us more information on that angle."

"Sounds reasonable. That has bothered me all along too. One of those loose ends that might unravel the whole thing, but it could be that they knew each some-how in another way. That would explain why Fielding didn't use the chain of command."

"If so, why didn't Lieman mention it?"

"That's a pretty good question. I say we call the chief in the morning and push it."

Then she said it. "Lieman is law enforcement."

Santiago said grimly, "That has occurred to me too."

Jason watched the flickering screen but the images flowing through his mind had nothing to do with the show.

In his head played the scene of two men opening the door of a bedroom and approaching a sleeping couple and taking out the husband but not the wife.

Bang, bang, bang.

It probably could have been him. Bursting through the door of his apartment would be simple enough, but he did wonder if the reason they'd tried another method didn't have to do with the fact the complex was so busy with people of all kinds coming and going. Both Fielding and Danni had houses, so escape was just a matter of getting out the door. Chad had been caught out on the street. Jason's room was generic with a queen bed that had a bedspread patterned with black bears and pine trees, and paneled walls to resemble what the average tourist might think of as a north woods lodge, but it did have a nice lovely window overlooking the same lake as the restaurant where they'd had dinner. He'd left the drapes open so he could gaze out over the water because he was really, really tired of watching television in general.

Full moon. That seemed appropriate somehow.

He got up and prowled the room, restless and edgy. He could usually feel a case closing in, and if ever that was happening, it certainly seemed to be this one. Resting his hand on a table by the window, he stared out.

It was dark—not cold, not yet, not even here, but it looked chill and black out there under the silent, brooding trees. . . .

There was a shadow by the steps that led downward toward the dock. He saw it at first as just something obscure, his brain busy with the whirlwind of the past few days, his attention only abstract until it was caught by the way the figure slipped past the tall pines and disappeared.

No one walked like that unless they were being *stealthy*. In fact, very few people were out and about at this time of night, especially here. *Couldn't a person get eaten by a bear or something out here in God's country?* Jason glanced at his cell phone and it was past twelve.

Shit.

No part of him had believed they would actually be followed, but then again, his car had blown up and Danni was dead. . . .

Time to go. He slipped on the shoulder holster but kept his weapon in hand before he left the room. The air smelled like pine and water and it was hell-and-gone different from Milwaukee.

He'd knock on Ellie's door, but it was very quiet and someone might hear. Much more without sound than what he was used to at home, with the people who worked later shifts coming and going and the busy street beyond the apartment complex. Maybe it was just as well he was a city boy and couldn't sleep without some sort of background noise.

There was one advantage to cell phones. He pulled his out, leaning against the wall in a shadow, hoping the illumination didn't send off too much of a signal, and sent a text.

Man outside. Weird.

Enough for a warning. He crept around the end of the building and wished he'd pulled on a sweater or something. Not that he wasn't sweating already. The light breeze was cooling it on his skin but he would be less noticeable if he wore something dark.

His back scraped along rough wood siding intended to be rustic, but half dressed it wasn't comfortable, though he doubted the company that built it intended to have someone edging along it without a shirt.

He held his weapon, walking carefully around still fully leafed-out shrubs that rustled, and hoped the slight breeze would be a reasonable explanation to anyone who might notice. He wasn't nervous, which always surprised him. Even the night he'd been shot by the Burner he hadn't been particularly nervous, just focused, and that it had gone wrong hadn't been because he was jumpy.

Cool, actually. This was what it was all about.

A twig snapped behind him and he whirled, but he saw the slim silhouette, recognized it, and lowered his weapon. MacIntosh was unmistakable even in the dark, and he nodded as she came around the edge of the building. The glint of her .45 was visible in her hand.

She said one word so hushed he almost missed it. "Where?"

He gestured with his gun to the right.

The soil smelled acrid. He stepped through the wood chips in the decaying mulch in the flower beds, skirted the walk, and ducked back into a corner. She joined him a moment later, and he had to say he admired always that she didn't see the need to ask a litany of questions immediately, which he found refreshing in a female. Sexist? Maybe, but at the moment he didn't care. . . .

It was enough she was a good shot and he knew it.

He held up a finger. *One suspect.* An unspoken message. At least he'd only seen one, but before there had always been two killers.

Ellie nodded, slipping up alongside him.

They'd been in this place before. Stalked and stalking . . . predators against each other. He leaned in and said next to her ear, "Interesting time of night for slipping through the trees."

Damn, her hair always smelled good. Like flowers. A strange moment to notice, but he did.

The night breeze whispered past. She murmured, "Got you. Let's go."

Jason eased against the siding, knowing he'd have

splinters in the morning—provided he lasted that long—and then he rounded the side of the building, gun extended.

MacIntosh shone a powerful flashlight designed to deflect direct vision and the person trapped in the beam whirled around.

A kid. Jason took a second to inhale. *A kid. Holding a fishing pole. Don't fire.*

He could swear the figure he'd seen was a lot taller. . . .

The pale-faced boy stammered at the sight of their guns, and a bucket in his hand fell with an audible thud, water splashing out of it. "What . . . what? I'm . . . I was f-fishing for bullhead. I know the sign said no night fishing . . . you aren't supposed to . . . I'm sorry. I'm sorry, man."

"Jesus." Jason lowered his weapon and felt ridiculous. "He's like . . . twelve."

MacIntosh at least had the grace not to laugh. "Tall enough to look like a man. And someone recently blew up your car. Aren't you cold without a shirt?"

He sent her a derisive look. "Pretty cold, yes. I don't think he is who I saw."

"You aren't jumping at shadows?"

"I might be, but—"

The first shot was surreal. It actually brushed her hair, the smooth strands moving in a linear motion as the bullet thudded into the building. Jason registered what was happening and shouted to the kid, "Down."

The kid with the jigs and the pole was faster than he was, dropping flat. The second bullet nicked Jason's arm. Older, wiser, and he now understood that particular burning sensation, he plunged downward next to an already prone Detective MacIntosh. The walk was cold and smelled vaguely of old, wet leaves.

"Where are they?"

"I can't see anyone." Blood was seeping out of his bicep but he could still use his arm. Not broken. That was something anyway.

She said, "You okay? I think you're bleeding."

"I know I'm bleeding," he responded furiously. "I can't fucking believe I've been shot again. Metzger is never going to let me off medical leave. Just wait until I find the son of a bitch."

The term "hell in a handbasket" seemed appropriate.

Quite frankly, she had no idea what a handbasket was, but hell was another story.

Hell, currently, was lying on her stomach outside an old motel in rural Wisconsin, with nothing but a coat thrown over her sweatpants and T-shirt, barefoot, weapon drawn, with no target because it was so dark if a person was in hiding, and so light otherwise because of the moon. Some sort of plant was tickling her nose but she was a little afraid to raise her head in case she drew more fire.

Ellie had no idea where the shooter might be. Obviously Santiago was hit, and there was a civilian—a child no less—in the mix. That was a law-enforcement nightmare.

It really wasn't a surprise, but her partner knew swearwords she didn't even know existed. A steady stream of them came from his mouth, albeit under his breath as he rolled to his side, leaving a glossy trail of blood across the mulch and rocks. The full moon was pretty, but unfortunately it illuminated the scene a little too well.

"Where is he?" she asked urgently, waving a leaf out of her face. "Any idea?"

"He? Could be some bloodthirsty female. I think you just discriminated against my gender." The way the words came, it sounded like her partner was gritting his teeth. "Hey, kid, stay down," he shouted, but it probably wasn't necessary since doors were opening in the units around them, lights popping on behind the curtains.

Ellie rose up cautiously. She'd scraped her knee, or something had happened, because it throbbed. "He's got to be running."

"There you go again." Santiago caught her arm and jerked her down against him. "No. Give it a minute. Let's get our bearings. We have no idea where the shooter is, and if it is the guys we are looking for, there are two of them. I knew snipers in the military that could take out a target at a pretty impressive range."

That was not necessarily good news. "We have a lot of civilians to consider."

"Yeah, well we might want to consider ourselves too." There was a sheen of sweat on his face; she could see it glisten in the moonlight. His arm tightened like a steel band around her waist and she could feel the warm seep of blood from his wound through her clothing. "This is not the time to go all hero cop, Ellie. They want me, and probably you too, and all these people around will cramp their style. Stay put for a minute while we decide what to do."

Staying put was not really an option. For one thing, he was bleeding enough she was concerned and she was fairly sure—but only fairly—that whoever had planned on the ambush was right now figuring out how to escape.

"Police officer," she said loudly. "Can someone dial 911?"

"I already did." It was the kid, prone in a bed of mums just beginning to go brown. "It's an app on my phone."

"Thanks," She meant it. They could use backup.

"Listen," Santiago said urgently, getting to his feet next to her and pulling her up with surprising strength for a man who had just been shot. "Over there. I can hear them. They're running. Come on."

There was a reason people were afraid of the dark, Ellie decided as they sprinted toward the parking lot. For one thing, it was cool, and even with the moon, murky under the trees.

There was also a choice they seemed to blithely skip by in the movies. Running full out required that a weapon be dangerous in your hand, or holstered, and neither was conducive to much in the way of speed, and in Ellie's case, she was barefoot.

Somewhere a car door slammed and an engine gunned.

Her partner outdistanced her, wound and all, by at least a hundred feet to the parking lot, mostly because it wasn't paved and the gravel hurt her feet.

The car was just backing up, brake lights flashing, and she had the slightest glimpse of a face as the man turned and reversed with a vengeance that caused gravel to spurt loudly. The car narrowly missed the back bumper of a small compact.

"Stop!" Santiago hesitated only about one second before he fired, ostensibly at the tires, but despite the full moon it was hard to get a perspective. As she ran up, the car lurched into forward motion, the lights from the headlights swinging across the woods as they sped out of the parking lot onto the small county road that led toward the highway.

"License plate," he said and took off on foot again, as if he could catch an SUV . . .

There were three deer, faithful citizens of the state of Wisconsin, infamous for their tendency to be startled by passing cars, causing unfortunate collisions of nature and machine.

Ellie just caught a flash of gray first, a ghost of a fast-moving shadow, and then there was the screech and thud. The second animal ran full on into the side of the car, which had swerved enough to clip a white pine and then skidded sideways, half off the road, the first deer on the hood, still kicking. The sound of breaking glass and the groan of crushed metal signaled it had not been a light accident.

There was a third deer, bewildered, hesitant at the edge of the woods, that stood stock still as if it didn't want to abandon its fallen comrades, but then took one look at the bloodstained man dashing up with a gun and turned and leaped gracefully back into the woods.

She would have run too.

It had happened within the space of about two minutes.

"Get out of the car, motherfucker," Santiago yelled, gun leveled as he circled the side of the car. In the silvery light, the dark river down his arm and smeared on his chest looked barbaric. "Out! I'll shoot you through the glass."

The airbags had deployed on both sides, giant puffs obscuring the front of the car.

The passenger-side door opened and a man slid out, chest heaving, onto the pavement. The suspect had blood on his face, but as far as Ellie could see, everyone around her had blood pouring all over the place and the shock effect was gone.

"I'll get the driver." Santiago was on his way, his voice sharp.

"Go carefully. Hands where I can see them," she said sharply to the man on the road. "I'm a police officer, but I think you already know that."

Not a minute later, in the act of cuffing the injured suspect, she heard the shots. Two of them.

Ah, no.

This night just kept getting better and better.

When she got around the back of the car she saw that her partner had hauled the second man out of the vehicle, which was currently at a skewed angle with the headlights crazily pointed about forty-five degrees upward, the buckled hood decorated with what seemed to be a full-grown buck, antlers and all.

Santiago had his weapon pressed to the man's temple, his knee in the middle of his back. She didn't catch all of it, but just bits as she ran up.

". . . not in a good mood right now. Get that? Nod if you do. Move otherwise and I'll just blow you away."

Splayed on the ground on the side of the narrow road, the man grunted, probably in direct response to the pressure of Santiago's weight. Dark haired, Ellie registered, and dressed in a Windbreaker—also dark— and his hands were pale against the pine needles scattered everywhere. "Hey . . . Okay," she said in an attempt to at least diffuse some of the potential violence. "We got them. Relax a little. I think enough people have been shot lately, let's break the trend."

Jason glanced up at her, but his eyes looked unfocused. "These two are probably the ones who targeted three good cops. If I killed this asshole right now, would you tell anyone?"

The question stopped her cold, the woods around them quiet but yet alive, like there were a million listening voices out there, a legion of judgment weighing her answer.

Luckily the sound of sirens in the background spared her the need to respond.

Chapter 23

It was all slipping away.

She could feel it happening, like the sickening roll of a ship in a violent storm. He hadn't touched her in two weeks now, wouldn't return her calls, and when she'd finally just gone to his door, his sister had answered and said he was out of town.

The look of disapproval in the other woman's eyes was duly noted but she didn't care too much about that. Pride had never been her downfall. There was only one way to truly get what a person wanted in this harsh, unforgiving world, and that was to take it.

"When he returns, tell him I came by with news from Vivian, will you, Mae?"

"You can tell it to me and I'll relay the message." She stood here, all high and mighty, blocking the doorway.

The bitch.

She forced away the thought of what she could do. If another woman close to him disappeared . . .

No, she couldn't wipe that haughty look from her face permanently, but she would give odds she could shake her. Carefully enunciating the words, she said coolly, "She's divorcing him. Called me long distance last evening to ask me to break it to him. He'll get the papers from her lawyer."

"I am sure you shed some crocodile tears over that news, Helen."

"I have no idea what you mean by that, Mae, but she's my friend, and I want her to be happy. Sometimes things just don't work out, you know."

Mae MacIntosh said, "You might want to keep that in mind."

"**I shot the** damn deer. Get over it."

Ellie looked at him like she wanted to strangle him, which Jason might welcome because he hated hospitals. Like he really *hated* hospitals. Stark white walls, that antiseptic smell, the hushed sounds of the shoes of the nurses . . . Just put him out of his misery now. His partner said accusingly, "All I know is that I was apprehending a suspect and heard two shots. You about gave me a stroke."

He defended himself gruffly. "That buck was still alive, but I could tell he was really hurt, at least had a broken leg or maybe two . . . and you know, it seemed like the right thing to do."

"Did it?"

"He was suffering, dammit. That was at least a ten-point buck, too. First shot might have gone off a little since I was favoring my left hand. So just to be sure, two shots."

"That's your story?"

"MacIntosh, the air bag was in the way. I couldn't have aimed for the suspect. If one of those bullets hit him, I'd be sorry, of course. Ballistics would show I shot blind through the windshield. If I'd wanted to nail him, I'd have done it from the driver's-side window. For any injuries he incurred, I am deeply sorry."

"Neither bullet hit him."

"Now that's disappointing to hear."

"How come I get the impression you cared a lot more about that deer than the man you might have hit?"

"Because you are starting to know me pretty well." The conversation was mostly for the nurse who unwrapped the bloodstained cloth from his upper arm. Jason asked, "Seriously, no witnesses to them shooting at us?"

Ellie was pale, which was accentuated by the blood on her clothes, which were pajamas—that blood being his, or he hoped so—and she shook her head. "Just the kid with the fishing pole. And his back was turned to the gunmen because he was staring at us since we scared him half to death. Who else would see anything? It was late. All sane people were asleep. But we caught them."

He was sitting on an exam table in a room in the emergency department of some regional hospital in the middle of the boonies and in a pretty unhappy mood at the moment. His upper arm throbbed like hell. "I think you just implied I might be lumped into the insane category, MacIntosh. Thanks. And we caught them? Only thanks to errant wildlife. Otherwise they would have gotten away."

It galled him. The idea of that kid with his bucket and fishing pole caught in the crossfire. Fine, target cops. Cops could fight back. Don't endanger a kid . . .

"Did you think you would be in any other category?" Ellie looked unapologetic. "Both the driver and passenger, by the way, are in the hospital. But there were guns in the car, now in the custody of the state police. If they can be matched to any of the murder scenes, it looks like we've got our guys. At the least, we have them for assault with a deadly weapon for the attack on you, and fleeing the scene of a crime, not to mention resisting arrest."

"It's something. Are they talking?"

"How would I know? I'm here with you." Her dark blond brows rose. "Besides, this is not our jurisdiction. We'll get a chance once they are transferred down to Milwaukee."

She had a point.

"I'm wondering . . . how did they find us?" Her gaze was direct.

"That is a pretty good question. How did they blow up my car? They have long arms, it seems." He winced as the nurse got out a syringe. "Okay, whoa. Hey, do you need to do that?"

The woman was older, a little stout, dressed in pink scrubs. She said in a pragmatic tone that was no doubt a result of working a night shift in the ER, "You have a bullet wound and from those scars, it isn't your first either. My needle scares you? I think you can endure a little prick, Officer."

"Never say little prick to a man," he muttered. Truth was, he didn't like needles. He never had.

The nurse laughed. Ellie gave him a look of reproof, which he ignored.

"I don't suppose there is any chance the parking area at the motel has surveillance cameras?"

"Why would they? To watch the deer wander by?" Ellie shook her head. "Besides, you know they'd be disabled. Our enemy is more careful than that."

Our enemy. She was right there.

"I'm starting to think he is a genius." He exhaled and closed his eyes as the nurse gave him an injection in the upper arm. It wasn't bad. It was just the sight of the needle that bothered him for whatever reason. Maybe he needed to go see Ellie's shrink.

"The doctor will be right in."

He nodded, but his gaze was fixed on Ellie as the door closed behind the exiting nurse. "They are tracking your car somehow. You could have a passenger in the form of a GPS device. Either that or they are sophisticated enough to be able to track your phone. The Henleys have deep pockets, and so do the people they are in bed with if the money-laundering theory is true."

"Here's the problem with that theory. They didn't know you'd be leaving with me after the explosion. You wouldn't have either if I hadn't been physically right on the scene. What about Metzger?"

"What about him?"

"I don't think it is my car."

Whatever the nurse had given him started to kick in. He was pretty sure he was still in pain, but starting to not care as much already. "You think the chief took a potshot at us an hour or two ago? I think if I'd seen *him* out my window, I might have recognized that big square head. Was he pulled out of that car and I didn't realize it?"

Ellie didn't share in the joke. "No. I'm wondering if his phone is the one that might be compromised. He called to ask where we were and I told him. A few hours later, they show up."

"I bet he sleeps with his phone, MacIntosh. I'm doubting that's the case."

"Yeah, but a certain DEA officer visited him right after all this started. All Metzger had to do was get up to talk to someone at the door of his office, or leave the room for any reason if his phone was out on his desk. Whoever is running this seems to be a step ahead of us all the time."

"Oh, holy fuck." Jason's tongue felt thick. "Remember I told you Danni was going to call the chief?"

And the next morning she was dead.

"I remember *now*." His partner's face was set. "Did she?"

"I don't know."

A grim truth.

"That makes two connections between his phone and the shootings. With what just happened to us, maybe three. I told him you'd had dinner with her." Ellie stood up, her bloodstained coat moving around her. "I might place another call to him myself. We could be totally off base, but there is a way to find that out."

"Over the phone suddenly seems like a bad idea."

"Don't worry. I'll actually call the night-duty operator, leave a message to call me back from someone else's phone and to have his swept."

"I wonder if Chad Brown called him. Me too." He stopped, wondering if it was a bad idea, but said it anyway, "We going to talk about it?"

"About you threatening to shoot someone right in front of me in a manner that could be presented as self-defense if I didn't point out it wasn't?" Her hands slid into her pockets but she didn't flinch from the question or try to pretend she didn't know exactly what he was asking. "We probably should, but let's postpone it to when we aren't so tired and you didn't just get a big dose of a narcotic painkiller."

Would he have done it? Even he didn't know. It was damned tempting though. *An eye for an eye . . .*

The door opened and a man in scrubs came in carrying a file. "Are you Jason Santiago? I'm Dr. Jackson. Let's see what we've got here, shall we?"

Ellie went out the way the physician had come in. She glanced back over her shoulder. "I'll be outside."

Carl got the second call at exactly 1:10. He was travel weary and unwinding, but unable to sleep yet, so he was still up, feet propped on the generic coffee table in a hotel by the beach, watching a late-night show and paying attention to about half of it.

His head hummed, his body was weary with fatigue too, but he was not quite ready to let the day go.

He glanced at the display on his phone. Unknown number.

But he recognized it. He'd always been good at that; it had gotten him through school. Photographic memory. He'd sit down to take a test and could recall the page in the textbook almost exactly. He'd never pored over notes or worried too much about the lectures in college, he'd just read the books. Usually, it had worked pretty well, and this was the same person who had given him the connection between Brown and Crawford.

"Lindsey."

"You have a good memory, Lieutenant. Did you see my sister?"

"I did."

"Is she okay?"

"Not cooperative, but okay."

"You are asking a lot of her." The throaty voice was exactly as he recalled. "How was my nephew? They stayed at my apartment right after the shooting for a few days. He would wake up screaming. He's not quite two years old, you know."

Carl did know. That tiny peaceful figure in the crib had left an indelible impression. In his mind's eye, it was still there. "He seemed to be sleeping very soundly when I saw him. Listen to me, you need to stay out of this. Whether Joanne gave me valuable information or not, she and I agree on that one."

"I'm going to give you a clue. Do you have any idea of how a conspiracy works?"

"Lindsey . . . how much do you know?" He had to

admit a rush of adrenaline shot through him. "Don't poke your nose into business that is better left off to the police."

"I know enough. Now . . . conspiracy?"

"A pretty fair idea," he amended, "but define it for me."

"Lots of bad people with the same goal. That's a conspiracy."

"I'll buy that. Any reason we are having this dictionary discussion?"

"This isn't a conspiracy."

"This . . . being what?"

"This is someone putting out a fire. You know how a fire starts, Lieutenant? A single spark. Then you have to kick the coals, but sometimes they scatter, and before you know it there are all these small blazes going and you have to pick and choose which one might turn into an inferno and turn you to ashes."

"Is the fire we are talking about something to do with the Henley family business being tied to drug running?"

"Actually, no."

No? That was not quite the answer he expected.

Carl rubbed his jaw. "Mind telling me what then? I'm just not following. You weren't clear the last time we talked and you aren't clear now."

"I'm trying to help."

"I know, but it isn't working so far. Like when you called about Danni Crawford? She's dead now, by the way. And your sister wouldn't offer me anything."

"I've already said you are asking a lot of her."

"I'd like to save her life. And it seems to me you are asking me for something, but not being very clear about it."

"What about Angelo Terrance?"

The name Lena had given him. Now they were getting somewhere. "Okay . . . I don't know. What about him?"

"Ask yourself this: is he yours, or is he theirs?"

The call ended. Carl held the phone in his hand and stared at it as if it would give up secrets it did not even hold.

Incredibly, the phone rang again just a few minutes later.

"Carl . . . we have a problem."

Metzger? This wasn't good. "We do?" Carl wasn't normally sarcastic, but it was pretty damn late. "I thought that was why I was in Florida."

"Go move Fielding's wife right now. That's an order."

"This time of night? Why?"

"I'll explain later. Let's just say Santiago and MacIntosh are headed back here. As far as I can tell, all hell just seems to be breaking loose. Anything you can do to fix it, I'd appreciate."

"Fine." Carl was still dressed, so he got up and reached for his keys.

"I want Joanne Fielding in our protection just as soon as you can get there. And you watch your own ass, got it?"

"I can't promise she'll cooperate."

"Then arrest her."

"For?"

"Make up something."

Serious stuff. Carl contemplated the parking lot of the motel, but it looked clear and he closed the door quietly.

"What am I supposed to say to Joanne Fielding when I pound on her door at this time of the morning?"

"That she isn't safe unless she comes with you, and by the way, the locals will meet you there, because I am taking no chances. Did you know that Santiago was shot this evening up north?"

He didn't, but then again, he was going to guess MacIntosh hadn't called him because it was pretty late. Or early, depending on how a person viewed the time.

"Again?" Carl pressed a button to unlock his car.

"Arm this time. Flesh wound. I doubt he's a happy camper, but you know, I'm not one either. Use this number if you need to reach me. I'll explain why later."

"Okay . . . Joe, I have a theory."

"That is music to my ears, Lieutenant. I want to read about it in an article titled: *Milwaukee Police Department Solves a Recent Rash of Homicides Involving a Threat to Its Own Officers*. Catchy, right? Tell me about it later. In the meantime, please call me back when we have a material witness and her son secured and safe. The title I don't want to read is: *Murders in Florida Related to Serial Cop Killings in Wisconsin*."

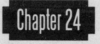

Chapter 24

The door creaked.

He heard it, but then again, he heard things in the night now. A scrape that turned out to be a loose shingle. Or the screen door he forgot to latch, gently bumping the side of the house in the soft breeze off the lake.

This wasn't the wind.

The real mistake was thinking he could actually sleep. He couldn't. He hadn't in weeks.

So when the door opened, he knew it.

The creak of those old hinges. That noise was familiar. He heard it every day when he came inside, but it was different in the middle of the night. Cold and eerie, especially as he lay there in his bed, his eyes focused on the ceiling.

Someone was downstairs, moving around.

* * *

She'd spent the night pursuing would-be assassins and errant deer, explaining in her pajamas the situation to the state police and trying to be taken seriously, and then there was that pleasant stint at the hospital.

No one could call her life boring, anyway.

Ellie ended up driving back to Milwaukee with a wounded man who wasn't known for his social graces in the first place and was half doped up on morphine. Going back to the motel had not seemed like a good idea, so considering the circumstances, she'd decided south was her best choice. Once at Bryce's empty house, she led Santiago into one of the vacant guest rooms, told him firmly to go to sleep, which really wasn't necessary since he was weaving on his feet, taken a long, hot shower, and then had managed to grab a few hours of sleep herself before her phone beeped.

With a Santiago-worthy curse before answering, she said, "MacIntosh."

"I want you here by one o'clock." Metzger could be as charming as her partner. "Grasso is bringing in Mrs. Fielding and I want you to be the one to talk to her."

"I thought she was in Florida and had already been interviewed."

"She was, she has, and I want her interviewed again."

Ellie had shot him a text with their location at the new number he'd given her so he knew they were back, but a part of her still resented the order as she rolled out of bed. Her knee ached from when she'd twisted it trying to keep from being shot, but it did seem like a small price to pay. "Why me?"

"Hamish and Rays are both men, and have already interviewed her. Grasso doesn't seem to be able to get anything out of her except an impression she is scared, which by the way, I believe. Therefore, Detective, you. Like her you are young and female and I think she could use a friend right now to tell her troubles to. You seem like a good fit. Strong-arming her hasn't worked at all."

Still a little mystified, she said, "Okay. What do you think we will accomplish, sir?"

"Let me put it this way: I have gone over the past very eventful week or two, and have determined one thing. I have not left my phone anywhere unless I have a very bad memory and I have a very good memory. The only other person I know who has touched it is Joanne Fielding, who asked me if she could borrow it at her husband's funeral. That she had left hers in the car didn't surprise me under the circumstances because one would expect her to be distracted, so I of course said yes, and she wandered away to ostensibly call her uncle who had gotten lost twice on the way to the funeral home. Now that I look back on it, Ms. Fielding had it out of my sight for about three to five minutes. I'll grant you that I don't have one bit of evidence, nor do I quite understand her motivation, but maybe you can find out for me if she put a device in it and why."

That was how Ellie found herself walking into an interview room, notebook in hand, with a cup of coffee—she needed it—to sit down opposite Joanne Fielding just before two o'clock in the afternoon.

The woman sitting at the table was very pretty, or

would be if her eyes weren't ringed by shadows and her eyelids puffy as if she'd been crying. Long dark hair, pink silk blouse, minimum makeup, and white capri pants. She looked, and probably was, travel-worn.

They already had something in common.

Ellie offered her hand. "Hi. I'm Ellie."

The other woman took it, her fingers cold and light. "Can you explain to me why it seems like I'm being questioned when just last night I was told I was in danger?"

Ellie sat down across the generic table. "It has come to our attention our communications could have been compromised and you had talked to Detective Grasso, who in turn talked to Chief Metzger. Considering there was a murder attempt—and this would have made the fourth killing of a police officer—last evening up in northern Wisconsin, we thought it best to remove you from harm's way. Luckily, the detective was only shot, and will recover."

"Oh God." Joanne Fielding sank back and rubbed her forehead with her palm.

"Yes, I'm with you there. Tell me about Garrison Henley." Ellie gave her most sympathetic smile.

"Why?"

"Because this all comes back time and again to that family. Now we are getting tips from someone close to them." That was a stretch, but maybe worth it. Ellie set aside her pen since suspects found it disconcerting when she wrote down what they said, but it wasn't her purpose here to intimidate. So, no notes. "Do you know Angelo Terrance?"

"I don't really know him, but *of* him. He works for

Henley Enterprises. He was hired after I had already quit. He handles some of the finances of the company but also Mr. Henley's personal schedule."

"One of our detectives received information that he was under investigation by the DEA. Did your husband know something that might help their case and that is why he tried to contact them?"

Joanne looked genuinely bewildered. Glossy dark hair brushed her shoulders as she shook her head and her thin hands trembled on the table. "My husband contacted the DEA? I didn't know that. My husband's concerns with the Henley family were purely personal, Detective."

"He thought your son was really Garrison Henley's child, correct?"

Joanne looked as if Ellie had just struck her. Her answer was barely audible. "He accused me of that, yes."

"That must have been difficult."

"Would you have enjoyed that particular conversation?" A ghost of a smile touched the other woman's mouth.

"No." It was easy for Ellie to be truthful on that score. "Why did he suddenly decide, when your son is almost two years old, that there is a question about the paternity?"

"We were having some marital troubles." The admission came out reluctantly. Joanne looked at the table. "He swore he wasn't going to pay support for a child that wasn't his. I loved him but he could be very self-righteous sometimes."

Well, at least that cleared up one point Ellie had

never quite understood. "Okay, I get that. I am sure Garrison Henley could afford it much more than your husband could on a cop's salary. Do you think he obtained information that could implicate the business, given we think Mr. Terrance, who works for the company, might be under investigation? Did David call the DEA to put pressure on the Henley family to just agree to the paternity test?"

"Like I said, I had no idea he ever called the DEA."

"Do you know anyone named Lieman?"

"No."

Ellie blew out a breath. The answer was there . . . somewhere. She said as neutrally as possible, trying to ignore that the room smelled like a thousand cups of stale coffee. "Let's go back. So your husband asks for a paternity test and Garrison is decent about it and agrees and admits it could be his."

"This is extremely embarrassing for me, Detective."

"I am not here to judge you, Joanne. I'm here to try and find out what is going on so you and your son can be safe. Just last night someone shot at me. I assume you remember that is not the most pleasant experience in the world. They hit my partner, and he isn't peaches and cream on a good day, so just imagine his mood right now. Help me sort this out and we both win. I think you are in this, and in deep. All roads lead back to your involvement with Garrison. So he says he'll take responsibility but then his father lawyers up and tells him absolutely not, don't do it. Do I have all this correct so far?"

"Maybe I should have a lawyer myself."

That made Ellie sit back with a flicker of hope they

were finally getting somewhere. "Mrs. Fielding, we are trying to stop a runaway train here. What makes you think you need a lawyer?"

The other woman looked pale now. "I . . . I . . . don't know. This feels like an interrogation. And you don't know Ely Henley. He is an extremely determined man. Garrison did what his father wanted because he's young, but he isn't stupid."

"I should think, considering the brutality of your husband's murder, you might just want to help us. We flew you back from Florida under police escort in case there was any danger to your life and that of your child. I hope you remember we are the good guys. Do we agree on that point?"

"I agree you'll try and help me, but I am not sure you can protect me."

Fair enough. "Why is that?"

"Detective, I don't know about the drugs, and I don't know about the DEA, but I do know that Ely Henley has a lot of people in his back pocket. He is charismatic, wealthy, and ambitious. If he is tied to any of this, you are going to have to dig deep and step around land mines. I worked for him for two years and he is a force to be reckoned with. Garrison said yes to the test, Ely told him no. That was the end of it. As I didn't want the test in the first place, it didn't break my heart. Quite frankly, that is all I have to say."

Ellie felt brutal, but there was very little choice. "Let me ask you one more question because I think if you answered it honestly this could break our case. If you don't I am going to be forced to hold you, and I think the charge would be conspiracy to murder. Is there any chance you tampered with Chief Metzger's phone?"

Any hint of remaining color drained from Joanne's face. Even her lips went white. Her voice wavered. "I definitely want a lawyer."

Jason wasn't all that big on libraries. He liked to read well enough, though normally he kept it to humorous and political books—he absolutely shunned big, complicated literary novels, no doubt of the kind Grantham was writing. He saw enough angst and betrayal as it was just in the course of his daily life.

But here he was, in a small soundproof room with Grasso, a little high on those damn painkillers again, though this experience with being shot was hell-and-gone better than the last one.

Sort of laughable to be able to make the comparison, but truthful enough.

Grasso checked his watch. "We only have the room reserved for an hour and I had to be very persuasive to get that. I hope he shows soon."

"Persuasive. You wordsmith, you."

"Wordsmith? And *you* are making fun of me?"

"I heard it on late-night television and have been dying to use it in a sentence." Jason sat at the table, picking up a pen and sliding it through the fingers of the hand he could still use. The other one was fairly numb, his arm in a sling. He quit kidding. "I hope he shows soon too. Metzger has pull—I should think so—but these undercover guys aren't necessarily accessible."

"The field supervisor named the place. I just made the arrangements." As usual Grasso was stylish in his suit and tie, his hair perfectly combed. In contrast, Jason was fairly sure he looked like crap warmed over, because that was essentially how he felt.

Just as he opened his mouth to reply, someone rapped on the door and opened it. "I'm sorry . . . I'm looking for the Marquette study group."

Code for: This is Lieman.

Grasso said, "You've found it. Come in and shut the door."

The undercover thing always felt stupid, Jason thought, but these guys did a unique job that required certain skills he did not possess. He was about as subtle as a tsunami but apologizing for it seemed redundant. Agent Lieman—they had never even been told his first name and it didn't seem like that was going to happen—was midthirties, wiry but not tall, with a pleasant-looking but unmemorable face, brown hair, and he was dressed like Grasso in a suit, tie, and polished shoes, though he didn't carry it off nearly as well.

He looked like an accountant, and in fact, Jason learned in the next minute or so, he actually was one.

"Forensic accounting," Lieman said pleasantly as he took a seat at the table. "I worked for the FBI for a couple of years but then was offered the job with the DEA. Look, guys, I know your chief was adamant I come in for this, but I am going to tell you now, if you compromise my investment in a case that has taken me almost two years to get to a point where we are about to arrest out some serious criminals, then the government of the United States will be very unhappy and I might wind up dead. I just want to make that pretty clear up front."

Jason's feelings on the subject were that they had some pretty serious criminals they were trying to apprehend as well. "How the hell can we possibly compromise your case? We don't even know what it is."

"Then why did Fielding call me?"

Grasso said, "You know, that is why *we* wanted to talk to *you*. We were hoping you could tell us."

The three of them stared at one another for a long, excruciating minute. Jason was the one who broke the silence. "I think maybe we are at cross-purposes in some way. Let me clear up our angle. One of our officers called you. We only know that because you came in and told the chief after he was killed. After that, two more officers were killed, and we have two suspects in custody that could be professionals, except they aren't talking. We think maybe it is linked back to the Henley family and a possible drug connection. Joanne Fielding isn't really cooperating either, by the way, but we are fairly sure she had some part in making the line of communication from the Milwaukee Police Department accessible to whoever is hitting cops left and right. Our case in a nutshell. I just gave it all to you." He smiled, but there was no warmth in it. "Your turn to give something back."

"My turn? All I know is that Fielding called and left a message on my phone that could have gotten me garroted in my office if anyone else had heard it." Lieman was testy, his eyes hard.

Jason might be a little high, but he was not an idiot. Comprehension came in like a welcome guest with a warm handshake. "You are working for Henley Enterprises inside?"

"Yes. I can divulge that much, but I had to clear it."

Still, the whole thing was crystal as mud. "You won't tell *us* without thumbscrews but Fielding knew this? He was a patrol officer."

"I have no idea what he knew." Lieman ran his hands through his hair. "Do you see why his call made me nervous?"

"How did he have your number?"

"You tell me."

"What was the exact message?" Grasso's tone was sharp.

Lieman gave it up with obvious reluctance. "All he said was: *I know Henley's dirty little secret.* He left his number and asked for me to call him back. I couldn't for a day or two, and by then he was dead."

"That's helpful." Grasso turned, his hands in the pockets of his perfectly tailored slacks. "Do you think this is about the drug angle?"

"I hope not, but those are dangerous people. You have three dead police officers, and I am just as concerned as you are, but you do realize hundreds of people are dying in drug-related activities, right? With what I am doing . . . three is nothing. Every single life is important, but only three? I'm trying to save a lot more than that."

"Well, fuck," Jason said with heartfelt frustration. "So none of us know. You don't happen to know Angelo Terrance, do you? We had a tip the DEA is on him, and—"

"And?" Lieman put his elbows on the table, his gaze intent.

"Oh shit." Jason's throbbing arm faded into the background as everything else zeroed into focus. "*You* are Angelo Terrance. Ah, man, Fielding wasn't calling the DEA, he was calling someone close to Henley. Don't you guys get this? We aren't looking at this the right way. Let's go over it again."

Ellie was at her desk when Santiago came and planted himself in a chair. He didn't look too good, but then again, maybe he should have looked worse, considering the previous night. It did look like he'd showered, since his normally tousled blond hair seemed relatively tidy.

The report she was working on was certainly an interesting one. Lake resorts and midnight gunfire and spooked, helpful deer . . .

"What would you do," he said with his usual careless drawl, "if you were rich, pretty influential, knee-deep in some iffy business ventures with people who can be fairly dangerous, fucking around on your wife, and someone threatened you?"

"Now there's an interesting question." It certainly caught her attention.

"You know, I think so too. It could be why I am asking it."

Ellie considered it. "I am none of those things, especially the wife part . . . I don't have one, though I understand it is now possible in a few states were I so inclined. Can you be more specific?" She closed her screen and put her chin in the cradle of her hands.

He didn't look exactly smug, but it was close. "I have absolutely no proof at this point, but I am going to bet every dollar I have—which is not a lot, by the way, but let's focus on the all-I-have-part—that Garrison Henley is not the father of Joanne Fielding's kid."

"Oh good." Ellie gave him an admittedly contemptuous look. "Thank you for restating what she'd already told us. I talked to her a few hours ago. She said the same thing then."

Santiago leaned forward intently, his good arm planted on her desk. "Ellie . . . I have a kind of crazy idea. Care to hear it?"

She wasn't sure. His expression gave her pause and he almost never called her by her first name. It must have just slipped out. "What?"

His blue eyes were electric. "Did you know that the Republican Party has been tossing around the idea of Henley Sr. for governor?" Santiago looked almost diabolically elated. "He has money, clout, and charisma, the works."

Pretty much what Joanne had told her. "I know all that."

"Though the drug rumors have surfaced, even Lieman says the business is so tightly run he hasn't been able to get warrants yet and he has been working the case for almost two years. At the moment there is nothing in the way of Ely Henley getting a nomination. Except maybe Joanne."

"Joanne? You mean in case she claims Garrison is

the father of her child? She doesn't. Her husband may have thought so, but—"

"Not Garrison. Ely."

She sat there, letting it sink in. *Ely Henley? Really?*

Santiago shook his head and went on emphatically. "Hey, no one gives a shit if his son fathered a child with someone he wasn't married to. It happens every single damn day. But if you are *already* married and screwing your son's girlfriend and want to be governor, it makes you look pretty bad. Allegations like that have screwed more than one career."

She didn't disagree. "You think Garrison's *father* was having an affair with Joanne?"

"You do remember she worked there for a few years."

"Yes."

"Good-looking older man who is your boss? Yeah, that's never happened. Oh, she was having it on with Garrison too, or he wouldn't have first said yes to the test. You know, I can't say that I blame Fielding for flipping when he figured it all out, and for maybe bowing out of that picture. And it explains why Garrison was open enough to a paternity test, but his father said hell no, don't do it, son. Those things are pretty fine-tuned as I understand it. What might come up is that our good friend Garrison is as innocent as the day he was born, but that a close male relative is the papa. The American people would hate that. Bye-bye Mr. Governor."

Joanne's reticence came to mind. "I suppose that is possible."

"Henley would want to keep it quiet. He has motive, and he has the money and unsavory connections to pull it off."

"We have no proof of this."

"No. But one blood test will do it. Then the whole game changes. Besides, I'm going to guess the two assholes the deer caught for us will talk when they realize we've figured it out."

It was possible, but Ellie doubted they could be traced back to Henley. They were most probably part of the business running money through his stores. If she had to call it, neither one was in the country legally. "They are just hired thugs. They won't know if we've figured it out or not."

But this theory was plausible . . . she just wasn't sure it was going to be easy to prove. "Even if he is the father, it is one big step from trying to squelch a scandal to three dead police officers."

"It occurs to me that whoever he is in bed with financially might benefit greatly by having a governor in their pocket. Whether he asked for help or not to tidy up this little mess, maybe they took the initiative. Lieman has indicated this is one big case."

"Henley must have threatened Joanne."

"Ya think? Of course he did. But you see, now we have two men in custody, we have Joanne, and we have Lieman. Or will eventually when he can talk. Henley is in some deep shit."

She murmured, "I hope so."

As irreverent as ever, Santiago said, "My arm completely agrees with you. Hell, I'm having trouble lifting my beer. I wonder if I can sue him for that. Let's go."

Chapter 25

The house was on fire.

He'd tried to stop it, but the old boards were like tinder and went up quickly. Finally he jumped out a second-story bedroom window, hit the porch roof, the wood scraping his flesh, his breath leaving his lungs, before he rolled and fell the rest of the way onto the pine needles and dirt.

Acrid air scorched his throat once he could draw a breath. He could hear the crackle of the flames, the hiss of the hungry inferno, and feel the blistering heat of it.

Then he saw her. Standing in the swirl of smoke, her expression hard and unapologetic, demonically lit by the blaze, her hair wild, and when she turned and walked into the darkness he wondered for a moment if it was all some sort of macabre dream.

No, it wasn't. He knew that as he struggled to his feet.

This was a hell of his own making.
God help him.

They probably were a mismatched set, Jason decided when the door of the Henleys' ostentatious house opened and a middle-aged woman who managed to ooze elegance in a pair of tan slacks and a silk scarlet blouse looked at them as if she'd rather have had a dead cow wash up on her neatly paved walkway in a sewer flood.

Grasso was as tailored as ever in a neat white shirt even without his tie, pants unwrinkled, and Ellie was pretty even with the hint of fatigue in her face, her smooth hair shining. Jason figured he might be the one who raised that perfectly plucked eyebrow. True, he hadn't done much more than put on a clean pair of jeans, and because he still had on the sling he despised, he'd just pulled on a white T-shirt and slung a denim shirt over the whole ensemble. Shaving also hadn't been much of an option considering he could barely move his arm, so he'd decided to forget it.

Scruffy cop, pretty cop, rich cop. Okay, he fit his part well enough.

"Mrs. Henley."

"Lieutenant." She inclined her head at Grasso but it was stiffly, her gaze slightly hostile.

"This is Detective Santiago and Detective MacIntosh. Can we please speak with your husband?" Grasso was polite but his voice held an inflexible edge.

"He isn't here." Mrs. Henley wanted to close the door. They could all feel it.

Ellie held out her badge even after the introduction. "When do you expect him?"

"He and Garrison went down to the marina on Lake Michigan. We have a boat there. The weather is going to be too cold to take it out soon and we're going to close it up." She narrowed her eyes. "May I ask why you are here again?"

"The slip number would be helpful."

Mrs. Henley obviously knew something was up. "It's that urgent?"

Grasso said smoothly, "It could be. I assume you want to help us."

"Don't assume anything."

Now there was the cold voice of a woman who could make a great governor's wife, Jason thought. It got under his skin. He said bluntly, "We need to ask him about three murders and see if there is probable cause to arrest him. Two suspects are already in custody who might testify, and my painkillers are wearing off from where they shot me last night." He added without any finesse at all, "Give us the information we want right now, please. If he's innocent, it won't hurt anything. If you think he is possibly not quite so angelic, then that makes you an accessory after the fact if you don't speak up. Got it?"

Indignation tightened her features. He could swear she almost said *how dare you*?

With impressive politeness, she asked, "What is it you think he might know?"

To Jason's surprise, it was Ellie who said, "Is it possible he might be able to give us information on Joanne Fielding's connection to your family."

Nicely done. No accusation. Just a blunt statement. "My husband?"

Holy shit. The woman knew. Jason saw it in her face. He was right, but then again, it was all a little wrong, so it was impossible to feel justified, so he just asked as quietly as possible, "Ma'am, if you could just give us the slip number, we'll just get out of your hair. Seems fair enough, right?"

She gazed at him, her eyes disillusioned. "You know, it does seem fair enough, Detective. I am sick of his shit. Let me tell you exactly where to find Ely."

"**Lake Michigan is** the largest single lake contained in one country in surface area, though Lake Baikal in Russia has more volume. It is the fifth-largest lake in the world. Michigan has an average depth of 286 feet, and is 307 miles long." Ellie had read up on it before her move to Milwaukee. She was a lot more used to small lakes surrounded by woods with clear water and the typical game fish.

"I guess they left the part about the science lesson off the brochure when they were advertising this tour." Santiago gave her one of his usual sardonic stares as they walked along the pier. The breeze ruffled his already unruly curls. "I might have skipped it if I had known. Is there a test at the end? I think I left my notebook behind."

Coolly, she rejoined, "You weren't officially invited on the tour. Metzger said specifically for you to go home and stay out of it. That you want to be here is your own decision, and for your information, my official stand on it is that you should maybe still be in the hospital."

He ignored the comment, which did not surprise her. "I grew up here and I could have saved you some research time on LM. Here it is in a nutshell. The lake is big. Use your eyes. Big."

"The simplistic approach." Grasso's gun looked stark against the pristine material of his shirt in his shoulder holster. "You are good at that one, Detective."

"I try."

The water smelled faintly briny, like the ocean, but there was a distinct freshness that was different, Ellie thought. And he was right, *big water*. With rows of expensive boats all bobbing gently in the light wind coming in from the northeast, which might have been why she wished now she'd worn a jacket. The city lights gleamed over the rippling black waves, making diamond-bright moving reflections. The marina was surprisingly busy considering the sun was going down, reddish against the horizon, sending out fingers of brilliant crimson.

Pretty picture that was postcard worthy. She could see the allure. If she had the money, she'd like a nice yacht and to relax with a glass of wine on deck on a sunny day in a place like this.

"I should have gone into a life of crime." Santiago was gazing at a beauty of a boat with clean lines and a massive hull and what looked like a mahogany deck. "Holy Christ, some of these boats are worth more than my apartment complex."

There were times in every police officer's life that

that thought surfaced. Not usually with any serious-
ness, but it did seem to be a disparate lifestyle. Ellie
had to agree, at least a little. "I was kind of thinking
the same thing, but being able to look in the mirror
and like what you see isn't a bad feeling either. Do
either one of you have the slightest idea exactly where
we are in terms of the boat owned by the Henleys?"

"Just ahead." Grasso pointed.

"That one?"

The unmistakable sound of gunfire was her answer.

"Oh fuck." Santiago muttered the two words and
Ellie saw the glint of his weapon as he jerked it out.
Grasso was already on the move, heading down the
docks, and she sprinted after them both, cursing whatever gene made men faster than women. It didn't help
that the world was a flash of masts and moving boats
and the sun was going down quickly enough to wash
the scene like a fine sheen of blood.

Man down. She saw the figure before she heard
Grasso utter the words, and by then she'd gained on
Santiago, no doubt because the idiot should be at home
in bed. Water churned and she saw a boat—large and
low—with a running engine, start to move, as if it was
leaving the dock.

Grasso stopped at the fallen figure, but she caught
a glimpse of the spreading pool of blood and she went
past at a dead run, letting him deal with it.

"Police." She shouted it but the motor wasn't exactly quiet and apparently the boat was still moored,
because the entire dock shuddered enough she felt the
impact as whoever was at the helm tried to leave without untying it.

Was that even possible?

Maybe. The surface under her feet moved again. Not much, but there was a screech from the metal pieces that held the moorings, and she fought to keep her balance.

There was no conscious decision. Ellie jumped for it, going sprawling onto the back deck, hearing the groan as the anchors for the ropes began to tear free. Behind her someone shouted. As she was just getting to her knees another jerk sent her back down and a cleat flew by her head in a lethal hiss and broke the actual back window of the yacht itself.

The vessel rocked, the engine gunning into a high pitch, and she was suddenly sliding as yet another lurch seemed to free them from the dock. Almost immediately the boat felt lighter and whoever was steering throttled it successfully out of the marina before turning the boat to face open water. Buoys rocked on either side as they passed.

Black water, the roar, and then she was skidding to the edge as whoever was in charge hit full throttle, slamming her into the railing, which she gripped with one flailing hand. Spray splashed her face.

She was suddenly being hauled off across the lake on a speeding boat in the dark.

Big water.

With a murderer.

This roller-coaster ride surely had to end soon, she thought as she tried to slither to a more advantageous position, but whoever was at the helm really, really wanted to put some distance between himself and that body on the dock.

That was when she saw the hand. White knuckled, gripping the lower part of one of the railings.

You have to be kidding me.

What? It was impossible, but she could swear that someone had followed her onto the vessel—almost successfully anyway—and was clinging . . .

Last she checked, this was not a James Bond movie.

Expelling a breath she slid forward, probably right into the line of vision of the person driving if he bothered to look back, and hoped she was making an intelligent decision. One swift glance back showed that the back window of the boat was indeed shattered, so she shoved herself upward in one swift move, leaned over the railing, saw just who it was—not a surprise—and grabbed his arm to try and haul him on board. She hissed, "Are you insane?"

"No, just infirm. God, he's hauling ass out of here." The words were almost inaudible, and Santiago was washed in spray, his features glistening, hair soaked, his face barely visible. She knew nothing about inboard engines, but his position seemed pretty dangerous. He shouted, "This sling, I can't get out of it. Maybe I should just let go."

The volume of his voice was loud, but there was no choice. And he was right, the boat was picking up speed, but at least right now they weren't that far from the pier. There was no way she could pull him up, no way. Had they not been moving, maybe, but only maybe.

And no way he could swim. Not with one arm.

But if she let him go, there was very little doubt in her mind that he might drown.

"I am going to kick your ass," she said through her teeth, watching the waves froth up over his back as the boat picked up speed. "I mean kill you in your sleep, pillow over your face, poison in your coffee, bomb in the shower—"

"Does this mean we'll be sleeping together?" His face was wet, frosted with spray from the wake, and she now had her feet braced against the rail."

What would go first? Her hold or his? Right now she was only helping him hang on. If she had to take the entire burden of his weight, she had no doubt either she couldn't do it, or his shoulder would dislocate.

Then he must have fought free of the sling because his other hand came up to grip the railing. She had a fair idea of the pain because of the expression in his face, but he yelled, "Go! Stop the damn boat. You can't pull me on board."

Ellie was still not sure he could swim, but at least he had both hands on the rail and he was right in that she couldn't haul him onto the boat.

He was still an idiot, but he had a point. Ellie let go of his wrist and sprinted toward the cabin, drawing her weapon. Shattered glass crunched under her feet but she managed to keep her balance, the sound covered by the sound of the craft. Her hair whipped around her face.

They were headed toward open water.

Not good.

Any internal conflict over whether or not to shoot was resolved right there. Ellie did not know how to pilot a boat like this on one of the largest lakes in the world, and as far as she knew, her partner was still dragging along behind. She could see the silhouette of the man at the helm of the boat, his hands on the wheels, the eerie red sunset in the background . . .

She hefted her weapon in her hand, released the safety, and opened the door into the cabin. "Police."

His head whipped around and he muttered something. Young, nice looking, but his face was pale, shell-shocked, and wet as if streaked with tears.

Not Henley senior . . . no way. Early twenties at the most, dark hair, and not surprised. It had been a hope only that he hadn't seen her jump on board.

What was she dealing with at the moment? He stared at her gun, but his hand was still on the throttle. Ellie stood, feet braced, a panic she didn't want tightening her throat. She ordered with harsh urgency, "You're under arrest. Stop the engines please. Now. Or else we might add manslaughter to the charges. I'll shoot you, I swear it."

All she could do was hope Santiago was still holding on.

"My father is dead."

Definitely Henley junior. "We can talk about that, but for now, halt. Or I will fire."

Then she did. Not at him, but into the side of the cabin, the sound incredibly loud, a punctuation to the threat. The young man flinched and to her relief, with a push of a button he killed the motors and she almost lost her footing again as the craft abruptly slowed.

*   *   *

"I didn't kill him. I was going to . . . betray my mother . . . with *my* girlfriend . . . how could he? But I didn't. She did." He swiped his shaking hand across his face.

Ellie was going to have to make sense of the babbling later. For now she kept her weapon extended and advanced, grabbing him by the shirt. "Whatever you've done or not done, you *are* to help me now, got it? I need you to assist me to get someone into this boat."

Chapter 26

The train pulled into the station and he handed over his ticket when the doors opened.

There was nothing left for him. He needed to go. Needed to start over.

"Headed?" The porter asked it briskly.

"Minneapolis."

"That is what your ticket says, sir. Welcome aboard."

Carl found it amusing to watch Santiago try to defend himself because he wasn't sure who was more fuming mad, Metzger or MacIntosh.

At least MacIntosh tried to keep it under control, but Metzger was full-out furious.

"You could have compromised the entire situation. Do you realize your partner had to enlist the help of a murder suspect to haul your sorry ass into the boat?"

Santiago, drenched, shivering, still somehow managed to look unrepentant. Carl wasn't sure how he pulled it off, but he did. Metzger had given him his coat and he pulled it tighter with his good hand. The other one dripped blood. He even argued. "She jumped on the boat. She jumps like a girl, by the way, so I thought I could manage it. Henley just happened to take off at that moment. Not a bad decision, just bad timing."

"I jump like a girl?" MacIntosh waved a hand in evident frustration. She was also wet, a muscle in her cheek jumping. "Are you kidding me? For your information, I wasn't the one being towed behind a speeding boat."

"I missed a little."

She said lethally, "I won't miss when I take my side-arm and—"

"That's enough," Metzger interrupted, stepping between them.

"I was trying to help. Jesus." Santiago actually did look a little sheepish.

Around them lights swirled and there was even a police boat from the harbor patrol anchored just off-shore, though Garrison Henley had brought the boat back peacefully enough. He also sat on a bench, sans jacket, his head in his hands, under arrest but not cuffed yet. His face looked like it was carved out of marble.

"Yeah, you tell yourself that you were a lot of help when they treat you again at the hospital for the wound you tore open hanging on to that boat." Metzger turned away, his gaze razor sharp. "Let's clarify all this if we can. What happened?"

"I think he and his father finally had a frank discussion about that paternity test." Carl was willing to step in and gestured at where a crime scene tech had drawn an outline of the discarded weapon on the pier. It had been bagged and taken away, but the white lines showed where it had been dropped before Garrison Henley had jumped into the boat to take off. "It is just a guess, but Joanne probably told him the truth."

"It was two years ago." Santiago might look like a drowned rat, but he was still thinking, shaking blood off his fingers. "What set him off?"

The kid could hear them. He looked over and Carl would swear he exactly recognized that wounded look. He'd had it himself. The disillusionment, the realization your parents had betrayed you, but in his case, *his* parents had not done it on purpose. The car accident had been just that, an accident.

Not so much with Henley.

Maybe that was why he'd liked Garrison the first time they'd met. A meeting of like souls.

"My mother told me." Garrison Henley said it with frigid civility. "She knew about it all along, or suspected anyway. I wanted to vomit. Was I sleeping with my father's mistress or was he just fucking my girlfriend? You know, it all starts to blur. Then she marries a cop and has a kid and it belongs to one of us, but no one knows who. I'm trying to decide who I should hate more, him or her. Then I finally talk to him about it, and he admits it. He doesn't deny for one minute he urged her to go out with me so she could come with us on vacations and come over to the house and no one would think anything about it . . . that son of a bitch. He did it to me, but he did it to my mother too."

"So you decided to kill him?" Ellie MacIntosh looked a little worse for wear too. Her hair was windblown and her jacket splattered with blood that probably came from Santiago. Someone had turned on spotlights by the boat slips and her expression was grim and unforgiving.

He shook his head. "I didn't do it. I brought the gun, but I didn't do it. Check it."

Metzger said with a very fierce measure of authority, "Then who did, son, because someone killed your father."

The dead body was undeniable. Carl had been the one to call it in, stuck with the corpse until the crime scene unit and medical examiner arrived. They were nearly done, and the body had been zipped into the bag no person ever wished to occupy, and loaded on a stretcher.

"It wasn't me." He swallowed, his Adam's apple bobbing. "I did bring the gun, we were arguing, and . . . and I wanted to kill him, but someone else fired the shot. That's why I jumped on the boat and tried to run. First off, I didn't want to get shot too. Second, I didn't want to be found standing over his body with a gun." Garrison looked at all of them with disillusioned eyes. "My father does not always keep the finest company. I assume that is why you all are here in the first place, correct? Maybe it finally caught up with him."

MacIntosh said, "You told me 'she' killed him. Your mother?"

"No." He shook his head.

"Joanne?"

"No." The young man's voice was a whisper.

And Carl knew Henley was telling the truth.

Morning after hangover.

It felt a little that way, like he'd tied one on with the best of them. Jason blinked and his eyes even felt scratchy, but the truth was, he hadn't had one drink the night before. Grasso had driven him first to the hospital emergency room to have his wound stitched back together, and then to his apartment. He'd crashed like a dead person, which he was lucky he wasn't.

He assumed MacIntosh had gone to wherever her boyfriend had chosen to remove himself from harm's way. Probably a tender reunion. He didn't want to think about it too much.

So now they were in Metzger's office, rehashing his less-than-stellar performance the evening before. A botched rescue attempt that made it necessary for *him* to be rescued, when he wasn't even supposed to be there in the first place. Great.

And the chief was still pissed.

"This convoluted mess just keeps getting better and better."

"Yes, sir." Jason tried to be as polite as possible.

"Shut up, Santiago, before I suspend you."

He sat up a little straighter to try and appear sincere, though honestly, he hurt all over. "Yes, sir."

"I said don't speak. It will remind me you are here, and quite frankly, you don't want that. The only reason you are sitting in that chair in this room is because this is somewhat of a debriefing and you know what went down. Are we clear?"

Morning. The smell of doughnuts and coffee—not good doughnuts and good coffee, but it was familiar and somewhat comforting. Jason almost fell into the trap and answered, but at the last minute refrained.

"You see, you can be taught." Metzger turned to the table. "Lieman says it was a sponsored hit from Henley's questionable business partners, and the good news is, the DEA is moving in to make arrests. Being married to a drug cartel is lucrative, but dangerous. As soon as his partners saw him going down for the hits on Fielding, Brown ,and Crawford, they did not need him testifying. Our lovely medical examiner did the autopsy this morning, and she confirms the bullet came from a rifle, not the handgun being waved around by Garrison Henley. His hands tested negative for powder residue also. The kid is telling the truth, and we let him go about an hour ago."

Ellie, wearing a tan jacket over a white shirt and navy slacks, her blond hair in a straight shining fall around her shoulders, asked, "What about the two men in custody who fired at me and Santiago?"

"One is still in the hospital from the crash, and the other one is out on bail, which tells you a lot about who he works for since it was set extremely high. Ballistics can't match their weapons to the other shootings, but we all know they were probably the team that did it, just professional enough to ditch the guns. At the least they will be deported. We don't know who they are because their identification is falsified. We have to hand this over to the federals."

Jason had to admit it frustrated him, but he managed to not make a caustic comment.

Grasso took a sip of coffee before he said, "Where is Joanne Fielding?"

"Being guarded by U.S. Marshals until we can ascertain the threat is gone."

"Good idea."

Metzger turned to stare at him and Jason wished he'd remember to not speak. "Since that comes from an officer of the law who has had some extremely questionable ideas on how to do his job lately, I am not going to take that as high praise. All of you, go home. Get some rest. I am going to say as far as we are concerned, this case is closed."

"Are you kidding me? I liked Danni Crawford."

"Do I look like I'm kidding, Santiago? Several investigations are colliding here. We've been told to back off." Metzger's gaze touched on everyone in the room, one by one. "So, back off."

Carl thought about it long and hard on his way home.

Then he called.

Lindsey answered after five rings. He was a little surprised she hadn't tossed the phone. "Lieutenant."

"How did you know it was me?"

"No one else has this number."

"You are lying. You knew I'd track you down. Did you kill Ely Henley?"

"What on earth are you talking about?"

He laughed softly. It was a warm afternoon and he was in the kitchen, the sun streaming in through the big windows. "You checked into me, didn't you? Looked into that case five years ago and found out why I was transferred from homicide."

"Explain to me why I would do that."

"Because you thought that I, of all people, wouldn't push it if you did the same thing. Vigilante justice. I'm going to tell you there is always a price."

"It's an interesting supposition."

"Is it a wrong one?"

"I like you, Lieutenant Grasso. But you'd never be able to prove it in a thousand years beyond a reasonable doubt."

He had the feeling she was right. "Where did you go? One of the other boats, I expect. If I check into it will I find out one of your law school friends' family has a vessel nearby?"

Lindsey was quiet before she said, "Did you know Henley coerced her? No, not rape, but emotional rape if you ask me. When she found out she was pregnant he got very edgy and the bastard threatened her if she said anything about the affair. He was worried it might affect his life. I'm going to tell you he didn't deserve to take another breath. Lieutenant, it all comes down to one thing. He bragged that he'd made sure she and his son weren't touched the first time."

"Good of him."

"Wasn't it? The *first* time? I happen to love my sister, and I love my nephew. She can't live that way. I read about your past case, and quite frankly, you circumvented the law."

"I don't know about that."

"Oh, but you do. You took out two guys who didn't deserve to live but would probably only have minimum sentences. I happen to know a little bit about how the judicial system works. Good-bye, Detective Grasso."

The call ended and Carl couldn't decide if he wanted to laugh or swear.

What goes around, comes around . . .

Chapter 27

The first really cold day. Frost on the ground like a sprinkling of powdered sugar and there were ice crystals on the stones of the walk in splintered patterns.

In her life Ellie had done difficult things, but this one had to rank up there.

Her grandfather was out back, fiddling with his truck, not the new shiny one parked in the driveway, but the old one he kept by the shed and used to haul wood and various other bits of cargo that might scratch the paint of the vehicle he always complained about being entirely too expensive.

He'd heard her pull in—she knew he had—but had gone back to work with a wrench on something in the engine. When she got out and shut the door of her car, putting her hands into her pockets as she walked up, he waited until she was close to speak to her.

"Can you hand me that screwdriver, please? The one with the red handle. I'd appreciate it."

She bent and retrieved it, putting it in his outstretched palm. "This one?"

"Feels right."

The breeze had that slight narcotic bite to it, almost sweet with the threat of winter around the corner. But first the leaves would drift down into piles of brilliant hues, the plants would eventually all fade and go to sleep, and the animals that didn't hibernate would leave fresh prints in the snow . . .

"I need to talk to you," she said quietly. "Maybe when you are done, we can go inside."

He withdrew from the engine and took out the metal bar holding the hood, but his profile was remote as it slammed shut. "Where is your young man?"

She wasn't sure if Bryce, in his middle thirties, would like to be called a young man, but then again, that was better than old man. "There was a bit of a problem in Milwaukee but he's back there now, working on his book. Did I tell you he has an agent now in New York?"

"That's pretty impressive."

"He's a pretty smart cookie." Ellie grinned as she used her grandfather's favorite expression, but it faded fast. She did *not* want to have this upcoming conversation.

He wiped off his hands. "This old tin can will wait. Nothing I can't do in the morning. Besides, it's getting cold. I never used to feel it, but these days I can't stay out like I used to. We liked to camp well into November when I was younger; go deer hunting at three in the morning when it was so cold the breeze would slice you in half, but I am past that. Let's go inside."

At least he was acting perfectly natural, though she had a feeling he knew why she'd come.

The house was warm and smelled faintly like wood smoke from the fireplace in the corner, and he bent over and shoved in a piece of wood from the bin next to it before he went into the kitchen to wash his hands. The silence between them hung like a cobweb in the spring laden with morning dew.

He spoke first. "So you all were investigating a pretty prominent man, but someone killed him."

"Ely Henley, yes."

"He had people killed to cover up his affair with some young woman and their love child?"

"It looks that way."

"At least the woman and child weren't harmed."

"No. It appears he was an ambitious man, and there are monsters, and there are worse monsters. He is part of the former group." She kind of wished she'd accepted Jody's offer to come along, but in some ways, this was a private moment and her sister had a way of taking over a conversation.

"At least it's over."

"I agree." Ellie sat down at the table where she had eaten cereal and pancakes . . .

She couldn't go there. That child wasn't having this conversation. Detective Ellie MacIntosh was having it.

Finally she said, "Grandpa, tell me about Vivian."

"So, that is why you are here," he said, sparing her the declaration as he sank heavily into an opposite chair.

"That is why I am here."

"It's her?"

"The skeleton? I'm going to guess it is your first wife, yes." Ellie found his resignation a comfort in some ways, but unsettling in others. She wished he'd offered coffee. He always offered coffee, but not this visit apparently. "Auntie Mae gave me a letter Vivian had written her well before she supposedly left you. I had a handwriting expert that the department uses compare the signature to the one on your divorce decree. Mae also got that for me from the safe deposit box the two of you have for the family papers. The law firm in Chicago where the papers were supposedly prepared still actually exists, but the attorney whose name was used never practiced there according to their records. It would be my guess someone, like a clerk, was bribed to make up a false document. The signatures are not a match."

He sat there, silent. His hands, always so strong and capable in her memory, looked thin and blue-veined where they rested on the arms of his chair. "I see."

She chose her words carefully. "As soon as I learned you had been married before I was surprised no one had ever mentioned it to me."

"Why? Is any man proud his wife left him? It was water under the bridge, Eleanor. Why would you need to know?"

If only that was the case.

It was difficult to articulate, but she said, "Can you just tell me what happened? If she didn't sign those papers, someone went to a lot of trouble to make it seem like she did. If you look at it from a perspective of a law-enforcement officer, that is suspicious. Mae was able to tell me a little about her and she said Vivian had an older sister who has since passed away, but who also always claimed that she never heard from her again after she left northern Wisconsin."

"I killed her."

Ellie froze. From the top of her head to her toes. Those were not the words she wanted to hear, and yet the ones she dreaded she would. Like a nightmare moment, when something rustles in the dark . . .

The clock in the corner sounded very loud in the resulting silence.

But then she shook her head. "No, you didn't. I've thought about it too much to believe that. The day you showed me the grave, I sensed you knew who it might be, but you were   stricken. Maybe that was why I didn't want to let this go. So you could have the answer. Tell me."

"I didn't mean literally killed her, Eleanor," he clarified quietly. "But it is on my head, just the same. I've always worried that was true."

"I need you to explain it to me."

He nodded, just once briefly, suddenly looking a decade older. "Vivian had a friend . . . close friend. They went to school together. A pretty young woman who used to come to the house often so they could gossip and have coffee. I really didn't think much about it, but it got to be this girl was about everywhere I turned. We would run into each other in town often. It was a very long time ago. I was a young man, and to be truthful, when I realized what was happening, I couldn't decide if I should be flattered or irritated. I finally said something to Vivian and she just laughed and told me it was my imagination."

Ellie had seen pictures and yes, he'd been a very *handsome* young man. "Did you discourage her?"

"No. I didn't do anything about it. However, I wasn't the only one who noticed. People started to talk. When Vivian left me, everyone thought it was because I was having an affair. I believed it was because she thought the same thing."

Obsession was not a modern invention, nor was stalking.

He went on. "I was furious at first. After all, I had mentioned to Vivian that Helen was starting to make me uncomfortable, but it wasn't my fault." His expression was pensive, melancholy, and he sighed. "Anger is a powerful emotion. I suppose since everyone thought it was true, and I was humiliated and unhappy, the rumor became a reality."

Ellie digested the information, at least able to see it in an abstract sense, not in terms of her grandfather, but maybe in terms of that young man in the pictures. "So you became involved with her?"

"And realized quickly it was a mistake. Helen was quite a determined young woman under her serene exterior."

"Helen?" The sickening lurch came back. "As in my grandmother Helen?"

"No." To her relief, he shook his head. "It was quite a common name back then. Helen Streeter was her name. There are two reasons I have always worried she was responsible for Vivian's disappearance. The first is that the rug in the bedroom was missing when I came home to find my wife had left me. Yes, she'd packed a suitcase and taken some of her clothes, but I couldn't imagine why she would want that old rug."

Good point.

"And the second?"

"Was that this woman tried to kill me one night. I'd told her a few days before I wasn't going to marry her, divorce or no. At the time I couldn't sleep anyway and I smelled the smoke in time."

"*She* burned down the original house?"

"I saw her leave from my bedroom window. I tried to put it out, but it was an old farmhouse and it went up pretty quickly. I had to actually jump for it. That night I *knew*."

Ellie tried to remind herself that yes, as he'd said, he'd been a fairly young man. "Did you pursue legal action against her?"

White brows lifted in an arch of disbelief. "Really? I'd lost my wife first, and then my house, and I hadn't helped it all by behaving like a fool. To be honest, I didn't know what to do. So, I committed the worst sin possible. I did nothing. I couldn't prove anything. I had a missing rug and a house that caught fire and my word against Helen's that she was ever there. I was guilty and miserable over it, and I just wanted to walk away."

She knew what had happened then. He'd moved to Minneapolis, eventually gotten a teaching degree, met her grandmother, married her, and then finally come back to Wisconsin.

"What happened to this Helen?"

"I have no idea. Her entire family moved away while I was gone."

The wind sighed past the eaves in a low, whistling song. Ellie offered, "Do you want me to try and find Helen Streeter? I can't promise you anything, but I could give it my best shot."

"That was a long time ago and I do admit I think vengeance does lie with the Lord. At our age, who knows if she is still alive? I do know I want to give Vivian a proper grave."

"So then I find Ms. Streeter."

For the first time since Ellie had pulled into the driveway, her grandfather smiled in a faint curve of his mouth. "If anyone could, Eleanor, it would be you."

For a man not known for giving compliments, that was a nice one.

She rose to leave, but stopped and turned. "Answer this for me. If someone else hadn't found the body, would you have called me?"

Her grandfather looked at her somberly and told what she thought was the complete truth. "I don't know. In my place, under the same circumstances, what would you do?"

She didn't have an answer.

And that was the answer.

Epilogue

Interesting office. Jason liked art, he just didn't own any. It was hard to imagine he would have the sort of taste to effectively pick out something that would not look just as at home on the wall of a gas station.

Jason walked in and saw that the woman who greeted him was tall, with sleek dark hair cut short, and a build he would term statuesque if he actually ever used that word.

He didn't. He knew it, but he didn't usually say it.

He tended to say things like *she was built like a brick shithouse,* but he wasn't sure she'd be flattered.

She didn't flip through a chart or anything. She didn't even have the classic notepad. The doctor just motioned him to a chair and smiled in a very generic way. "Mr. Santiago. Please have a seat and tell me why we are having a conversation."

"Detective Santiago." He sat down in a leather-covered chair and clasped his hands, elbows on knees.

"Is that how this works? We pretend it is just a conversation?"

"We can pretend, but I would be better if you were simply honest . . . shall I rephrase? It seems like you prefer we are extremely candid. Why are you here?"

"It is recommended, by the city of Milwaukee, that after being shot in the line of duty, I seek some sort of counseling. The first time it happened, I decided I would take their therapist of choice, but it was kind of a waste of my time, so I declined to return to that therapist. I declined to go to any therapist, but it turns out I don't have much latitude there. Kind of pisses me off, really."

"The first time?"

"Twice in the chest. This is just a scratch."

"But still . . . a second shooting. It sounds like that might be traumatizing. Was it?"

"I think I would vote that it ticked me off more than anything. I was about to return to duty."

Dr. Lukens had slightly almond-shaped eyes and they regarded him with an almost disconcerting directness. "It sounds like you like what you do. Being a detective then, for you, is a rewarding occupation. What about it, would you say, appeals to you so much?"

If there was anything he despised in this world it was sitting around talking about his feelings. But Metzger had made it crystal clear he had to be cleared by a professional to get back to the job. Hence this evaluation.

He wasn't sure if asking Ellie for the name of her shrink was a good idea or not, but he liked the irony of it.

"Well, for one, when people shoot at me, I get to shoot back. A real advantage, don't you think, Doctor?"

"I suppose that is true enough, but that could be said of the military too."

"I was in for four years before I became a police officer."

"I see. So apparently you like order in this world and are willing to risk your life to preserve it."

Jason rubbed his neck and stifled a wince. His arm was healing nicely, so sometimes he forgot it was still pretty sore. "I don't know if I have ever looked at it that way. I do know I am not suited for sitting in a cubicle all day, or driving a trash truck, or wearing a suit and schmoozing clients of some kind. All of those occupations sound boring as hell. When I get up in the morning, I never know what is going to happen that day."

"That extends to possibly being shot in the line of duty, quite obviously. Do you think you have anxiety over it possibly happening again?"

"Performance anxiety?" He probably shouldn't have said it, but couldn't resist the grin. "Me? Not one of my problems."

"Do you often use flippancy to deflect questions that make you uncomfortable, Detective Santiago?"

"I *always* use flippancy to deflect questions that make me uncomfortable." He relented then, because this interview was pretty important. "No, seriously, I'm not anxious for it to happen again, because quite frankly, it really hurts. Do I wake at night sweating over it? No, again. I'm not built that way, I guess. I think I can reliably say I will handle dangerous situations exactly the same way I handled them before either one of the incidents that resulted in me being shot."

Dr. Lukens said dryly, "Maybe a little more caution might be in order."

"Hey, I might have been shot, but too much caution can get you killed."

"I will keep that in mind. Tell me, then, do you feel you are ready to return to duty as soon as you are cleared on a health basis by your physician?"

"Absolutely."

"No other problems? Nothing you wish to discuss?"

He shouldn't have hesitated even for one moment. But he did, and she caught it. Her gaze sharpened. "Yes?"

"This has nothing to do with my ability to serve the homicide division of the Milwaukee Police Department, okay? But maybe I need to talk to someone about it."

"You are in luck. That happens to be what I am here for."

Man, this was really actually hard to say. "My partner is your patient."

"He is?"

"How many homicide detectives do you have seeing you? *She* is."

Her saw her connect the dots. Georgia Lukens cleared her throat. "Not everyone tells me what they do, Detective, and virtually every single patient comes here for a different reason." Before he could speak, she lifted her hand. "And don't ask me what hers is.

Just as what we say here is strictly confidential and only between the two of us, so is every word she and I exchange."

"I wasn't going to ask." He was telling the truth. He blew out a short breath. "We were just assigned together early this summer and I have a small problem with her. Or maybe a big problem. I'm not sure which it is, but a problem for sure."

"Perhaps you should talk to your supervisor about it."

"Yeah, well, it isn't that kind of problem."

"Define it for me."

Well, he had a slight problem there too. However, he had to admit, there was something freeing in being able to talk to someone who couldn't tell anyone else what you said. "I find her attractive," he said bluntly. "Like I have some seriously impure thoughts that involve both of us sans clothing and communicating with body language only. Got it?"

"I do, actually." Dr. Lukens laughed softly. "You have an extremely direct way of expressing yourself, Detective. So you have sexual feelings about Ellie MacIntosh. That isn't surprising, if it makes you feel better. When men and women are put together on a constant basis, relationships often form. The single most likely person a spouse is going to cheat with is a coworker. She is a very pretty young woman and shares your passion for law enforcement. I think I might be more surprised if you didn't feel that way."

"Well, for your information, I'm not all that happy about it." An understatement.

"You don't like the vulnerability."

"It's just plain counterproductive. She's involved with someone else, and the last thing we need, either of us, is for me to make decisions in a dangerous situation based on me wanting to protect her."

There. He'd said it. It was kind of interesting, but he was relieved to just blurt it out and get it all off his chest.

"Ah, so these feelings aren't just sexual."

"I'd appreciate it if you left the word feelings out of every single statement you make."

"Yes, I get that impression about you." Georgia Lukens tapped her fingers on her desktop for a moment. "I'm going to tell you what, Detective. In my evaluation I am going to say that I think you are certainly emotionally ready to return to your job whenever your physician clears you on the basis of your health."

That was an enormous relief. What he didn't need in his life was a bad evaluation from a therapist that would shoot him in the foot with Metzger.

"But?" He could read people. That was what made him a good detective. He was already halfway to his feet, but correctly interpreted her expression.

"I think you could maybe benefit from another session or two."

"Don't you all say that to keep your clients?"

"I suppose some of us do if you are lumping me into some sort of category, but can I ask you if you disagree?"

"My last girlfriend was getting her Ph.D. in psychology. I've been analyzed half to death, trust me."

"And I remind you of her?" Lukens looked amused.

"You both have great tits."

She was unfazed. "Thank you. Yet, still, you didn't answer my question."

"Do I have unresolved issues?" He shrugged. "I'm pretty sure I do, but introduce me to a perfectly adjusted person. It isn't possible, because there is no such thing."

"I can't say as I disagree, but we aren't aiming for perfection, just maybe more clarity."

"I'm not positive I want more clarity. This world can be a very bad place and I see that clear enough already. What I do is try to take some of the badness out of the equation."

"But what do you do for yourself?"

"Drink beer, watch a little porn now and then, not the hard stuff—"

"Crack jokes to cover your feelings." The interruption was mild. "Yes, I said that word again, but you must acknowledge that all day long, and even all night long when we dream, we feel something about every minute that passes, whether or not it is irritation over a traffic delay, or appreciation for a good meal, or sadness because someone we know was hurt or betrayed, or maybe even that has happened to us."

"Dwelling on it doesn't do anything to change it."

"A healthy attitude."

He spread his hands. "You see, I'm fine."

"I am not sure I would go that far, but you certainly are functional in my opinion as a law-enforcement officer." She pointed to a door with a discreet exit sign embossed on a gold plaque. "There is a separate exit to preserve the privacy of my patients. It was a pleasure to meet you, Detective Santiago."

"You too." He meant it. If she was going to get him back on the job, then she was currently his favorite person on this earth.

He had no idea what prompted it, maybe the warm fuzziness he felt toward Dr. Lukens at the moment, but he paused with his hand on the doorknob and surprised himself by saying, "I'll think about another session."

The evening was cool but clear, and on the news they had promised a true harvest moon later. Ellie sat on the back deck and sipped a very smooth Merlot, her body relaxed.

Bryce had grilled some lamb chops and served them with small roasted fingerling potatoes and chilled asparagus with aioli. It had been delicious and she had eaten with true appreciation.

"So, are you going to tell me?"

The quiet question made her glance up. Bryce settled into an opposite deck chair, his gaze full of speculation. Even though it was getting pretty chilly his feet were bare and there was just a hint of ragged white on the hem of the worn jeans that hugged his long legs.

"The prosecutor isn't going to go after Joanne for anything. There is a pretty solid argument she was coerced and the threat was obviously real."

Three dead police officers and another one wounded. Yes, the threat was real.

"Ambition is a very powerful motivation." Bryce sounded more philosophical than surprised. Ever the scholar, looking in on human behavior was more an exercise in curiosity than something that required his participation. "I also think Ely Henley, like so many powerful men, tends to forget he can actually be held accountable. I'm sorry for his son, who will have to live with this for the rest of his life."

"Me too." She took another sip of wine. Stretching out her legs, she surveyed the indigo sky. "I love fall. The air smells different."

"Ellie, not that the Henley case isn't interesting, but I was really asking about Helen Streeter."

Like she didn't know that. Was she ready to talk about it? Maybe.

"She's still alive. Up until a year or so ago, she lived alone in an apartment in Saint Louis, but she's in a county nursing home now. I talked to the director and it seems she has some lucid moments, but it isn't reliable enough, or so I was told, for me to take the time to make the journey to question her."

"And what would be the point?"

That was actually a hard question to answer. She could emphasize the woman had probably murdered her grandfather's first wife, but it really was over half a century ago. The only benefit would be an affirmation that they knew the truth.

"I could give my grandfather some peace."

"It seems to me that he came to terms with it long ago. I am not saying in any fashion he is fine with what happened. I am just saying the reality of it is not going to change anything for him. You are the one who needs to hear a confession and it doesn't sound like you would get a reliable one."

Santiago had told her almost exactly the same thing. Ellie stifled a defensive comment. "Helen Streeter never married. Worked as a clerk in a law office for most of her life, which I find intensely ironic. Her only sister died in a car accident in her late thirties."

"It doesn't sound like a very fulfilling life."

"She didn't deserve one."

"I doubt that anyone would disagree with you."

She changed the subject, because he was right. Essentially that case was closed. "Grasso is being permanently reassigned to homicide, or at least that is the rumor."

Dark brows went upward. "What about Santiago? New partner for him, or new partner for Grasso?"

"Metzger hasn't said anything yet to me."

"Either way it will be interesting. Santiago has some challenges attached to him, not the least of which seems to be his ability to get himself into situations involving bullets."

"If I may play devil's advocate, first of all his job involves some danger, and it seems to me I've gotten you in one of those situations and myself in more than one, so can we discount that aspect?" Then, curious, she asked, "Which one of them do you like better?"

"Me?"

"Santiago or Grasso? I respect your opinion, though to be honest, it is up to the chief."

"An interesting one, but okay. Grasso. He's a fairly complicated guy, in my opinion, on the outside, but not so much so on closer inspection. He's driven, and he doesn't really have a big agenda. He likes the job—maybe even lives it. His ghosts aren't the bad kind, but he has them."

The bloodred spread of the sunset was appropriate to the conversation. "And Santiago?"

"Is a fairly uncomplicated man on the outside, but that's deceptive." Bryce took a sip of wine. "I am going to guess his ghosts would make a person wake up sweating in the middle of the night. If I can go a little further, I would speculate they both would disagree with me if they were sitting here right now."

She would guess exactly the same thing.

"I didn't renew my lease." Another change in subject.

Bryce processed it without a blink. "That's progress."

She had to admit she gazed at him in exasperation. "Somehow I thought you'd be a little more effusive."

"And scare you away? No."

This was where she should protest he wouldn't scare her away . . .

But he probably could.

"So, I'm moving in."

"Looks that way." Bryce turned and looked at the sunset. "What are you going to tell your grandfather?"

"That I found a new place to live. No details supplied."

"I meant about Helen."

She'd known what he meant . . . the entire world was evasive with her, wasn't she entitled to be so now and then?

Slowly, she said, "I think he doesn't want to know."

"We all aren't hunters, Ellie. Besides, it sounds like he's been dealing with the guilt for a long, long time. He doesn't need the answer. He has known it for half a century."

That made sense . . . she knew it to be true.

"Okay. So what's next?" She considered the ruby liquid in her glass.

"We debate over whether or not you like the couch in the living room."

"I think the couch is fine."

"Then I think we should just relax and worry about the details another day."

That could be sound advice.

She hoped she could take it.